Masque: Choices

A Gaston Leroux Phantom of the Opera Romance series

-Book One-

Caridad Martin

Masque: Choices© 2014 Caridad Martin
The Gaston Leroux Phantom of the Opera Romance Series, Book one
All Rights Reserved

Isasi Press

ISBN-13: 978-0692363249 (Isasi Press)
ISBN-10: 0692363246

Distributed by Createspace
www.Createspace.com

First Printing: May 2015
Printed in the United States of America

Acknowledgements:
Cover art by Jesh Art Studio
Teaser by Mishael Austin Witty author of A Shadow of Things to Come
Photography by Reinaldo G. Walker
Thank you to Gaston Leroux for writing a story that is for all time. I hope to have done your work justice.
Thank you to Joel Osteen for his weekly inspiration.
And most important Thank You Lord for granting me your favor.

Dedication

For Thorin who is Light, Love, Laughter

Author's Note:

Throughout the 19th century in France, unlike in England, when referring to a titled noble by the title alone the style was not to capitalize the title as in, the comte, the vicomte, the marquis. When the noble was referred to by the full title, the style was to capitalize the title as in, the Comte du Villiers. I have used this style throughout the book.

Contents

Prologue

Paris Opéra, Box five, 1878

The voices wafted up slowly, only to crash as they reached him. He could feel the tedium piercing his mind, slacking every muscle in his body. He massaged the back of his neck, straightened his posture and leaned forward slightly, straining toward the stage, but remaining just out of sight in the opera box. He picked at the red stains under his nails. His pipe and favorite blend lay in his coat pocket. He wished he could smoke his pipe just now, but the rising smoke would give him away.

The chorus girls were attractive, but undisciplined, the men dull and cocky; mediocre singers, all seventy-eight of them. He sagged in his seat, popped another bonbon into his mouth and slowly sipped at his champagne. He stretched his long legs and kicked off his slippers, placing his feet on a small stool in front of him. With care, he untied the mask covering his face and placed it on the stool next to him. Fresh air hit his face and he inhaled deeply. Everything was as he liked it in his opera box. He would leave a tip as always for Mme. Giry, and even add a bit extra for a pair of new ballet slippers for his concierge's young daughter. A tapping sound brought his attention back to the stage.

"No, no, no," M. Legafe, the choirmaster, squeaked. He tapped the baton on the music stand. "You are not watching me. From the beginning, Mesdemoiselles, Messieurs. Maestro, if you *please*."

The pianist blinked quickly and began to play once again.

M. Legafe smoothed his mustache with one hand and held up his baton with the other, gave the signal, and a cacophony of voices filled the opera house. *Once again the managers ignore my advice about the lack of talent in the chorus, and with the usual catastrophic results. They waste their money, my time, and irritate my hearing!*

A small figure approached from the left wing and the voices trailed off. All heads turned toward the young girl entering.

Ah, a distraction. Looks about eighteen. Pretty enough overall, wheat-colored hair, a mite too flat in the chest, not tall enough, and her dress—looks—shabby, even from up here. From which nest did they drag this little songbird in from?

"Ah, impressively late, Mademoiselle. Charming,

if you were at a society ball—but you're not!"

The latecomer's cheeks bloomed with color as she barely squeezed in between two girls. She cleared her throat and said in a soft voice, "I apologize, Maestro, it is just now I was asked to report to you. I was in the office of Messieurs Debienne and Poligny."

Typical. Every girl they hire for the chorus has the same mundane good looks…and this one will have the same mundane voice. I will send a short note to the managers expressing my boredom with their newest choice.

"I see." Legafe scrunched up his face and eyed her as if he were inspecting a moldy piece of bread. "So it is the fault of our dear managers, Debienne and Poligny, that you are late. May we continue? Your gab is taking up our precious time."

"I thought I should apologize," said the girl, her cheeks again showing her embarrassment.

"Come now, your name, Mademoiselle?"

"C…Christine…Monsieur."

"Do you happen to have a surname?" He cleared his throat and blew out his breath dramatically.

She raised her head slowly and looked directly into the man's eyes. "It's Daaé, Monsieur."

Up in the opera box, he sat up, planting his feet firmly on the floor. *Daaé! Did she say Daaé? Could her father be Alphonse Daaé?* He had heard the violinist play many years ago when on a break from his work at the Palais Garnier. A tiny angel stood by Daaé's side and accompanied his music—and what music that was—music from heaven. *This young woman would be the child with the short golden hair that entranced the entire fair with her singing.* He had stood so far back in the crowd, that he had not realized the child was a girl. Alphonse Daaé had impressed him that day by refusing to take any of the money the public offered, as if he had been playing for God alone.

"So, Mlle. Daaé, since you like being the center of attention…" He looked around at the chorus for approval, but just found bored, fed up faces. "Let us hear you sing on your own."

"Oh no, Monsieur, I couldn't," Christine protested. She grasped her hands in front of her and rubbed them.

"You can and will, Mademoiselle. Maestro…from the beginning…the…ah…the *Ave Maria.* If you are any kind of singer, you will know that one!" He smoothed his mustache again.

"I really…"

"Step out and sing!" he shouted.

The girl swallowed hard and stepped out from the group. She grabbed a handful of cloth from the sides of her skirt, opened her mouth and began to sing.

From the moment the first sound escaped her lips and wafted up to his box, he could tell that her voice had been trained by a pedestrian teacher— ignorant of what he'd had in his possession. For the same reason, M. Legafe would not recognize her gift.

Since that fair, he had not heard a purer sound in song. His eyes almost closed in pleasure, but the plain, heart-shaped face was the perfect background for that voice. He would not miss a moment of this double delight.

"I see we need a lot of training, Mlle. Daaé. Rusty, but there is…"

"Shut up and let her sing, you idiot." The sound reverberated throughout the stage.

The chorus gave a collective gasp.

"What the…" M. Legafe looked around the opera house, but he saw no one, all the seats were empty. He looked up into the rafters—only Buquet, a stagehand, stood leering as he looked over the new girl—and that voice was certainly not his.

"It's the ghost, Monsieur," said a slim dark-haired girl dressed in a long white tutu peeking out from behind the right wing curtains on the stage.

"What? Nonsense," the choirmaster replied.

"But it is," the girl insisted.

"Let the girl sing!" Again the voice was everywhere at once.

"Please Monsieur, let the new girl finish her song, or…there will be trouble," the ballerina insisted.

"This is all pooh! Bah!" M. Legafe hesitated, but signaled to Christine. "Oh, go on, finish." He swallowed and nodded to the pianist, but the blanched musician was squinting and looking up into the boxes.

She did not wait for the music to start and

continued to sing the *Ave Maria* a cappella.

He leaned his head on the back of the chair. Unwillingly, his eyes fluttered closed before tears escaped his eyelids.

This is the voice I have been waiting for all these years. I never imagined—Daaé's child. Awkward, that it's a girl. Regardless, I will train her voice correctly, make her a diva, the best opera singer the world has ever known. My own, my very own, beautiful angel to instruct and to perfect.

Chapter 1

Paris Opéra, fifth cellar, 1880
Choose!

"Tick-tock, tick-tock, the hands run 'round the clock. Which hand chases which? Tick-tock, tick-tock, time to make *your* choice," he chanted. Erik tapped the watch in his hand and said in a melodic voice, "Well, my dear, do you choose the scorpion or the grasshopper?"

Christine dried her hands on the wrinkled skirt of her dress, and out the corner of her eye glanced toward the chamber door. She opened her mouth as if to speak, but she sucked in her lower lip instead.

"The hands won't stop. Choose now."

"You want me to choose between life and death?"

"You might not think it from the looks of me, but I do not like death or dead things, not at all. I like living things around me. I want a living wife not...well never mind *that*." He was dressed all in black. His face was covered with a black half-mask. His thin lips and skeletal chin showed.

"Why do I have to choose at all? I do not like scorpions or grasshoppers. Could I not pick a cow? I had a cow when I lived in Uppsala with my father." Bravely, she tossed back her hair as if she hadn't a care. If she could distract him, he might change his mind and abandon his mad plan.

"Now you are just acting silly, child. I do not wish to make you nervous, but that boy in there is running out of time. And you want to tell me about your cow?" he chided her softly. Erik turned away slightly from the little window to face her. "Well?"

She grew pale on hearing his words and wrung her hands again. They were getting hot and swollen from the constant rubbing. She could not afford to make a mistake. Right after Erik kidnapped her during her performance on stage, Raoul, her fiancé, had come to the fifth cellar to save her. Somehow, he had found Erik's house by the lake and fallen into the torture chamber. Trapped there for hours, it was he who needed her to save him now. Earlier, when Erik was in his room and Raoul heard her nearby, they talked a little and his voice grew stronger. She held hope for his life as he called out to her from the desert-like over-heated room. How could such a vital young man be dying? Raoul was only a year older than her twenty years. With Erik standing by the door, she did not dare speak to him. Hope of rescue was now dwindling to nothing.

"Please put out the light in the room. It doesn't matter if he stays in there, but put out the light. We could go to your library and play cards. Or I could put my head on your lap as you read to me."

He arched a brow. "Cards? Too late for cards or reading now, my love. Why it is almost eleven o'clock, and we know what that will mean." His veiled grin made her shiver.

"If you turn off the light, we could go for a carriage ride in the Tuileries. You know how very much I love to take a ride with you."

He looked at her through narrowed eyes. "It is rather unkind of you to think of carriage rides at this time." He adjusted a knob. "I do believe he could do with a glass of water just about now." Erik smiled benevolently as he turned away from her for another peek through the small window. "Perhaps," he said with his back to her. "I should just make the choice for you," Erik suggested, his voice as soft as silk. He could have been discussing her preference for honey or jam.

Her eyes wandered to his right hand; he had long fingers suggestive of his height. He wore his usual gold ring on the index finger, with the figures of a scorpion and a grasshopper. Each creature had the tail of the other in its mouth. She wondered if it was the grasshopper that chased the scorpion or the other way around. Her world was turning upside down, but one thing remained true. The man she loved was running out of time.

Erik's golden eyes followed hers, and he turned the ring so that it spun around on his bony finger. "A small gift from the little sultana…for past services rendered." He chuckled lightly.

Pleading, she searched for his eyes. "Which one is doing the eating, Erik? Won't you tell me?"

"Why, if you knew that, my dear, it would spoil everything. You would know the answer to my riddle." He tilted his head slightly and smiled at her as a patient teacher smiles at a young, dull pupil. "What fun would that be then?"

She winced at his dry cackle.

Christine wrung her hands again and dried them on her dress. She was wearing a simple blue morning dress, one of the many dresses in her wardrobe. When she was in his abode under the opera house, he insisted she use only what he provided for her. "I don't know…Erik, please, please stop this game and turn off the light!" She tried not to let desperation creep into her voice.

He walked to the chamber and partially opened the small window to where her fiancé roasted like an animal on a spit, and looked through it. He made no comment, but she saw the slightest smile ghost his lips. "What was that, my dear?" He turned to face her again. "A game? You mentioned something about a game?"

"I beg you. Stop this now," she pleaded, making

every effort to hold back the tears that would set off a tirade.

He looked through the window again, and his lips thinned out into a semblance of a smile. "Yes, the vicomte does seem to be playing a game, perhaps it is charades. Oh! He just fell onto his side and…"

She gasped involuntarily.

He stared at her with steel eyes, then turned back to the window. "Oh dear girl, what a jolly idea you had. This is going to be fun. Wait—wait, mouth opens and closes." He laughed and slapped his thigh over and over like a clopping horse. "Wait. Is he clawing at his throat? I wish you would look. They could use his talent upstairs."

"Stop torturing him, Erik!" she yelled, covering her ears with both hands. "Please, please stop."

"This boy plays the most intriguing game of charades. Is it a fish?" This time his smile was almost genuine, and his eyes glowed with merriment. "His tongue just fell out of his mouth—a snake? He's rolling from side to side—I can't guess. Would you like a go?" He waved his hand, motioning for her to come up to the window. She recoiled from the hand, a slow wail escaped her.

Raoul must be near death. It is over. She knew what her answer had to be. The time for hope of salvation was gone. Raoul could not escape and save her and so she must save him. She blinked back tears. There was no choice she had to save Raoul's life or lose her own in mourning.

"The scorpion, Erik! I choose the scorpion!" The words erupted out of her mouth, and she rushed to the little table where he kept the two caskets with the figurines. She opened the lid to one and swiftly turned the scorpion.

He did not move; his eyes glazed, fixed on nothing. She was certain, at that moment, she could hit him over the head, and he would not notice. If she could...and get away with Raoul. She looked around...nothing. Erik pulled a lever on the wall and a loud hiss, coming from the chamber, filled the room.

"What is that?" She feared the worst. "What does that noise mean, Erik?"

No answer.

"Erik, can you hear me? Erik?" Feeling braver, she pulled on his coat sleeve urgently. It was a little forward, but she had to get Raoul out of that room with the hiss. "I choose the scorpion...I will be your wife."

Erik turned to face her and blinked slowly as if just woken from a deep sleep. He looked down at her hand and laughed his terrible laugh, devoid of mirth or joy. It made her skin crawl to think how he had developed that laugh. She removed her hand. She remembered the first time she heard it, she had not known to whom it belonged, but she had shuddered deep inside. She hated that laugh. Joseph Buquet's body was found not too long after, the sound of Erik's laughter had resounded throughout the Opéra halls.

"Oh, but she is clever. My darling girl is brilliant, indeed. That was a jolly good choice! Paris loves you; they applaud for you." He brought his hands together in a thunderous clap that made her jump.

She grabbed his sleeve. "Let him go free, Erik. Please," she said, her voice jagged.

"Well…yes, of course. Did you not hear his cooling shower? I hope it is not too late. You did take your time with your delightful game. Imagine wanting to play games when the poor boy was going through his agonies…well…I must tell you that some people do not recover well from their…um…visit to the desert," he said, walking through the partition that hid the chamber from the rest of the house. "Not at all."

A few moments later, the wet vicomte lay on the floor just outside the torture chamber. Erik stood over him with an imperial stance. Hands resting on his narrow hips, he observed the young man with detachment as if he were an interesting specimen. He tapped the young man's head with the tip of his toe, but the head just lolled. Her heart crumpled at the sight of Raoul.

Raoul de Chagny was semi-conscious, his face was blotched, and he was coughing softly from the cool cellar air hitting his dry, scorched lungs. His sunken eyes blinked but did not open fully. A low, pitiful moan escaped his lips. Shaking, she knelt by him, careful to use only two fingers lest Erik become jealous, and stroked his wet but still overheated forehead. Raoul's hands shook uncontrollably. He had tried so very hard to save her. Christine schooled her face into a look of indifference, hiding her desire to gather Raoul in her arms and press him to her, cooling him with her kisses. She looked up and saw the fury return to Erik's eyes and she withdrew her hand, knowing that the touch had been a mistake.

"Now, now, my dear, that will not do." He grabbed her arm roughly and pulled her up away from the vicomte. "It will not do, you are to be Erik's wife," he growled, dragging her away from the torture chamber and toward the little parlor next to her bedroom. He left her standing by the door. Erik walked back to the body, slowly bent down, and hauled the vicomte through the long hallway, away from the torture chamber by the feet, passing the music room then the library in turn. He let the young man's head bump repeatedly against the floor as he went. Christine felt each thump and lifted her hand to her heart.

Erik's eyes bore into her as he pulled the vicomte's dead weight past the little parlor where she stood immobile, then past the kitchen which was across from Christine's bedroom. He continued across the parlor in the direction of the main door. Perhaps, he would take Raoul across the lake in the boat. Just as his hand touched the door, they heard a two bell alarm. With a quick change of directions, he pulled the body back across the parlor and into his bedroom. "Go into your room and stay!" he ordered her. "If you choose to share anything with our visitor about the games we played, there is nothing that will stop me from snapping the boy's neck." Her eyes opened wide at the threat, and she ran into her room locking the door behind her.

"Erik, let the vicomte go," a bold voice called out from the doorway. From the keyhole in her door, she saw a short, dark-skinned man in strange clothes, come into Erik's parlor. Hope rose and vibrated in her. Did this strange little man have the ability to save her and Raoul?

Chapter 2

The Foreigner

"Where are your manners, Hafiz? Won't you at least greet me?" Erik said to his visitor. A look of feigned innocence grazed his face. A mocking bow followed.

"I know exactly what you are up to." The short man looked up at Erik. He looked nervous but determined.

"Once again you have circumvented my alarm and my locks. A true daroga. I must work on that."

"Where are you keeping the Vicomte de Chagny?" Hafiz asked.

"I am *not* that boy's keeper, so why would I be aware of his goings and comings?" Erik replied.

"You must release the vicomte and the girl." The dark-skinned man walked into the parlor and looked around him nervously. "Where are they? You must bring them out."

"Who? Who is it I must bring out, Hafiz?" he asked, mocking false innocence.

"Don't play with me, Erik! You know I'm talking about the Vicomte de Chagny and his fiancée, Christine Daaé."

"Ah Daroga, how you presume of our friendship. First, you enter my home without permission, and then you dare to dictate whom I may have in my home." A smirk spread on his lips. He decided to extend the game a little longer by inspecting his nails carefully as Hafiz glared at him. He couldn't call him or anyone else a friend. Hafiz was his oldest acquaintance and he knew him to be a good-hearted, honest man, if such an absolute existed. Over twenty years earlier, Hafiz, as daroga, chief of police, had been sent to find him in the Nijni-Novgorod fair and extend the Shah's job offer. Erik returned with him to Persia as the court illusionist. Eventually, his talents became known and he built the Shah a magnificent palace, with a torture chamber similar to the one where he had tortured the vicomte. He had used all his knowledge of illusions as he built the palace to create confusion and deceive the Shah's enemies. The palace had hidden doors that led to chambers, which led inside walls, in an elaborate deceptive maze prepared for his employer's safety. The Shah seemed to appear in the oddest places in the palace and at the same time was seen signing a document in front of foreign dignitaries. The Shah praised Erik's efforts but feared Erik's intimate knowledge of his new palace. In recompense for his job, the Shah asked Hafiz to blind Erik, but fearing his superior mind he decided that the magician's death was the better choice. He asked Hafiz, his chief of police to kill Erik. Hafiz was offended by the duplicity and warned Erik. The Persian used his position as daroga to help him escape. Hafiz was found out and thanks to his father's social position was not imprisoned or sent to Erik's torture chamber. The Persian lost his employment, home, possessions and was exiled with a small pension.

Erik travelled on to Constantinople with the Persian on his heels. He went on to build the Sultan a palace which rivaled the one in Mazandaran. Once this palace was nearly complete Erik noticed the wind turning in the same direction. This time, he assigned a value to his work and took his pay from the royal vaults. From there he had thought to return to the Tonkin pirates he had met as a youth while in South East Asia, but his feet suddenly yearned for cobblestones beneath them and he returned to Paris.

The Persian followed and took the apartment he still lived in at the rue Scribe. He knew other Persians who were also in exile and recommended Erik's skills as a master mason. Hafiz explained away the mask as being protection from the Shah's assassins. Erik built houses for Hafiz's Persian friends. In each house he was asked to build an escape route or a special room where the family could hide if the Shah ever sent his henchmen. For Erik this was the most normal time of his life.

After some time he heard that a grand opera house would be built in Paris. Having grown bored with building the plain little houses with the secret passages and rooms, he applied for a chance to work on the opera house project. He bid and won a contract to work in the troublesome flooded cellars. When Erik descended to the fifth cellar he found a lake that was eight to ten feet deep in some places. The dark, the musty odor, the coolness of the cellar gave him such comfort that he broke into song. The perfect acoustics cemented the deal, Erik was home.

He began to work on the opera house foundations, creating a maze of double walled tunnels the workers could go through to work despite the surrounding lake. He told a few of his workers that M. Garnier had asked for a secret house to be built for his use under the opera house. Aside from their regular pay Erik added a generous compensation for their discretion. The masons worked under his direction until they had built a beautiful home by the shore of the underground lake. The front looked like the surrounding rock face. It was approachable through the back by the foundation tunnels and in the front by boat from the lake. For the first time, he commiserated with both the Shah and the Sultan, as he dispatched the masons who knew too much to be left alive. Erik sent their compensation to their widows.

Foolishly, he thought to have escaped his inquisitor when he built his house by the lake five floors under the Paris Opéra. Hafiz's policeman's nose led him to his door within a month of moving in. The other man's personal loss for his sake, had tied Erik's own hands since then and had made him subject to innumerable queries and visits over the years by the Persian. *He thinks me buried away from humanity. How very shocked he will be when he learns of my impending marriage.*

"Where are you keeping them? You cannot play these games with other people's lives Erik! Do they still live?"

Tired of the game, Erik said, "I will indulge your curiosity on this happy day and I will let you in on one of Erik's secrets, but be careful not to pry too much. You wish to see Mlle. Daaé you say?" He walked to her bedroom and softly rapped on the door. "Christine? Please come join us."

She emerged from her room still wearing the wrinkled light blue dress which complimented her petite form. A sigh nearly escaped him. He never tired of looking at her. Her large, hazel eyes looked to him nervously, her full lips were thinned out and compressed. She walked straight, keeping her posture as he had taught her. He extended the long fingers of his gloved hand to her and she placed hers on them. The top of her head fell well below his shoulders. Her hand trembled in his and he squeezed it slightly.

She had listened to every word spoken between the two men. Who was this man and could he save her and Raoul? His skin had a dark, even tone lined by age. He wore a dark suit with an olive green waistcoat; a black kamarband belt and an astrakhan cap—a foreigner.

"My dear, this is M. Jenaad Hafiz Esfahani, an old friend of mine from my days in Persia. He was daroga, or chief of police, there. It seems he knows you already." Erik sucked his teeth. "Somehow Hafiz, has gotten the notion into his head, that I am holding you here against your wishes."

On closer inspection, she did recognize him. Erik had chased her and Raoul at the opera house. This was the man who had pointed the way to the rooftop, away from Erik's trapdoors. On reaching the rooftop, she had opened her heart to Raoul and confessed her inability to break Erik's hold on her. She told him of visiting Erik in his underground home and she confessed what she had done. It still shamed her, when she recalled the way she had callously, ripped Erik's mask off to satisfy her curiosity. She shuddered from head to toe, when she thought of what she had discovered beneath the mask. Erik would not allow her to leave with the secret she had discovered, but from somewhere in her depth she had found the courage to do the best performance of her life. To gain her freedom she agreed to be Erik's betrothed and wear his ring from that day on. Raoul had been dismayed by her story, but not by her actions. At the end, he had lifted her chin and kissed her under the statue of Apollo's Lyre swearing to save her from Erik and love her forever. Her heart had belonged to Raoul alone from that moment on. She wondered why this foreigner, who now appeared to be Erik's friend, had helped them back then.

She dropped her arms to her side as Erik's arm circled her waist.

"Would you enlighten my friend Hafiz as to our plans?"

He was probably around Erik's age or older. Erik had called him a friend and the man had not denied it. Was he part of a master plan to trick her or was he as trustworthy as he appeared to be? If she was wrong, Raoul would pay the price. Her best chance to help Raoul survive would be to listen carefully and play along. The short man's lively green eyes held hers. She could not risk Raoul's life. She needed to buy time if she was ever going to extricate herself and Raoul from all this.

She offered the stranger her hand and added her best operatic smile, but said nothing. She felt a light pinch at her waist.

"Mlle. Daaé, just call me Hafiz, and I beseech you, open up to me. Is this man forcing you to remain with him? Speak up now, and be frank with me," Hafiz said, staring intently into her eyes. "You are engaged to the Vicomte de Chagny are you not?"

"Monsieur, that engagement was but a childish game. The vicomte and I have known each other since childhood and have never given up the habit of playing silly games. You must not take us seriously. I have promised myself, to Erik." Erik held her lightly but possessively by the waist.

The Persian scrutinized her face, eyes darting from her to Erik. "Mlle. Daaé…"

Erik's hand subtly tightened around her.

"Please, I have already explained myself, Monsieur. Erik and I are to be married. As Erik's friend, we will invite you to share our joy."

"This is not a game Mlle. Daaé, I can be of help…"

"I thank you for your kind offer," Erik interrupted him. "I will welcome your assistance in preparing for our nuptials."

"What?" The Persian's green eyes flashed to Christine's face. She held his eyes as bravely as she dared.

"Expect me in your apartment tomorrow. We want to be married as soon as possible. Is that not so, my dear?" Hearing those words made Christine's knees wobble and her smile dip. Erik must have noticed, because he drew her to him and, with his support, she re-pasted the smile on her face. She managed to nod her agreement when the words would not come out.

"I will leave you now…I beg your pardon, Erik. Everything seems to be as you say." The Persian did not sound convinced, and his eyes continued to roam the room.

"Your visits are always...singular, Hafiz."

With a grim set to his mouth, the Persian said, "I take my leave then. Mlle. Daaé, Erik."

Both men bowed formally to the other. The shorter man left through the back door he had come in through. When the man was out of earshot, Erik exclaimed loudly, "Damn him! Let him try that tunnel again. He will think twice about entering Erik's home uninvited!"

"Please...a seat." Her thoughts returned to Raoul. Was he recovering? She thought it was best for Raoul that she not make inquiries as to his health. Erik took her to the divan and she almost collapsed onto it.

He paced in front of her. She followed him with her eyes, making sure to keep her emotions guarded. Had she been right not to trust the foreigner? She knew that now she would never escape Erik. Christine suddenly felt exhausted. She had doomed herself to a life with this madman and covered her face with her hands.

He slapped her hands away from her face. "Do not try to hide from me. You will never hide from me," he cried. "It is Erik who will hide from you."

Two years earlier when she had first arrived at the opera house, A strange voice had offered to coach her voice and her ambition prompted her to accept this help. As her maestro, he had hidden from her as he corrected her singing, seemingly from Heaven. She had called him her Angel of Music remembering the old Swedish tale her father had told her. He admitted to her that he was indeed the angel her father had promised would come to her. Eventually, her voice reached heights of perfection she still could barely believe came from her mouth. She could see herself as a future diva at the Paris Opéra, all thanks to her dear maestro, her Angel of Music.

He paced in front of her again and it brought her back to the present. Raoul! It was a risk, but she had to know. Keeping her voice as disinterested as possible, she asked, "Erik? What will you do with Raoul?"

"He is no longer your concern," he shrieked. He gasped and seemed to check himself, licked his lips and continued in a more even tone, "I…I will return him upstairs. A stagehand is sure to find him—or not."

"Do as you will. I want to go to my room and rest for a while." She could feel his eyes on her. This was always the case when he thought she couldn't see him. She no longer needed to see him, to feel his eyes burning into her, searching for the love she couldn't give.

"Good idea. You have exhausted yourself with all your silly games tonight." He helped her up and guided her to her room. "Take a long bath and sleep. This way you will be fresh tomorrow. We have much to do with a wedding to plan. It was splendid of you not to make that grasshopper hop! The trash collectors in Paris would have been busy tonight; picking up bits of bodies." His lip nearly curled but drooped in the end.

From the glow in his eyes, she feared he would laugh again, but he just turned away and walked across to his own room, his shoulders slightly rounded; perhaps he too was exhausted. Christine lay on her bed, too tired and shocked to cry. She rested her head on her pillow and closed her eyes. She fell into a dreamless sleep.

She awoke to the sound of his music, and sat at the edge of her bed, listening to the beauty of it. He was playing one of the songs he had taught her to sing. She had the odd feeling that she should be worried about something, someone, but at the moment she couldn't think of what it was. She gave a little shrug and walked out toward the music.

His long form was hunched over the piano. As always, he wore a finely tailored black suit, and yet his clothes always managed not to fit him. His long dark thinning hair was pushed straight back, away from his face, held neatly in place by a black ribbon. His mask, as always, was in place, covering from just above his eyebrows to his upper lip. Although his majestic eyes were hidden from her, she knew them well. It amazed her, the changes his eyes could make all within the space of a breath. They were the color of liquid amber hardening around a steel core.

Christine knew what lay under the mask. She didn't like to recall the day she had ripped the mask from his face to satisfy her curiosity. He had taken her to his home by the lake, five floors below the stage and played music for her. It was the first time she knew him to be a man and not just a voice. She had felt the same feelings of peace she felt now except for her curiosity. Her imagination led her to believe that because of his voice, he must look like the depictions she had seen of the Archangels⁻perfect men with huge luminescent wings. That was where her curiosity made her pull the mask from his face. The horror of his face paralyzed a cry in her throat. She shuddered at the memory. Erik nearly lost his mind because of her brazen act. He cried and besought, professed his devotion and cursed at her. Then he groveled, imploring her for the tiniest dole of affection. Her tender heart broke for him. It was in fear that her dear maestro would hurt himself, that she had acceded to remain with him in his home a while. After a fortnight, he returned her to the stage. That had been just a few weeks before he found out about her plan to run away and marry Raoul and kidnapped her. His wretched sobs were still etched in her heart. Yet, she never feared for her safety. Hungry for the melodious sound, she looked for a chair, to sit closer to the music

Chapter 3

Restrictions

"Are you awake?" he asked, shook her shoulder softly. "I have taken the vicomte upstairs," he told her, scrutinizing her face. She sat up in the bed, instantly alert to news about Raoul.

"Did anyone find him?" she asked, making sure to keep the concern out of her voice.

"Did you expect me to wait around?" He snorted.

She shook her head. Christine hoped he had left Raoul in an area where someone could find him and not up in the rafters or in a utility closet, but it was better not to ask.

"Come, your breakfast is ready," he said, his eyes watching her steadily.

"I'll be there in a moment." Sadness over losing

her chance to marry Raoul combined with hope for his safety. At this very moment, he might be resting in a comfortable bed, cared for by a doctor. How she wished she could be the one to find him, to care for him. She stopped her futile reverie and went to refresh herself in her bathroom. She went to her wardrobe, grabbed a dress and pulled it over her head, not bothering to notice the color or the material. She wore no corset, but the dress fit her perfectly. With a few strokes of her brush, and a twist, she pinned her hair up. She was ready for breakfast. She took her shawl; it was always chilly in the mornings under the opera house, even in his kitchen.

In the kitchen, Erik took out a chair for her and she sat at a small table. This would be the first time she had a meal outside her bedroom. During her previous stay, Erik had taken her meals to her room with a tray. He placed several dishes in front of her so that she might choose. Christine chose fresh peach, hot bread with butter, cherry jam and a thick slice of ham. She felt his eyes on her and began her meal. Before she was halfway through she noticed that not only was he not joining her, but that there was no place setting for him. "Erik? Are you not eating with me?"

"I want you to enjoy your breakfast," he said curtly. With that, he marched out of the kitchen. *Well, that is one way to get rid of him!* She suddenly felt ravenous, ate every morsel on her plate, and had a second peach before her thoughts returned to Raoul.

After breakfast, she sat on his divan in the main parlor, reading a book. Erik left his room and joined her. He was impeccably dressed, a pinstriped charcoal gray waistcoat breaking up his customary black.

"We must talk, Christine." He did not look at her, but kept his eyes averted. "By choosing the scorpion you chose to be my wife," he reminded her.

"I know." She stared sideways at his mask. The mask gave him a normal profile.

"What a noble sacrifice you have made, I hope he appreciates it," he said with a tight jaw.

"I said I would and I will keep my promise."

"You no longer have a choice!"

"You make it sound like a penance."

"Is it not for you?" he asked, an ugly twist to his mouth.

She got up and turned away from him, not wanting him to see how much of a sacrifice this was for her. She did not wish to hurt him needlessly, but her life was effectively coming to an end. The man she loved was lost to her and as her husband, Erik might not allow her to sing in public again, keeping her voice for his private enjoyment. If that was the case, she would have to obey and swallow that bitter pill too.

If only she could have shared a few more kisses with Raoul. A few ardent kisses from the man she loved was all she would have in her lifetime. Marrying Erik was a penance, but saving Raoul's life was worth all her losses. She blinked back tears.

"Christine?" Erik's voice was now softer. "I want you to be happy." He held her by the elbow and turned her to face him. "I know you accepted to be my wife just to save that boy's life...still...I don't want you to be miserable." He sought her eyes. "I...I won't force anything on you that you do not desire."

"What do you mean?" She wondered just what he expected from her. She had not thought he would want a real marriage. Cold fear crept along her spine. Would she have to see him without the mask?

He drew a deep sigh and, looking away from her, said, "I will accede to any restrictions you wish to apply to...our union."

"What do you expect from me, Erik? As your wife, I mean," she questioned him, worry stealing into her voice.

"I want us to share music, and books. I want to spend time with you, to take you out for rides. I want to do the same things any other husband would do with his wife." He glanced at her, his hands knotted at his sides.

She blushed even before she spoke. "You have not mentioned...intimacy."

"I do not want you to die!"

"Then it is not a goal for you?"

"You do not know me well yet, but you will...given time." With his gloved finger, he stroked her arm just above her wrist. "I just want you to be my wife, my companion."

"I do not want any form of intimacy…I can be your wife in every other way…but I do not want to…" she blurted out, feeling heat all over her face and averting her gaze from him.

Barely raising his head, he muttered, "I want a living wife, and I am but a corpse! You alone have seen the monster that I am. I would not expect you to…no, no never that!" He stood up and strode away from her to the fireplace. "How could I ever expect such a thing from you?"

"I hope I was not harsh. It is not my wish to hurt you, but I had to speak plainly."

His hand spread on the fireplace mantle, holding him in place as he shuddered. "How could you think that I would…expect…?" The skin along his jaw line flushed. "You say nothing. Do you fear that I would force you?" He gaped at her. "Against you will?" Savagely, he raked his fingers through his sparse hair.

"Erik, you must understand…the danger of having a child," she faltered. "It could have your…your…" He was shaking his head wildly before she finished. His shame was so palpable, that Christine found it difficult to continue.

"No, no, no, this hideousness," he faltered. "This abomination. It must end with me. There can never be a child." Again, looking away, he continued, "Though it shames me, I must inform you, that you need have no fear on that account. As I am incapacitated."

"What do you mean?"

"I...I cannot function as a man, in that sense. Your fears are futile." His jaw color deepened.

"Is it because of your face?"

"Sweet girl, can you not tell that it is not just my face?"

She gasped. "I...oh..."

He cut her off roughly. "We need not speak of this again as it is a moot point."

She was astounded by his disclosure, but quietly sighed in relief and took a seat. He would not steal into her bedroom to claim his marital rights. Hesitatingly, she asked, "Do *you* have any restrictions?"

"Just one...no, two...you are never to contact that boy again."

She breathed deeply. "Of course not. What is your other restriction?" she asked candidly.

He walked across the room and sat next to her, grasped her by the shoulders and made her face him. "No one is to know."

"That we are married?" she asked incredulously, looking up at him. He was close to her now, and she could smell that peculiar, unpleasant, Erik smell. She could not pinpoint just what it was, but she did not want to inhale deeply. It reminded her of bad things.

With his face only inches from her, he continued, "No one is to know about my affliction. Let them think we are man and wife...that you are fully my wife.

"Would I make *that* a topic for conversation? I

see no need to involve anyone else in our affairs." Christine managed to wiggle out from his grasp and walked away a few paces. Her heart broke for him. For a man to admit to that type of problem he must feel miserable.

Her freedom did not last. He patted the seat next to him and she walked back obediently and sat next to him.

He cleared his throat. "Does your restriction allow for...an occasional caress? I would wear my gloves of course. I only want...only so I may place my arm around you sometimes. Would you be agreeable to that? There would be no need for your hands to touch me. My own mother only did so a few times...unless I dreamt it." He shook his head as if to clear it of an unpleasant memory and looked to her again. "I seek some measure of...companionship from my wife. That would be part of it, yes. To hold you a little as I can do nothing more," he added reassuringly.

Christine noted his dejected posture, he was shrinking into himself and she could not reject him further. If this masked man with the cursed face, was to be her husband—though not through her free choice—she would spare him some kindness. "I could not in good conscience deny you companionship." She got up, leaned over and softly brushed her lips against his forehead, though it looked dry and withered, her lower lip hit the mask, dislodging it a little. She was surprised his skin felt ordinary under her lips. He did not say another word and remained unmoving where he was. She walked away to her room to be on her own.

She sat on her bed, going over the day's events, feeling as if the world were slowly crashing in on her.

She looked up and noticed he stood at her open door. He entered the room, looking more like himself, walking tall, menacing, and said, "Everything is agreed to, we will talk more this evening. You rest while I go out and make arrangements so we can hold the ceremony within a week." He turned away, leaving Christine to absorb the fact that her impending wedding to her Angel of Music, the Opéra Ghost, would take place in less than seven days. *One week and then I will be his forever.* At that moment, she promised Raoul that a secret corner of her heart, she would remain faithful to him. She took out the photograph she had hidden in her dresser and, holding it close to her, finally allowed the tears to come.

Chapter 4

The Wedding

"Does your restriction allow for…an occasional caress," he had asked, terrified of her answer, and then she had leaned over and placed her lips on his forehead, leaving a soft kiss that he could still feel. She had treated him as if he were an ordinary man and touched her lips to the yellowed shriveled skin on his forehead. *I should not have allowed it!* But the pleasure of it made him shiver.

He meant only to test her, to push at her resolve. Christine touched her lips to his skin and had not dropped dead at his feet. *How? His mother had said…* Erik felt perspiration bathe his body and his heartbeat quicken. His knees felt so weak he could not stand for a while. *A kiss.* Never before had he known this pleasure, this decadence‾his first and last. *A kiss.*

Now, he would beg for her crumbs every day of his life if he had to.

He was ecstatic and sad, and happier than he had ever been. He wished and wanted so many things at once that his head was a jumble. Erik also felt thoroughly exhausted. It was 11 o'clock in the morning; he still had to go through the rest of the day. A busy day was ahead, full of wedding preparations.

Somehow, after turning his back on him for so long, God was going to allow him to marry one of his angels. He chuckled, remembering that when he had first seen her, he had thought her looks mundane. Her looks were extraordinary, her figure perfection, her lips full, and her eyes half a dozen shades, with a baffling, delicious slant to them. Her hair was a golden honey blond with warm, earthy undertones. And her voice was made to serenade God himself. She did not love him, but that took nothing away from his ecstasy and since no one had ever loved him, he did not expect it

Erik ran through the tunnels until he was gasping and out of breath. He had left the opera house, heading toward the rue Scribe, and was let in by Darius, Hafiz's servant, who looking alarmed, called for his master. Erik paced the small living room in Hafiz's home.

"Stop it. You will wear out my carpets. And don't think I will not charge you," the Persian said.

Erik stopped in front of Hafiz. "Daroga, she kissed me!" he exploded. The Persian looked perplexed.

"Oh God, yes! She...she kissed my forehead. Here," He pointed to the spot she had kissed. The Persian looked horrified that something like that could happen. "Kissed me of her own free will. Her lips touched me. Here, here." He pointed at the spot again. Now do you see that she cares for me? Do you see that she is willing to marry me?"

The Persian quirked a scraggly eyebrow.

He had made a blunder! He knew it was not lost on the Persian that he had not said, "She *wants* to marry me."

"Her kindness is boundless...but you know, I hope you know that you cannot force...yourself on her."

"I was not meant to be with the living. She would die if I inflict myself on her." Life had just made a turn in his direction and he had to be less excited, more careful—everything was at stake. "A living wife. A companion for a short while, before I die."

The Persian sighed. "You are asking that girl to give up..."

He paced in front of the Persian. "A few months at most. We both know I am at the end...how long can my heart hold out. Constant pain grips my heart, threatening to shred it to bits. Even I, deserve a little joy before my wretched life comes to a close. The desolation alone is killing me."

"Who will want her then?"

"You have no idea what I brought out of Constantinople. She will be rich when I am dead. Plenty will want a rich widow."

"If I accede, Allah will call me on this," Hafiz said, more to himself than in answer.

"I call on you, my benefactor, and my judge, to grant me mercy! Every day I grow weaker. A month or two of happiness, that is all, then she can bury me and be free."

"Two months, you say?" Hafiz closed his eyes to Erik's nod. With a deep sigh, he asked, "What do you need of me?"

"I am putting this situation in your hands. You pay whom you have to, pay their asking price, offer a bonus if you need to, but I want to be married to her this very Saturday. I want it legal and binding. There is to be no question in her mind or anyone else's as to the legality and solemnity of the vows we are to take. She would want a priest. Go to a small, run-down parish, one that looks down on its luck—the one in Esbly for instance. Pay the priest there to come here. I want the ceremony performed in my home, and it must be registered in the parish records. Let him bend the rules. If not by heaven he will be compensated by me." He looked into the Persian's eyes and added with a sly smile, "Offer him enough that the priest is willing to pray *even* for me!"

"Erik!" Hafiz frowned.

"Oh Hafiz, you have lost your sense of humor."

He withdrew a bag of money from his cloak and handed it to the Persian. "Here, whet the holy man's appetite." He walked away, and in a barely audible whisper over his shoulder, he said, "He will come if he is hungry or greedy enough. Also, I want a discrete photographer. We will record the event."

"Here, you will need these." He put a packet of his and Christine's papers into the Persian's hands. Before taking her, he had taken the precaution of removing all of Christine's personal possessions from her room at the opera house. If she agreed to marry him, she would need all her papers as was the case now. Had she refused him, nothing would have mattered in their quarter of Paris.

Father Jules was early. Hafiz saw the old priest hurry down the street holding on to his wide-brimmed hat. He avoided a couple of carriages, and despite his *soutane* impeding him taking longer steps, he managed to cross as quickly as possible. Hafiz noted that even though he was plump, the priest was quick on his feet.

The day before, Erik had been insufferable, going over the minutest detail with him. "Are you sure the priest will come?" Erik had asked.

"With the amount of francs you are paying him, Father Jules could repair the old rectory and build a new chapel for his church. Trust me, he will come!" the Persian countered.

The photographer, a young man in a light-colored suit, was already sitting in the rented horse-drawn *omnibus* with a blindfold on, nervously clutching his equipment close to him. Once Father Jules was sitting, Hafiz began to blindfold him as well. Hafiz warned them both about the mask and advised them how to act around Erik.

The guests from the opera house were picked up next. Everyone was blindfolded with a hood. After half an hour of driving around the city, they returned to the opera house and entered through the rue Scribe entrance. The opera house rat-catcher, dressed in mended black garments, met Hafiz just inside the entrance. Once past the gates, they both led the blindfolded group through the tunnel entrance Hafiz preferred. Hafiz kept the guests' blindfolded until they were inside Erik's house. As the former daroga of Persia, his old profession was in his blood, and doubt in humanity's decency was always foremost in his mind.

Since the first time Erik took her down to his home, Christine had gotten used to his pampering. He had given her simple and expensive trinkets, dresses, fripperies, fine perfumes, and even her own bedroom in his house. Hafiz had taken her to see a modiste that used to work in the House of Worth, to have a wedding gown made. The Persian demanded that the woman stop work on everything else and create the dress of Christine's choice. After much cajoling, he ended up paying the woman an indecent amount for her services and getting exactly what he wanted, that is to say, what Erik wanted. When they went to the jeweler's, M. Franz, it was a repeat of the same situation. M. Franz was convinced and acceded to make the rings in the style of Erik's choice, in four days.

Early in the day, Erik brought down from the opera house apartments, her best friend Meg Giry with her mother Mme. Giry, to help Christine get ready. The older woman had been Erik's personal concierge for years, whenever he used Box five at the opera house. He blindfolded them, then rowed them across the lake with their own dresses and fripperies in bags. She and Meg had been friends since she arrived at the Opéra. Meg pinned her hair up into a new style from the pages of La Belle Assemblée. Small ringlets graced her forehead. Mme. Giry applied makeup that looked natural and gave her a glow. The older woman used just a hint of rouge accentuating Christine's high cheekbones and lips.

Meg helped her into wedding dress. The dress was ivory silk on the bodice and the skirt was made of cream satin. It had a dropped lace neckline with a fitted bodice that was encrusted with lavender pearls. The back of the skirt was gathered in pleats and topped with a bow. The baleen stays showed her curves to perfection. The back closed with tiny opaque glass buttons in lavender. She was sure that her dress rivaled the one worn by the Empress Eugénie.

She dabbed perfume on her wrists and behind each ear. Her jewelry was already in place: pearl drop earrings and a pearl necklace accented by a diamond pendant—gifts from Erik. Meg and Mme. Giry left to ready themselves in the adjacent small parlor. With a hard swallow, she was ready to fulfill her part of the bargain. Christine allowed herself one last look at Raoul's picture before she took her vows. Once she put it away, she blocked out all her thoughts and feelings and walked out of her bedroom.

As Christine stepped into the parlor, she saw the arrays of flowers in vases, white bows and other decorations. The fireplace and doorways were festooned with flowers and long swaying ribbons. The room was beautiful and it was obvious he had gone through a great deal of bother. Among the guests, she saw several of the opera house workers standing around. She knew them as she knew many people at the opera house, but they were no particular friends of hers. Christine wondered why they were at her wedding; she knew Erik was a loner, and she did not know him to be friends with anyone. There was, as far as she could guess, only one explanation; these people were an additional guarantee against her changing her mind. They were easily disposable, and their lives depended on her saying, "I will" during the ceremony. She continued to look around her and noticed another group of men dressed formally, standing together in a corner. None of them seemed familiar. She was surprised, but assumed they were acquainted with Erik.

Looking around to the other side of the room, Mme. Giry sat with Meg and Little Jammes, another of Christine's friends. She guessed that Erik had probably purchased Mme. Giry's dress. It was a black natural form dress with a sprite of dark gray silk roses falling, from waist to hem. With her hair in curls piled at the top of her head, and the fabulous dress, the woman did not look like the opera house concierge; she *almost* looked refined. Meg stood next to her mother talking to Little Jammes, also a friend of Christine's. Both girls were from the Paris Opéra corps du ballet. They wore very fashionable gowns for the wedding. Meg had confided that her new suitor, the Comte Éduard du Veille sur Meux, had bought her the gown after her last performance. Christine had yet to meet the young comte who had recently come into his title.

Mamma Valérius was not there on her wedding day—it was best. Mamma Valérius' failing health had recently provoked a move from Paris back to the seaside at Perros-Guirec. There had not been enough time to bring her to Paris comfortably. Although she was not related by blood to the old woman, Christine was devoted to her and could not have loved her more. Mamma and her husband Professor Valérius, had taken her and father in when she was a child and after leaving Uppsala, wondering from fair to fair playing music. The childless couple had become family to them. When her father died, she had stayed on with Mamma Valérius, who was by then a widow. They were close and the old woman would have noticed her misery.

Christine's thoughts trailed when she noticed a man that she did not recognize. He stood in the dense shadows, close to Erik's group of friends. He neared Erik's height, but was much broader and dressed all in black like Erik liked to do. A young photographer stood behind a camera, adjusting it, he wore wire rimmed glasses so thick they made his eyes seem like peanuts. He gave her a shy smile.

Near Hafiz stood a rotund, older man wearing a brown priest's *soutane* with a white stole around his neck—a Carmelite perhaps. On the right of Hafiz stood Erik. He was standing with his back to her, his hair cut short and worn combed back, the straps from his mask visible from behind. She gasped, and her heart skipped with the realization that this was it— she was about to marry Erik.

As she approached him, she noticed that today, he wore a dark gray suit—not black. He wore a black mask. He did not turn around to look at her, and she felt disappointed by his lack of interest. When she walked up to him and stood by his side, she noticed he wore a lavender silk-brocade waistcoat. The mask he wore was not his usual one, it was decorated with a filigree scroll design in silver. He barely glanced at her and made unintelligible grunts when required to speak during the ceremony. For the first time,

Christine felt he might not love her as much as he claimed. Wouldn't he want to look at his bride? When they exchanged rings, his was a plain gold band, much like the one he had given her as her Maestro. Her ring was a delicate gold filigree band.

She noted that his hands shook and he had trouble putting the gold band on her finger. When their eyes met, she saw both dread and love reflected in his amber eyes. He closed his eyes tightly and seemed to rock when it was her turn to answer the priest, his lips drawn into a taut, thin line, his breathing ragged. She did not wish to make him suffer, so she gave her answers clearly when the priest asked her. He gasped at her answer. During the ceremony, she found out that his legal name was Emmerich Ménard. She had never thought of him as anything other than Erik.

Erik wanted to see her as she walked toward him, but could not make his body swivel. Already, he felt faint and was sure he would have lost his composure had he seen her walking to him in a wedding dress. They stood side by side in front of the priest. His state of nerves was such that Erik heard the ceremony more than participated in it. He stammered and mumbled his answers when nudged by Hafiz. He was so intent on maintaining control that he was unable to concentrate at all. He kept his legs taut, knees locked, so they would not collapse.

His thoughts carried him away in a mixture of haunting memories, his grip on reality suspended during the moments the ceremony lasted. At last, he heard Father Jules say, "*Ego conjungo vos in matrimonium in nomine Patris et Filii et Spiritus Sancti. Amen.*" He, Erik, the opera ghost, "*le mort vivant,*" assassin, architect, ventriloquist, illusionist, master of trap doors, pirate, and mason—was a husband and had a wife just like any ordinary man.

The couple received blessings, compliments and congratulations from those present. Several toasts followed, and slowly he returned to the world. He swallowed with difficulty, but was able to participate by nodding. Christine was his wife! It had happened with no deaths. It struck him fully that he had a living wife, for whom he was now responsible. The reality of his marriage exploded onto his mind. He exhaled loudly, and luckily he was near a chair and was able to let his legs go, and collapsed onto the chair. His heavy head slowly fell back onto the head rest.

Someone shoved another glass of champagne in his hand and he gulped it down. He looked around and noticed the guests. People! There were people in his home! He began to panic and reached for his lasso, then realized that they were the very guests he had asked Hafiz to bribe to come. His hand reached out for another glass. People, moving and talking surrounded him he would need more than just champagne to get through this.

She had assumed this would be a miserable day for her, but oddly, she found herself enjoying her wedding. Meg had cornered her, and like old times they had a chance to gossip about the other guests. Her friend asked her if she was ready for her wedding night. Christine felt her face become impossibly hot and Meg giggled. Christine changed to another topic of conversation.

His eyes followed her. He did not always make eye contact with her, but a tiny curl of his lip told her that he was pleased to have located her. Although it had annoyed her to no end at first, this odd habit of his did not bother her anymore.

She approached him and asked who his friends, still standing on their own were, but he shrugged his shoulders. "Just people I know," was all he volunteered, with an amused glow to his eyes. "What are their names, Erik? I will need to welcome them."

"You have no obligation to those people, Christine."

"Are they related? They look very much alike," she insisted.

"They are musicians at the Opéra Comique that is all. Do not concern yourself." he said curtly, sounding annoyed.

"Still…"

"They are inconsequential!" he said in a low fierce tone that left no doubt that the conversation was over.

Christine let the matter drop, not wanting his temper to get the better of him on their wedding day.

He cleared his throat. "Would you like to eat something?" he asked softly.

"Yes, I would," she smiled up at him.

Placing a possessive hand on the small of her back, he led her to a long table with the wedding cake, meats, cheeses, and breads. A variety of wines and cider was available at an adjacent table.

The wedding cake, a croquembouche, was a fine confection of profiteroles, three feet in height, coated with a caramelized-sugar covering. This wonderment was finished with pulled-sugar flowers in ivory and lavender. Erik pulled one off and fed her one of the puff pastries filled with chocolate-rum crème. Christine had never tasted such a delectable sweet. It was crunchy on the outside, and when her teeth broke through the outer crust, the chocolate-rum crème spilled over her tongue. Her eyes closed in delight, and watching her, his lips curled into a smile. She reciprocated by also offering him one of the small pastries. His eyes filled with tears, and blinking hard he turned away. Too late, she remembered his reluctance to eat in front of others. He served her dry champagne to offset the sweetness of the profiteroles and sipped from his own cup. When they put their glasses down, he air-kissed the back of her hand before she continued to sample the tempting spread.

Their guests also seemed to enjoy themselves, and the food and wedding cake slowly disappeared. The wine and champagne flowed, and the dancing started spontaneously when René, one of the opera house workers, took out a harmonica and played a folk song. At first Erik stayed away from everyone, but after a while he brought out his own instrument and accompanied René on the violin. At one point in the merriment, Pietro pushed her and Erik together to dance. It was an awkward moment; he stiffened as his hand first touched hers. His smell was overpowering, so close to her and she turned her head a little to lessen the pungent odor. She felt his arm encircling her waist, pulling her close to him and realized he was stronger than he appeared to be. They fumbled their first steps, but as the dance progressed, they fell into a rhythm.

Christine was amazed that Erik knew how to dance. She had always imagined him as a recluse devoid of all of the social graces. She recalled her dance at the masquerade ball with Raoul, his grace and flair evident while they danced—she pushed the thought away. Some of the other guests joined them or clapped to the music. Erik's friends stayed away from the dancers, remaining in a group of their own. She noticed that man dressed in all in black stood by them, but did not speak with them. She did not see them eat or drink and hoped they were enjoying themselves, but did not speak to Erik about it again. Christine and Erik danced for a while until she was out of breath, and then he sat her down and got her a glass of champagne.

The photographer made both of them stand in several positions. In one photograph, they stood next to each other, her head barely reaching his shoulder. In the next one, he sat as she stood just to his left, her hand on his shoulder. As their witnesses, Hafiz and Mme. Giry stood with them for still another photograph. Erik insisted on several solo pictures of Christine, with and without her bouquet. Christine insisted on a few more pictures of the two of them. Erik complained as she had assumed he would, but he stood or sat at her side as she asked. The last photograph was of the entire group—bride, groom, and their guests. For this photograph, only Erik's strange friends did not join them. The room began to be filled with smoke from the flash.

After all the photographs were taken, she took a seat and rested her feet for a while. A very pretty girl she wasn't familiar with, but had seen around upstairs, came up to Christine and complimented her on her wedding dress. She introduced herself as Mariele, a cleaner from the first and second cellar.

The two girls talked about the people dancing for a while, and then in a very confidential tone Mariele whispered in Christine's ear, "They that talk say y0ur new husband's got mo' money than a pig's got dirt. He got this house, by the Seine no less. I ain't no fool I, can hear water lapping on the river bank."

"I don't really know what he has or does not," Christine answered stiffly.

"He gave you that, din't he?" Mariele asked,

touching the pearl and diamond necklace Erik had given her. Christine pulled away from the girl's touch.

"This is a wedding gift," she said, annoyed, and placed her hand protectively over the necklace.

"That ain't no regular wedding gift. You'll pay the price for that big fancy rock on your back. Tonight, just close your eyes and spread…"

"Excuse me!" Christine interrupted her. *How dare she sit here, eat his food, drink his drink, and have the nerve to insult him? The gall of her!* She glared at the girl and strolled away from her.

"You a working girl just like me. No cleaner, but you ain't all posh, he'll get you on your back tonight. You'll see." Mariele spat behind her.

Erik was talking to Hafiz, but his gaze darted to her, concern creeping into his eyes. She did not want him to know about this incident, so she gave him a big smile and joined him, putting her arm through his. His eyes stole to Mariele across the room, then back to her.

Christine made the sign for tipsy and whispered, "Too much champagne."

When he was engaged in conversation again, she shot back a dark warning look at Mariele, who looked away. It took a while for the indignation to leave her. She kept looking around the room to see if anyone else was giving Erik strange looks. For the moment, her resentment toward him abated. It felt odd to have protective feelings toward a man who had kidnapped her, nearly killed Raoul, and forced her to marry him.

As soon as Christine let go of Erik's arm, Meg approached her. "What was that with Mariele?"

"That stupid girl had the nerve to say some horrible things about Erik." She felt the anger welling up in her again.

"You'll have to expect that, Christine…he is a very unusual man."

"I could see a stranger being obnoxious on the street, but she is a guest in his home. He invited her to our wedding!" Christine wailed.

"She only knows the gossip about him. Even I was surprised by your wedding to Erik. You never gave me a hint that you were involved with him. I thought…I thought your interest lay…elsewhere," Meg remarked.

"I am only defending someone who cannot defend himself!" she cried in exasperation. Christine stormed off, leaving Meg gaping after her, and rejoined Erik. He held her hand, and she drew up a little closer, seeking his touch.

Meg was smiling slyly at her from across the room. *How annoying friends can be!*

After a while Little Jammes joined Christine and, despite her previous upset with Meg, the three girls went on to gossip about everyone else in the room.

Erik asked her for another dance. This time there was no awkwardness and they danced several times until she whispered in his ear that she was tired. He stopped abruptly. "I have been selfish and thought only of my own pleasure. These people no longer signify, they need to leave so you can have your rest."

"Please Erik, don't be rude to them," she begged.

He sauntered away and snatched the harmonica from René's hands. "Stop what you are doing. You are leaving right now," he bellowed. She cringed and felt heat invade her cheeks. Hafiz immediately took up the blindfolds. The man in black helped Hafiz lead the guests out. Before she left, Meg made her promise to visit her soon as she was rushed from the room with the others. Strangely, Erik's friends were already gone.

Erik joined Christine on the divan and rested his head on the back "I hadn't ever danced with a partner before tonight," he said to her.

"I would have never known."

"We dance well together," he said hesitantly.

"I hope we do it again soon. I love to dance."

"Your little husband will keep that in mind." He smiled.

Neither said anything for a while. It was not a comfortable silence.

"I…I have…something to give you." Erik reached into his pocket and pulled out a small brown bottle.

"What is that, Erik?"

"From what I have read and seen, the only relationships that thrive are those between equals. Right now, I hold the upper hand in our relationship…that is why I was able to force you into this marriage." He saw Christine was about to speak, and he put up his hand. "You married me to save the boy. But, you did marry me. It is up to me to reestablish the balance between us. Here!" He handed her a small plain brown bottle.

"What is it, Erik?" She turned the bottle over in her hand, but it had no label or other marking.

"It is a poison. I made it during my time in Persia. It is fast acting, tasteless, and odorless." He paced in front of her. "Unfortunately, it *is* painful." He chuckled.

She looked at the bottle in her hand with horror, as if the poison could escape. Death!

"You now have the power to kill me, if I should grow mad and become insufferable…or a danger to you." He stared deeply into her eyes.

Hand outstretched with the bottle in her palm, she tried to hand it back to him. "Here, here…take your bottle of death…I will not be a party to your games. You should give me flowers and bon-bons on our wedding day not poison! Only you would think to play this game."

"It is not a game, Christine. And, I will remember about the flowers! Hide it where only you will know where it is."

"I don't want this at all, Erik. Please take it back!"

"A prosperous marriage needs two equal partners." His eyes grew dark behind the mask.

"Do you expect me to use it, Erik?"

"Good God…I should hope not. As I said, it is a very painful death. But…I…I want you to have some power over me."

"It is not fair to give me a weapon I could never use."

"Trust me, dear, if I hurt you enough, you will use it. When the boy was in my chamber, you would have happily used it to save his life."

"Not happily, Erik."

He leaned toward her. "I know, but you would have used it all the same."

He had lain on his coffin bed—such a bed as only he had—for hours, dressed in his wedding clothes; it felt more uncomfortable than ever. He had purchased it hoping to get used to the coffin, before he was finally laid to rest in it.

He was married, for goodness sake, so why did he feel lonelier than before? He had a wife, but he had no right to make her his. *I may not be able to have her as a husband, but she agreed that she would not deny me companionship.*

Erik jumped out of the coffin and made his way to her room. He knocked on her door.

"Erik?" She opened the door.

"I have been thinking; I believe that having your company falls well within the parameters of your restrictions and my request."

She looked confused and frightened. "What do you mean?"

"I am seeking companionship," he blurted. His lips compressed into a thin line.

The blood drained from her face. "But…but now?" She held her dressing gown closed with double fists and took a tiny step away from the door.

"Yes, it is our wedding night and I need it now. I will return in a few moments when you have made yourself comfortable."

A few moments later he returned wearing a salwar kameez, a thin sleep-shirt, and dark, loose trousers, covered by a robe. He carried a blanket with him.

The stricken, angry look on her face told him that she had misunderstood his intention.

Erik walked into the room, lay down on the rug by the side of her bed and stretched out. His feet stuck out of the rug.

"What are you doing?" she asked.

"Getting ready to sleep."

"There?"

"Yes."

"And that is all you want?" she choked out.

"That is all I can have," he quietly affirmed. "I did inform you about my condition. Surely we do not need to enter into that conversation again."

"Yes, I remember." A flush crept across her cheeks. "I…well…good night." She tucked under her sheets.

After a while she said, "That floor must be very uncomfortable." She looked over to where he lay.

"It is your company I seek, not comfort," he told her pulling the blanket over his shoulders. "I have spent the last thirty years of my life in relative comfort but alone. I hope to end that now."

"Take one of my pillows, I have too many." She tossed him a fluffy pillow from her bed.

"If it is your wish to part with one and it will not discomfort you…I thank you." He took the pillow and tucked it under his head.

"Good night, Erik," said Christine. She got into bed, still wearing her dressing gown.

Had he come in with another intention, he doubted if he could have gotten through the dressing gown with all the flounces, frothy lace and ribbons. It looked like an over frosted cake and was, in fact, more ornate than her wedding gown. He averted his eyes from the offensive garment. It was a gift she had received from Mme. Giry. If he ever got a chance to be rid of it, he would take it.

He watched her wriggle and try to get comfortable without taking her eyes off him. "Good night, Christine," he sighed. He checked the mask covering his face, faced away from her to reassure her of his peaceful intromission, and closed his eyes, his wife was allowing him to sleep only a few feet away from her. He would sleep on the rug by her side, like her faithful watchful dog, and guard over her. Never had he known more bliss.

Chapter 5

Honeymoon Cakes

Every day, Erik needed to keep the mask on while he slept in Christine's room. He also needed to keep the mask on while she was awake. From experience, he knew that if he kept the mask on for too long it would irritate his thin, sensitive skin, bringing all sorts of annoying ailments with it. Since the wedding a week before, he had kept his usual mask on all day and all night, and was beginning to feel the irritation. That morning, his skin felt warm, and in some areas a fine rash was beginning to develop. He could feel welts forming around the edges of the mask. If he kept it on tonight, his eyes would swell, making the deformity visible through the eyeholes.

He waited until she was asleep, and in the

darkness removed it freeing his face from its prison. The fresh air felt wonderful against his ravaged flesh. He placed the mask carefully over his chest, his hand, ready to place it back on if Christine should awake from her slumber. Even in the dark room he felt vulnerable.

His masks were made by the finest leather craftsman in Paris. Cost was never an issue when it came to the quality of craftsmanship he demanded. They were made of rose-tanned leather, so fine that it adhered perfectly to his unique facial contours. The leather in the mask was made of varying thicknesses and firmness. The area of the forehead, eyeholes and cheeks were the thinnest and most pliant, while the leather forming the simulated nose was thick and hard. He secured it with straps that buckled behind his head.

The mask had been his shield against people's cruelty. As much as he could not say he loved the mask, it was the one constant in his life, his steadfast companion. It had hidden his greatest shame, his face. As unbelievable as it was to him, he was now married to a beautiful woman. Erik had kidnapped Christine not just because she was about to run away with the Vicomte de Chagny, but because he could not face another day alone. He had been willing to blow up half of Paris to end his pain, fully expecting her to refuse him—to prefer death to being his wife. What time he had left on this earth he would spend by her side. Carefully, he returned the mask to his face before he fell asleep.

Three weeks had passed since their wedding, and they settled into a comfortable routine. In the mornings, he made her breakfast, which she ate alone. Afterwards, he began preparations for the midday meal which again she ate alone while he disappeared into the music room. She sewed during the time that he left her alone. She checked her wardrobe and made the necessary repairs on her garments. She even convinced Erik to give her some of his clothes for darning. He had, what was to her, the deplorable habit of discarding his damaged clothes and replacing them with new ones. Christine had always hated darning with Mamma Valérius when she was a girl, but now she welcomed anything that would keep her busy and keep thoughts of her past aspirations at bay. When all that could be darned was sewn, she found herself with an empty gap in the afternoon.

Needing to occupy herself, Christine came up with the idea of making her own *Salon du Thé*. She took it upon herself to bake and serve patisseries in the afternoon. All the pastries were made tiny so that he would have no problem eating with his mask on. In the afternoon, they met in the library and had a small meal. Christine began by pouring each of them a steaming cup of fragrant tea, usually jasmine or mint. She would then dish out her freshly made patisserie-fruit tarts, diminutive canelé, a variety of cookies, or petit fours. Usually they had two tea infusions, but at times she would vary their drink and serve hot chocolate or coffee. Erik drank and ate what she provided with an equal appetite.

His favorite teatime tidbit was her tiny molasses cookies. She could not make them often enough. He even took to raiding her cookie tin, looking for the tasty morsels at other times of the day. Before Christine began her *Salon,* she had no idea when he ate and it seemed to her that he could go for days without eating. She never saw any scraps or any indication that he had, in fact, eaten a meal. Now, his stomach would actually growl as he ate if the meal were even slightly late. "All these ghastly noises are due to your tardiness today," he would say. Erik would stand looking impatient, just outside his door, waiting for her to call him. Then he would cross the parlor, past her bedroom and rush into the library.

He had asked for her company as part of the marriage agreement, but she couldn't accuse him of being obsessive about keeping *her* company—as a matter of fact, she rarely saw him except at the appointed times. She found that he quite often stood by the edge of the lake and sang his most beautiful songs as if he were singing to an audience. Once, she even spied him taking a deep formal bow.

Christine was used to constant contact with other people. She was accustomed to the continual sharing and camaraderie of the Opéra performers. Christine was beginning to feel lonely. She missed her long talks with Meg, Little Jammes, some of the other ballerinas and the chorus girls. Since she had come to the opera house, Meg had befriended her and had become her confidante. The chorus girl and the ballet-rat found they had many things in common, principally their love of opera, performance, and a penchant for keeping company with some of the most notable gentlemen who frequented the opera house.

Erik's gruff tone and manner still frightened her at times, but she was getting used to his ways. She reverted to thinking of him as her benefactor, her Angel of Music as she had when she first heard his voice. Most importantly, he kept his promise and never demanded more from her than her company. Yet, she could not help that her thoughts often turned to Raoul. She wished that there was some way for her to see Raoul again, to know he was well and had recovered. He must be just as worried for her. If only she could send word to him. She did not intend to betray Erik, but her mind constantly rummaged through myriad possibilities for a brief contact with Raoul.

The evenings were spent together in the library reading and sharing music. Every day, she left herself time before going to bed—usually with Erik lying on his rug nearby—to write in her journal. Her life was not as eventful as it had been before she married Erik, and now she filled the pages with her thoughts and feelings rather than events. She also recorded any new recipes she came up with for a patisserie. It was a period of peace during which no ground was lost or gained during the marriage.

After her monumental sacrifice, to save Raoul's life, Christine felt she deserved a smidgeon of normalcy in her life. She appreciated that Erik was kind and civil, but she was not in love with him and never could be. Christine missed seeing the sun shine, feeling it's warmth soak into her, she missed Mamma Valérius, she missed her friend Meg, and most of all she missed Raoul. She wanted to be surrounded once in a while by people *she* loved.

As she sat in the library on a stool by Erik, Christine could not stop thinking of Raoul. If he was well, he might be combing the opera house halls looking for her. She pondered over what to say to Erik so that he would let her go above, while at the same time despising herself for her duplicitous thoughts.

Dear sweet Raoul, he had been so willing to challenge his brother for his right to marry her. Their encounters had been brief, but each one had drawn their hearts closer. His fervent kisses and lingering touches left an unforgettable mark in her. All she had left of that love was a picture of Raoul accidentally tangled in her clothing when Erik brought her things down. The picture showed Raoul dressed in a naval uniform, the ship he served on was on the background. He had told her that he had been thinking of her when the picture was taken.

"Erik. I miss Mamma Valérius terribly, and I really should be checking on her."

"You know I have taken care of that. I have sent a nurse to live with her. She is well cared for." He got up to serve himself a glass of wine.

"It is not the same, Erik. She must miss me."

"We will see about a visit sometime."

"Thank you. May I visit with my friend, Meg, today?"

He sat back at once, regarding her through narrowed eyes.

"Now, we are getting to what you really want, my dear wife. You want to go up to see him, don't you?" he growled.

Erik looked at her with a hard smile pasted on his lips. "Shame on you. Using Little Giry to cover your longings for the vicomte. How terribly you must miss that lout!"

"I really want to see Meg," she pleaded, not looking at him, afraid he could read her thoughts.

"My little Lyrebird, how the tedium of our daily life must drag on you," he said, his voice, overly sweet with sarcasm. His fists clenched tightly on the chair arms.

"Erik, please. Why do you have to keep me locked away down here?" Christine wanted to move away from him, but she knew that would feed his rage.

He walked over to her chair and loomed over her. "You are my wife. Mine! You have no business running around an opera house!" he yelled.

The same opera house you took me from! Her own temper was beginning to flare. "Yes, I am your wife, but I have a right to see the light, to visit my friend!"

"The only one you should need to see is me...me...me...your husband!" he ranted. Abruptly, he dropped to his knees in front of her, holding fast to her skirts. His voice barely above a whisper, he groaned, "I want your happiness above all, but I need your love."

"I...I am doing my best," she responded.

"Is it my face that makes...you...you...withhold your...love?"

She had to look away. She could hear the agony, the need in his voice, and it tugged at her heart. "I need time."

"Time? Is that all? And then you will love me? I will give you time...but swear you will love me then, Christine, swear it!" He buried his face in her skirts and began to sob. They were quiet, discreet little sobs, as if she were not supposed to hear them. He was agitated and very close to her, his odor wafted to her. For some reason, it reminded her of death. She had to avert her face.

"Promise me you will remember your vows."

"I will not forget my vows!" she said with all the sincerity she could muster. It broke her heart to see him suffer that way.

"Taken before a priest," he reminded her, his voice muffled in her skirts. Not budging from his knees, a low wail escaped him.

"I remember...Erik. But, when am I to be allowed up? I want to see the sunlight," she insisted.

In a flash, he was on his feet and towering over her, his eyes wide and blazing. "Not the boy, not the light!" he shouted, closing in on her.

He pointed to his mask. "This…this is what your future holds. Only this!"

She gasped at his words and ran away clutching at herself.

In a pained, cold voice, he called after her, "You will have to bury me before you see the surface light again!"

Christine ran into her room, slamming the door. It was not her fault he was deformed and unloved. She was trying her best to keep her word and be a good companion. And he had no right to keep her from the world just because she could not love him. To think of a lifetime living with him five floors below the Opéra, was inconceivable. *If he dies, I will leave him where he falls and run away as fast as I can.* Her eyes stole to the little bottle on her dresser, but she looked away quickly as she was wracked with sobs. She took Raoul's photograph from her drawer and lying on the bed, she wrapped herself into a ball holding Raoul close to her.

All night, Erik pounded on the piano keys, punishing the piano in the music room. He played hard, in violent bursts, repeating the same pieces over and over again. Not one song escaped his lips. She heard him play out his anguish and misery on the piano. She heard him beseeching her through his music, and she refused to come out and soothe his pain, thinking only of her anger, of his claim on her, and her loss of liberty and love. If she was never to leave the cellars, then she would not offer him her compassion. On and on he played; and then, a few minutes past midnight, she heard a discordant chord and the music suddenly stopped. She came out of her room and made her way to the music room. He was gone. All she had to have done was to sit on the bench with him. It would have eased his pain and everything would have been fine.

Christine knocked on his door. When no answer came, she pushed the door open. The room was dark except for the flicker of one almost-extinguished candle. Christine wasn't sure what she would do if he were lying in his coffin-bed. Still, she slipped into the semi-darkness. On one of the walls hung leather straps in various sizes. She dreaded to think what they had been used for. The coffin lay open in the middle and drew a little gasp from her. She spied Erik sitting hunched over on a chair on the far side of the room, rocking himself.

"Get out!" he shouted. "Leave me be. Go back to your room, go dream of getting away from me."

"No, Erik, I will not go away."

"I hope you enjoyed my *Don Juan Triumphant*."

"Is that what you were playing?"

"Did you not feel his pain? Did it not burn you?" he asked.

"Come with me…please," she insisted as gently as she could.

"I must find…my mask first," he moaned, splaying his fingers against his face and looking around. Reluctantly, she picked up the mask off the floor by the coffin, and handed it to him. After he placed it on his face, she buckled it for him.

She extended her hand and asked, "Keep me company?" making it sound more like a statement than a question. Erik took her hand and followed her to her bedroom. He curled up on his rug and immediately fell asleep. She tucked a pillow under his head and covered him with his blanket. For a while she watched him sleep, wondering if he should wear a mask to sleep. Was it uncomfortable or irritating? As she fell asleep, she remembered his face and she shivered, grateful he was wearing the mask.

His shirt sleeves were still rolled up from cooking breakfast. He cleared his throat and without looking directly at her asked, "Christine?" His voice sounded hesitant.

"Yes?" she asked between bites of toast.

"If you'd like, I'll take you to see Little Giry today." He cleared his throat.

"I'd like that." Her heart skipped a beat, but she managed to put another piece of toast in her mouth and chewed slowly.

"Would you be agreeable to us having our tea first?"

"Of course we will have our tea first. I can make an extra dozen of the molasses cookies and take it to Mme. Giry and Meg."

His lips compressed unpleasantly. *What now? Am I supposed to make those only for him? Keep the peace, Christine.* "Actually, I prefer to make those cookies only for you, so I'll make them a canelé or the petit fours? What do you think?"

"It would be best to keep your particular recipes at home," he said with a tilt of the head. "Do not take them the canelé or the petit fours. Those are for home. They may taste leftovers from yesterday's tarte."

The mask did not cover his smile and his eyes sparkled in the eyeholes. *He can be so obvious!* She sighed softly.

During the afternoon tea, they sat quietly eating and drinking their beverages. Christine brought the teacup to her lips and took a sip of the linden leaves infusion. She took a bite of a tiny glazed pear tart; a smile graced her lips as she recalled their conversation during breakfast that morning. She reached up and offered him the rest of her tart, a sliver that she slipped between his surprised lips. Erik got up, kissed the air above her forehead, and took the last two molasses cookies from the tin with him. *My poor Erik!*

Chapter 6

Visits, Visits, Visits

"Are you awake?" Philippe asked as he entered Raoul's darkened room, only to see his brother with the sheets up to his chin.

"Oh, it's you, come in!" Raoul relaxed. "I thought it was that..." He stopped to catch his breath. "...that nurse you sent me." Talking still fatigued him. He closed his eyes and took a few slow breaths.

"A beautiful woman is taking care of you, and you complain! Only you, little brother," Philippe laughed. The confident, masculine sound filled the room. He was impeccably dressed as always. Comte Philippe de Chagny was a handsome man in his mid-forties, with exacting tastes and a lifetime of having those tastes satisfied. His genuine concern for his brother was evident in his eyes. He touched Raoul's brow. "Good, you are still cool. Your fever had me worried."

"Did you see her tonight?" Raoul looked to his brother, his eyes beseeching him for a positive answer.

"She did not sing tonight and she left no notice of her whereabouts." Philippe had made discreet inquiries about the chorus girl his younger brother was infatuated with. He had come up with rumors, but no clear answers. The girl had vanished. Some people claimed to have seen her give herself in marriage to the Phantom. Others had seen her enter an unknown carriage. There were those who swore they had seen her body hanging lifeless from the rafters. He did not tell his brother any of the rumors. It was best that he regain his health first.

"Have you questioned…" Again Raoul ran out of breath and had to wait for his weakened lungs to take in air again. "…her friend Meg?"

"Meg, the ballet rat? No, but I will look for her this week." Philippe got up to leave. He smiled at Raoul with a tranquil look on his face, hiding his worry. "This week, I promise," he said facing Raoul. "Now, calm down and get better." Frowning, Philippe patted his brother's shoulder and left the room. *Damn Christine Daaé!*

To think it was he who first took his brother to the Opéra and who had proudly thought the young man a *rogue* when he first began his flirtation with the singer. Thanks to Raoul's infatuation with the singer, he had almost lost his life to that madman running loose at the Opéra. Whoever he was, he'd like to wring his neck and make a true phantom out of him. If she truly had disappeared, good riddance to her. His lover, the prima ballerina, Sorelli, had overheard Christine and Raoul making plans to leave the city and get married; she had informed him immediately. Perhaps Christine Daaé was in a better place than where he would have sent her to keep her away from Raoul. If somehow, she was indeed married to the ghost, it was just what that girl deserved for all the trouble she was causing. He hoped Raoul never set eyes on her again.

Erik helped her onto the boat anchored by their front door. After he sat her down, he picked up the oars and pushed off, rowing her across the artificial underground lake. The oar disturbed the water and a strange, mossy odor arose. It was not entirely unpleasant, but she was glad that it did not permeate their home. Erik had linked the gas lines from the opera house to many small lamps on the rock so that the underground cellars were lit in a perverse mimicry of the sun from dawn to dusk. The flames licked at the walls in a slow sensual dance. After a few minutes of moving away from the house, she could not tell Erik's house was there at all—the door cleverly hidden in the rock face and the shifting mirage caused by the flickering lamps. After tying the boat at the other side of the lake, they made their way up through the tunnels, then up the stairs, finally arriving at the living quarters of the opera personnel. Christine took the covered basket Erik offered her as they approached Mme. Giry's apartment. She felt him almost caress her cheek with his gloved hand. Christine turned to ask him how much time she had to spend with Meg, but he had disappeared into the shadows. All she could hear was an eerie rustle coming from his cloak and a lingering odor. She stared into the dark, empty hall, hoping to see some proof of his existence. There was no reason to feel abandoned, but she did. Quickly, she knocked on the door.

Meg hugged Christine and let her in. It felt wonderful to be back in the Giry apartment. In Meg's bedroom the two girls sat on the edge of the bed. Over the past two years they had shared many cozy talks in that room. The sunlight shining on the faded wallpaper was a comfort to Christine.

"I am so happy to be here, Meg. I have missed you," Christine confessed, looking, around the room. She grinned at her friend. Everything was so familiar, the overstuffed open cupboard, the worn pink damask bedcover, even Meg's messy dresser with all its jars. The two girls sat on the bed facing each other, holding hands. They both felt a little shy. The balance in their friendship had changed; Christine was now a married woman, while Meg continued to be a ballet rat.

"Was it hard convincing him to let you come up?

"No, he offered to bring me this morning."

"And he wasn't afraid you would run into…" Meg's eyes widened just a little.

"Well, he did come with me…but anyway, we're married," Christine smiled broadly.

Meg took the tray from her dresser and put the tea service on the bed. She served each of them a cup. Christine brought out a plate with slices of lemon tarte. Erik was not partial to lemons and allowed her to take what was left of that tarte. Meg took a mouthful of the pastry.

Christine noticed, sadly, that the sunlight coming through the window was waning. Next time she would ask him if they could come up earlier so she could enjoy the sun's rays longer. She felt Meg touch her arm.

"Mmm. This is delicious! Since when did, you learn to cook?"

"I still don't know how to cook, but I'm learning to make patisserie. Mamma Valérius used to let me make cookies and cakes when I lived with her." She shrugged her shoulders.

"You have a talent for it, Christine. This tarte is amazing," said Meg, reaching over for a second slice.

"Erik loves all my pastries. Actually, he has become quite possessive with some of them. I am to make them only for him!" She laughed.

"Oh my, if your pastries have your husband so in love with you, then you have to teach me how to make them!" Meg giggled.

The two girls sat back quietly, and basked in each other's company while sipping their tea and sharing the sweets Christine had made. She was pleased that nothing substantial had changed between them.

A tear escaped and Christine furiously wiped it away, shrugging her shoulders. She took out her handkerchief and dabbed at her eyes.

"Are you very unhappy?" Meg asked holding her hand.

Christine shook her head.

"Do you love Erik?"

"Oh Meg, how could I?"

"My poor friend! But I don't understand why you married him?"

Christine shrugged her shoulders. "Meg, I have a letter. Would you…would you pass it to…Raoul?"

"Christine! Do you think it is wise?" Meg looked about—uncertain.

"I need to meet him. Don't look at me like that. I just want to let him know I am well…in person." She wrung an embroidered handkerchief in her hands.

"This is a dangerous thing you wish to do…I don't know…"

"Please Meg, you must. Hope is all I have," she begged her friend.

"What if your husband finds out?"

"I will die, if I don't see Raoul ever again." She wrung and twisted her handkerchief into strange shapes. "I just wish to say a proper good-bye. Nothing else can happen."

"Then you need to explain to me why you married the opera ghost, or Erik as you call him."

"There isn't much to tell. When Erik kidnapped me from the stage during my performance as Marguerite in Faust, Raoul tried to save me and found a way into Erik's home. I don't know how he fell into a special room Erik has…he made me choose between marrying him and watching Raoul die. What else could I do?

At the end of her story Meg eyed her strangely. "I wish you had found another way to save the vicomte than to marry a man you do not love."

"So do I, but that day there was no other way. Raoul had moments to live. I had to choose Erik."

"Do you hate him?"

"I could never hate Erik. Thanks to his training of my voice, I was a diva, even if only for a short time. I owe him so much. I vowed to be faithful and I will."

"You have no other choice now, you married by the church."

"If you were separated from your Éduard…if he was tortured because he came to rescue you…"

"It's not the same. What we have is a flirtation. I know it will never amount to anything. He is not like the vicomte. He would not antagonize his family or risk his position for me," she said sadly. "I very much doubt that he would risk his life for me."

"Do you love him?" Christine insisted.

"Unfortunately yes, but I know he can never be completely mine. I just know it." A tear rolled down

Meg's left cheek. She wiped it off and laughed. "Silly me, crying over nonsense like that." She took the letter from Christine's hand and put it in her dresser drawer.

"I will give the vicomte your letter," she said. Tears still glistened in Meg'sfgba eyes, but she blinked them away.

"Thank you!"

The two girls embraced. Meg pulled back and held both of Christine's hands, a serious look on her face. "Christine, did you hear about René and Pietro? The two stagehands at your wedding."

"René played the harmonica—what about them?

"Pietro is dead!"

Christine gasped. He couldn't be, she had done exactly as Erik had asked at the wedding. It must be a coincidence.

Meg continued, "Pietro was killed three nights ago. René was found passed out by his body in the gutter by the old sewer entrance. They said he smelled of drink and had a weapon in his hand. Maybe they got into a fight."

Thank goodness it had nothing to do with Erik. Christine shivered.

"To think the last time I saw them…they were having such a good time." Pietro had been the one to push her and Erik together so they would dance. The news put a damper on her visit.

Just as Christine finished her sentence, Mme. Giry and Erik came into the room, deep in discussion. "Faust is bound to be successful. You could wait until it ends," said Mme. Giry.

Erik nodded. "I suppose, I should practice patience in that as well." Noticing Christine's flushed appearance, Erik turned his attention to her. "Are you all right my dear?" He eyed her crumpled handkerchief, but did not mention it.

"Erik, Pietro is dead, and they think René killed him. Isn't that just awful," she told him.

"Just who is this Pietro?" He gave Meg a brief, expressionless glance. The ballerina would not meet his eyes.

"*You* invited him to our wedding."

"I see‾he was a guest," he said, his lips thinning. "You really must not let gossip upset you, my love."

"Meg, why did you open your mouth?" Mme. Giry pulled her daughter up by the wrist, her face twisting with displeasure. "You do love your gossip don't you girl?" Mme. Giry eyed Erik, and bit her lip nervously. "You've done enough damage for one day, go to your practices now."

"I'm sorry, Maman, I'm sorry, Chris…" Meg looked from one to the other embarrassed.

"Go now!" She seemed to muster all the strength of her wiry body, and she pushed her daughter out the door. Meg nearly crashed into the opposite wall. "These young girls do love their gossip…I'm sorry she upset you, Christine," she said, eyes darting to Erik again. The old woman was visibly upset.

"I am fine, Mme. Giry. I just feel so sorry for his widow."

"All this unpleasantness is nothing for you to worry about. I will send a little something to help her out."

Erik took Christine's shawl and carefully wrapped it around her shoulders. He slipped his arm around her waist again. "We will take our leave now."

"That would be so kind Erik." She gave Mme. Giry a kiss on her withered cheek. "Thank you for having me I…"

"Come Christine, we must leave." He quickly steered her past the older woman without saying another word.

On reaching their home, Christine turned on Erik. "Why were you so rude to Mme. Giry?"

"Rude? I thought I was quite restrained in view of the circumstances."

"What circumstances? The poor woman looked scared for her life," she insisted.

He placed his hands on her shoulders. "You really must take these morbid thoughts out of your head." He chuckled.

She stared at him, her chin jutting out. "What is your plan, Erik? Do you want the Giry door closed to me so I would not need to go up again?"

He enjoyed her lack of fear. Christine did not

fear him as most people did. He had seen large men turn pale at a whiff of his shadow. It was amusing to see her small frame stand square to his larger one. "Would you like me to read to you?"

He wished he could feel her sweet moist lips under his. He gasped at the direction his mind taking. His sudden reaction to her startled him. He wanted to touch her so much his hands tingled. These thoughts and longings had to be buried, as he had done for years. Only occasionally in Persia had he allowed lust to guide him. With Christine, he must bury all perversion, eradicate lust from his thoughts. His body and face were not made for receiving or giving pleasure. The only thing he was capable of giving freely was death. He had what he had always wanted most, a living wife. What he had to drive into his mind was that there was not even the most remote possibility that Christine would ever be wholly his.

"You go choose a book and I will pour us each a glass of wine," he said, looking away and fisting his hands tightly to his sides.

"Erik, I asked you a question. Do you want the Giry door closed to me?"

"No, my dear, I do not. And I promise you, that the Giry door will *never* be closed to you." He turned on his heels and quickly moved away from her.

Erik sat on a chair in her room watching her. She lay on the bed engrossed in her novel. Even though he had slept there since their wedding, he always referred to it as *her* room. For Erik, it was an unprecedented privilege to be able to sleep near her, to sit by her as she went about her daily living. He had never shared this level of intimacy with anyone before. It was wonderful to be able to gaze at her when she was relaxed. Unfortunately, he had to disturb her peace. He cleared his throat in an attempt to call her attention. She looked up from her book.

"I have a request to make of you. Please remain in your room while I conduct business with a...an associate." His eyes rested on her as he spoke.

"Why?"

"It is business."

"Is it Hafiz?"

"No, just do as I ask my dear." Why did she always need to ask, could she just not obey?

"Why can't I meet your business partner?" she asked.

"This person is not my business partner...no, not at all. Stay here and continue to enjoy your book. You are too curious for your own good, my love." He could barely believe that he was explaining himself, giving excuses. Nor could he conceive that he did not feel his temper rising. He would have given a thousand explanations to keep her pleased.

"It is not that. I just don't like to be excluded." She gave him a sad look.

"Trust me, Christine, this is a necessity." Except for the time he spent alone composing, he now hated doing things that did not include her.

"I promise I will not leave my room." She smiled and turned back to her book.

"Thank you, dear." Erik bent over and kissed her forehead before leaving the room.

A moment later, she heard the click of her door lock. Christine got up to check. He had locked her in! It had been weeks since he had done this. She could complain about his lack of trust in her, but maybe he too was beginning to know her. She could not have stopped herself from opening the door just a bit and peeking.

Christine looked through the keyhole in her door, but only saw a flash of black pass by her door. She kept her ear to the door.

"M'sieur!" A deep man's voice with a common accent greeted her husband.

There was a banging sound, and then Erik said, "Count it!"

"You wouldn't have an extra cup of coffee?"

"Not likely, that I would have you drinking out of the same cups my wife uses."

"I just ain't had nothing hot fo'days."

She was shocked that Erik would deny his friend a hot drink when they had so much of everything.

"Count it in front of me," Erik commanded.

She heard the sound of coins dropping one by one. "It's all there," the man said. "When d'you want the next one…"

"We are done for now," Erik interrupted curtly.

A short groan of disappointment came from the man. "Just put me in the know for m'next job. My sister needs the *sous*."

"I want that whole business stopped permanently. Here, send her this. And get yourself some soup."

So the man did have business with Erik. She heard more coins drop. Erik was so strange. She smiled.

"She can feed her little ones good on this. Thank you, M'sieur." The man lowered his voice and said something, but she was not sure if Erik answered, then she heard no more.

Finally, she heard two sets of footsteps. One faded and one set approached her door. Her door clicked again. Christine flew back to her bed and tried to look composed. She buried her face in her book. She heard a soft knock on the door. "Erik?"

"Who else would it be, my dear? It is a good thing my visitor did not need your services as a hostess."

Slowly, she looked up from her book. "I suppose you took care of him as best you could."

"You said 'Him'. How did you know?"

"A lucky guess. I cannot see through walls."

"No, my love, of course not…but you *are* a good listener," he smirked.

"Oh, do stop teasing me, Erik!" She put her book down and grabbed him by the hand, leading him out her room. "Come on, let us go sing! And I think you are a most kind and generous man."

Chapter 7

A Good Book

Mme. Rémy, had been supplying provisions for the masked man for over a decade. The man had regular features and beautiful amber eyes. His wide brimmed hat covered most of his face, and he wore his hair unstylishly gathered in a ribbon on his neck. She always wondered why the attractive stranger never smiled or showed any emotion. He handed her his list, waited for her to put his package together, paid and barely nodded a goodbye. It took her months to realize that what she had taken for handsome features was in reality a flesh-colored mask.

Every two weeks, for the past ten years, he had come in and purchased the same items in exactly the same amounts, with no deviation—ever. Then, a few months earlier, he had begun to buy different items in varying quantities: cinnamon, vanilla, sugarcane. Two months ago his order again changed. He doubled his usual amount of flour and sugar, added lemons and dried fruits. When she questioned the change, he chortled and said, "I am now married, and my wife enjoys making me patisseries." She had never heard him speak a whole sentence before that day. Mme. Rémy, opted for discretion and merely congratulated him. He was the only one of her customers who never haggled over prices, and occasionally he even tipped her. She did not care if he had married his horse.

Erik made Christine her favorite breakfast— an omelet with onions, tomatoes, diced potatoes and mushrooms on a crusty baguette with a thick wedge of Camembert cheese melted on top. He pulled the chair out for Christine, and she took her seat at the small table. As usual, there was only one place setting. She chose a fresh pear from a fruit basket, cut it into small chunks, and ate the pieces with her hands. He leaned back on the sink, chuckling quietly as he watched her eat. He was dressed in his usual black pants and white button down shirt. His sleeves rolled up, exposing the soft, dark down on his forearms—his narrow shoulders tapered down to even leaner hips. Even though gaunt, his height made him an imposing figure. She smiled up at him and continued to eat her pear.

She looked up again, and asked, "Erik, why don't you ever eat with me?"

He adjusted his mask. "You would not want me to."

"That is foolish. Why do you think that?"

He sat on a nearby chair by straddling it and leaning on the back rest. "As a child, I was never allowed to go near the table when my parents were eating," he said in a flat, emotionless tone.

She was appalled. "Why would your parents do that?" she asked, fearing the answer to her question.

"I have told you before how disgusted my parents were by…by…my face."

"But, where were you supposed to eat?" she asked, facing him and putting down her fruit.

"In my room…I always ate alone in my room." He looked away from her, the old hurt returning to his eyes. "I tried sitting at the table once, but after my father gagged, I got such a beating for it that…well…I have never sat with anyone to eat again."

He got up and took the food from the oven. Christine sat forward as he put the omelet and baguette in front of her. "Go on, eat," he cajoled and sat by her again.

She had lost her appetite, horrified by the story he had just told her. "That is terrible." Her eyes watered, and she covered his hands with her own. "You were only a child." *When I have a child, I am going to love…* She stopped, remembering that in agreeing to marry Erik, she had given up motherhood in the same breath that she had given herself to him.

All her life she had dreamed, that one day she would be a mother that dream was now gone. She swallowed her disappointment.

He sat back down and continued, "It was the disgusted look in my mother's eyes…that hurt the most." His knuckles had gone white as he gripped the chair and his eyes looked far beyond the kitchen walls into the still vivid past.

"Here, have a glass of wine." She served him half a glass of their everyday wine from a jug on the table.

"It is much too early for that."

"Well, you look like you need it. I do," she said, pouring no more than two fingers of the wine into a glass for herself.

She was furious with his parents. What he had gone through, no child should ever suffer, especially for something that was not his fault in any way. *They should have loved him, despite any imperfection.* Her own parents, dead for years, had been loving. She missed them still. Even Meg, brought up by the strict Mme. Giry, had never been mistreated.

She could not erase the frown from her brow or the heaviness from her heart. She took his hands in hers. "I hate to eat alone, Erik, would you eat with me?" she gently coaxed.

"No." His voice rang out in a menacing tone. He got up and walked to the sink.

"I don't mind, so why not?" She put her fork down and walked up to him. He stepped back, but the sink stopped him. She approached him slowly and popped a small piece of her pear into his mouth. "We have tea together and you eat my patisserie."

"Those are small. I just swallow. Let me be, Christine." He turned his face away.

"I like it when we eat together," she said, smiling at him.

"I…I can't eat well with the mask on. I'd have to take it off, and *I will not* do that."

"You should be able to eat comfortably in your own home." Her fingers grazed his lower lip as she popped another juicy piece into his mouth. She watched his lips as he closed his mouth over the fruit and brushed her fingertips. She noticed that unlike the rest of his face, he had thin but comely lips.

Her hand graced his lips as she fed him. He stayed still, accepting every morsel, every scrap she put into his mouth, enjoying the occasional contact. His body reacted to her touch. If she looked down she would see how perverted a creature he was. She would know that by the simple act of feeding him a piece of fruit from her hand, he turned into a lustful animal. He stood very still, wishing to run, but not able to move.

Oh Christine, why can you not be mine? Why? Because you Erik, are made of death and she is living.

She was his wife, and that was more than he had ever had. It had to suffice.

"Before you brought me here, didn't you eat at your table?" she asked.

He shrugged his shoulders. "Before you came, I was barely alive," he whispered. *Now, I am too alive!* He had to solve his dilemma before she took notice. He tried to turn toward the stove, but she remained by his side.

He had told her that he was incapable of performing a husband's duty. She was about to find out he lied.

"I know what's under the mask."

"And you have endured the memory," he retorted.

His mother had also endured it. Since his birth, she had been disgusted by his deformity, but she had fed and cared for him. She had avoided looking at him as much as she could, and placed a mask on his face to save herself from having to look at his hideous features. Sometimes, after all his chores had been done and they were alone, she took pity on him and would pat his head, then feed him a sweet morsel. What joy those moments gave him, what a wonderful memory. She had never beaten him as his father had regularly done. She always tended to the wounds his father inflicted on him and that gentle touch had filled his need for love until the next beating.

"I worry about you not eating enough," Christine said. Her words brought him back to the present.

He felt her fingertips tease open his mouth. The sensation went straight to his manhood. He felt a piece of fruit slip into his mouth. If she touched him again, he would not be able to save himself. He turned away from her and began coughing.

"Are you all right? Erik?"

She hit him on the back with her palm. He nodded and she hit him again, harder this time. He loved her touch, her concern.

"Here, drink this." She handed him a glass of water. With his back still to her, he drank it down quickly.

When he turned around, she put her arms around his neck and held him. This had never happened to him before and he was confounded. Would she allow him to embrace her? Gingerly, he put his arms around her loosely and she tightened her hold on him. It was out of pity, he knew, but she felt soft and warm in his arms. He inhaled her body's delicious scent and his body heated. He allowed his fingers to roam and caressed her back. Losing control, a low moan escaped his lips. If he died right now, he would not mind spending eternity in hell because he had just been to heaven. She sighed against his chest, the heat of her breath worsening his plight as his body reminded him that he was very much alive and about to disgrace himself. He had to stop the dream before it turned into a nightmare.

"I…I better go lay down, you finish your meal," he said, pushing her from him, and headed toward his room. His dignity had been preserved but he missed having her in his arms.

Philippe sat by Raoul's bed, listening to his brother's tirade for the second time that morning. Had he known his young brother would get so excited, he would have never given him the letter. He had wanted to boost his morale not get him riled up. *Damn that girl!*

"That beast under the opera house still has her!" Raoul exclaimed, clutching Christine's note in his hand. "I dare not think what he may be doing to her," he added with a ferocious scowl. "I have to go to her, Philippe, I have to or I will go mad! He has fooled her into thinking they are married. Christine is so good hearted, so innocent, she will believe any tale she is told. Thanks to her father's constant storytelling, she is incapable of telling legend from reality."

"You are not moving from this house, Raoul." Philippe stood over him. "You're just beginning to regain your strength."

"How do you expect me to leave her in his hands? Christine is my betrothed," Raoul protested.

Philippe fought the desire to roll his eyes. "Do you really think you can face this monster, as you call him, in your condition?" Philippe chided.

"I can't ignore this!" he shook the letter in his hand. "We need to get the police involved," Raoul insisted.

"Before we do that, we need evidence that she doesn't want to be with him," Philippe said. "The note she sent you proves the opposite."

"Can't you tell he was looking over her shoulder

as she wrote? He commands what she writes, hoping to deceive me. She knows she doesn't need to ask for my help, that I would not entertain a plea to forget her and abandon her while she is in the clutches of a monster," Raoul assured his brother. Philippe shook his head, not convinced by his brother's words.

A knock at the door interrupted them and Philippe opened the door. "My Lord, it's the Marquis du Bourdeny," the footman told him.

Philippe smiled. "Ask Mme. Fortine to make sure his lordship is comfortable…and tell them downstairs to set a plate for him in the dining room." He turned to his brother. "Come on Raoul, Louis is here. Get dressed and join us in the parlor. You need a change of air."

Louis sat in an overstuffed chair with his long legs stretched out in front of him. He was a ruggedly handsome man, blessed with a naturally taut, lean frame. His thinning, grizzled hair made a striking contrast with his boyish face. Only the lines around his somber eyes betrayed his nearly six decades of life.

The marquis nursed a large brandy he had poured himself, his long fingers wrapped around the snifter to keep the liquid warm. The amber liquid swirled around the glass, letting the light reveal golden waves as he played with it. He sipped at his drink, savoring the calvados. Louis brought the snifter to his nose, and his thin nostrils flared as he took in the scent. The sharper Armagnac was more to his liking.

After greeting Louis, Philippe sat in a chair next to him, leaving Raoul to sit opposite to them.

"So how are you feeling, Raoul?"

"I feel stronger, but Philippe insists I stay in the house, as if I were a child," Raoul moaned, taking a seat. One of the maids came in with tea service and poured Raoul a cup. With a frown, Raoul motioned to the footman and his drink was promptly doused with a small shot of the brandy controlled by a counter signal from Philippe's hand.

"I agree, the fever broke and his color is back. But he is far from well yet." Philippe gulped his drink down. The footman immediately refilled the glass. "What brings you to Paris this time?"

"Can't I just check in with my godson?" said Louis, mock innocence in his voice.

"Mm..." Philippe narrowed his eyes at the older man skeptically.

Louis cocked his head to one side and grinned. "And since I am here, I might as well accompany you to the Garnier with a lady or two." He burst into laughter.

"For a moment, I thought you too had developed a fever," Philippe retorted, joining Louis in a hearty laugh.

"My fiancé was abducted by a madman at the opera house!" Raoul burst out, cutting in. "And Philippe will not allow me to rescue her."

Louis bolted to a sitting position, almost spilling

his drink, his eyes perking up in inquisitiveness. "Abducted?" he asked. "Small wonder your brother will not let you go, lad," he said with concern in his voice. "Have you seen him? What does this madman look like?"

"A monster…a monster that wears a mask…" Raoul's tirade was interrupted by a coughing spasm.

Philippe had Raoul's cup refilled with tea.

Louis turned to the older brother. "What is this about, Philippe?"

After their tea, Christine joined Erik in the library. "What are you reading?"

He took a deep draw on his pipe and slowly exhaled, letting the smoke spiral away and fill the room with the odor of fresh tobacco before answering. "Huh?" He lingered on the page, then slowly turned it.

"What are you reading?"

"A book," he said without looking up.

"Obviously, Erik!" she snapped. "What is the title of the book? You seem so interested it must be a really good book!" She got up and went around him.

As she neared to where he sat, he snapped the book shut, and tucked it into the side of the chair. "It would be of no interest to you."

She said nothing, but hated it when he made a little thing into a grand mystery. Curiosity pricked at her. She went over to the pile of books he had selected for her and took one without reading the title. Within minutes, she was intrigued by the colorful maps.

Just before bedtime, Christine returned to the library to choose a book to read in bed. She saw a slim dark tome peeking out from between the side cushions in Erik's chair. She bent over and picked it up. *The book Erik was reading!* Without hesitation, she placed it in her dress pocket and took it to her room.

Once in her room, she opened the little book and immediately felt her cheeks grow hot. Heat traveled all over her body as she turned the pages. Christine let the book on her lap close on its own. She made a little sound with her breath and reopened the book. Taking a deep breath, she quickly perused the pages to the end. Then, she looked through the book again, slowly this time. Twice she lingered, gaping at the illustrations, before snapping the book shut. Breathless and uncomfortable, she ran out of her room and tiptoed to the library with the book hidden in her pocket. She returned the book to the same spot in the chair, hiding it between the cushions. Just as she was leaving the library, Erik approached her.

"Are you looking for something to read, Christine?"

Oh no, he will know I saw it. She would not face him. She buried her head into her chest. "No Erik, I was just returning my book." She was grateful he didn't say another word as she walked away.

A week later she was still unable to erase the

images the book evoked in her mind. Were those poses even possible? Even when she was washing dishes, the images came to her. *If we were to be intimate—which will never happen—is that what he would want to do with me?* She shuddered in disgust, but her heart thudded against her ribs. If he was indeed incapacitated in that area, why did he read such books?

She began to avoid Erik if she could manage it and felt the heat rise to her face whenever she met his eyes. His graceful, skilled hands would sear her, when if by mistake, his fingertips brushed her skin. She imagined those same hands on other parts of her body, as she had seen in the illustrations.

One afternoon he offered her a ride on the boat around the underground lake. She jumped at the chance to clear her mind. They had taken leisurely rides a few times and she enjoyed going through the meandering canals and dipping under dripping tunnels. He rowed to a dark cavernous area he had never bothered to light with his lamps. Their only source of light was their own torch. The ever-present mist on the lake parted as the small boat cut through, leaving soft tendrils behind that caressed her skin. The soft touch brought back memories of Erik's book and she felt the too-familiar sensation of a warm face. She kept her eyes on the lake's dark water as if trying to discover a mystery hidden there, feeling very uncomfortable facing Erik during the boat ride. Christine had heard that men sometimes touched their own bodies in private. Did Erik do that after looking at the book? She mentioned a headache and with a pronounced frown, he rowed her back to the house immediately.

Christine drank a glass of sherry as she kneaded the dough for her pastry. She welcomed the exercise the stiff dough provided. *Erik probably looked through the book for intellectual purposes.* She beat the dough flat with her fists as she recalled the bizarre images. Taking a heavy rolling pin, she rolled the dough out. *Why would anyone want to do that...unless it was pleasurable?* The faces in the drawings were lax in ecstasy. She took another sip of her sherry.

Despite her marriage, she wanted to remain faithful to Raoul and was pleased that Erik's problem made that possible. Did Raoul ever read such a book? He certainly knew about kissing. She recalled the feel of his lips on hers, his hand at her back, pressing her against him. She had felt something then, but had no idea until...the book. *Did Raoul read that book?* In his last note to her, he mentioned their shared kisses. He had asked her to set a date for them to meet. She had not answered him or dared commit to a meeting yet. She poured herself another glass of sherry and took a seat at the kitchen table. The images from the book came to her mind vividly. Then unbidden images came to her mind, Raoul and herself substituted for the man and woman in the drawings not still drawings, but moving images. She nibbled on her lower lip as her eyes closed and she savored her thoughts as her thighs squeezed. The warmth spreading through her body made her dizzy, breathless. She took another sip, enjoying the images that came to her head. A sound made her look up and she quickly finished off her sherry, trying to ease the dryness in her mouth.

Erik sat alone in the library, worrying about his wife. He had noticed that during the past few days, Christine had taken to blushing for no reason at all. Whenever she faced him, her blush intensified. He wondered if her thoughts were of the vicomte and if her blushes were the result of guilt. He sensed his rage build. Was she remembering the boy's kisses? Was that all she had shared with the vicomte? He could not bear the thought of the boy's hands exploring her body. *I should have killed him.*

Earlier, he had found her in the kitchen tipsy, drinking sherry. She took one look at him, her cheeks turned bright red and she walked out avoiding his gaze. She forgot the patisserie in the oven and the sweets burned.

Their afternoon meal was late and it consisted of a day old lemon tarte. He asked her to make a second pot of tea and insisted she share it with him. He put his cup out again and she poured them both a sixth cup. As she handed it to him, she looked up at the bookshelves and flushed brightly.

"Are you all right? You look rosy," he asked warily.

"Oh!" She put both hands up to her face and felt the heat.

"Christine, you will tell me what is wrong right now," Erik demanded, scowling. He slammed his tea cup down hard enough to rattle the plate.

'I...am fine, I…"

"Nonsense!" he cut her off. "You have been acting very strange lately. I even found you at half-rats in the kitchen today."

She put her own cup down and got up to leave. "Oh pooh, I only had a glass of sherry. I'll be right back, I have to go to my room."

He grinned and said, "You are not moving from here, until you tell me what you are about!"

"You would keep me here against my will?"

"If I have to," he insisted. "Are you ready to explain your constant blushes?"

"Most certainly not!" she snapped, folding her arms across her chest.

"Then you will not go to your room," he said stiffly, crossing his arms over his chest, in imitation of her gesture.

Erik had to be joking about not letting her go to her room. Christine began to pace from one side of the library to the other. After a few minutes, she said, "I need to wash up in my room."

"If you have such a need, I suggest you speak quickly my dear." The command in his voice was not covered by the sweet sound of his timbre, or the curling of his lips. He stood by the fireplace facing her, hands at his back.

"I will go to my room now, excuse me." Christine turned on her heels and quickly headed for her room. She felt ready to burst and could envision the relief she would feel in a few moments. She relaxed her hips a little and readied her body. A few more steps and she would be in her bathroom. She smiled at the thought of her tiled bathroom and hurried her steps. Suddenly, she felt herself lose contact with the ground and her head went upside down, as he slung her over his shoulder. She cried in frustration. "What are you doing?"

"I told you, that you were not to leave the library until you told me what was wrong." Slowly, he headed back to the library. She bit her lips with every bouncy step he took.

Damn him! That's why he offered me those extra cups of tea.

The position he had her in pressed on her bladder, and she felt the urge to relief herself stronger than ever. He set her down in the center of the room. "Well?" he asked.

She stood facing him, drawn up to her full height, hands fisted at her waist. "How dare you not allow me my privacy," she accused and stomped her slippered foot. She begged her bladder to hold on. "You must stop this. Let me go to my room."

"You will be allowed to go to your room, but

only after you tell me why you have been blushing every time you see me, for no apparent reason," he retorted.

"Erik, I need to go right now!" She wanted to lunge at him, but just the thought of such an abrupt movement made her lose control momentarily and a few drops trickled down to her undergarment. She crossed her legs tightly, wobbling where she stood.

"What do you think about that makes you blush so?"

"Let me use the…privy," she cried, almost in tears. For a moment, she thought all was lost as a few more drops followed the first ones, despite her twisted legs.

"Are you remembering something? Is it something to do with the vicomte?" he taunted and stood before her arms crossed.

"Oh Erik!" Before she shamed herself completely, she turned away from him, lifted the front of her skirts and pressed against her private area as the need to relief herself overwhelmed her. It helped and she sighed in relief.

From behind her he snatched her wrists from under her skirts and held them at her waist, ending the necessary pressure.

"What are you hiding?"

"No, no, don't," she pleaded. She could not explain or fight him, but managed to twist and squeeze her legs more it did not help as much this time. She needed the direct pressure he was denying her. Her desire to release the pressure in her bladder was painfully unbearable. "Please, please, let me go," she begged him, not daring to struggle.

"Talk Christine. What makes my wife unable to look me in the eye?" he growled.

"Let me go, Erik!" she cried in dismay. Her lips turned white from the effort as a slight, but continuous trickle ran down her legs. Her pantalets soaked.

"I will know what you hide from me. Is it something you plan to do?" he snarled, his voice dark with fury. "I demand to know. Tell me!"

She knew he wanted her full surrender and would stop at nothing short of that. With her bladder slightly relieved, Christine shuddered as the worst of the feeling passed and the trickle stopped. She rested her head against his chest, exhausted from fighting her body's need. It was over and he had won. She had to escape and relieve herself right now, before the pressure built again. The embarrassment she would feel telling him about the book would be nothing, compared to her total humiliation due to what would inevitably happen in a few moments.

"All right, all right, I will show you. Just please, let me go," she pleaded.

He let her go, but remained by her side, watching her, ready to pounce on her again. With effort not to lose control, she reached up on a bookshelf, pulled out the tome he had been browsing a few days before and thrust it into his chest. "I found your book and looked through it. You horrible man."

He took the book from her and Christine rushed out of the library as fast as her soaked pantalets would let her. She looked back and saw Erik fist pressed against his mask's mouth hole, shoulders convulsing in mirth.

Damn him!

Chapter 8

Picture Perfect

"Concentrate, for pity's sake, or let us leave your lesson for tomorrow!" Erik banged his fist on the piano.

"I see no purpose. Why should I continue to practice if I am never to sing in public again?" Christine whined as she plopped down next to him on the piano bench.

"Pray tell me, Christine," he said impatiently. "Why wouldn't you sing in public again?" he asked perplexed.

"You mean you wouldn't mind…if I sang in public?" She looked surprised.

"What I would mind, is if you waste my time. I *do not* train parlor singers!" he countered in irritation.

"Oh Erik! When? When? Tell me when? Please?"

"I will return you to the stage when you are ready to replace La Carlota permanently. I may rage on about her, but she is a good singer. She does not have your talent, but her age and experience give her a presence you lack. Her repertoire is also vast, you must develop, and solidify yours," he said calmly.

"I promise to will work hard. As hard as you want me to." Her hands clenched in front of her as in prayer.

"Now, stop wasting my time, and start from the top. Second bar—*allegro*. That goes not only for your voice, my dear…but also your expression. Do you think you could favor us with a smile that reaches your eyes? Oh, and wipe that silly look from your face before we begin. One, two, three." His bony fingers stretched over the keys.

"Yes, Maestro!" she answered as she hugged him, causing him to stiffen in response. Christine pecked his jaw softly. He gasped and drew back a little, squaring his shoulders. Again, she had allowed her lips to touch his flesh.

A tinkling alarm sounded. Exasperated by the ill-timed interruption, he looked away toward the back door leading to the hidden tunnel entrance. Although he knew who it was, he left the music room and went to check the intruder's identity. "It's that Persian and he's already in." he called out to her from the back of the house. Erik cursed himself for putting an alarm in the tunnel used by Hafiz, but decided that a surprise entry would have been worse. *Damn that Persian!*

What he had to do was to block off that entrance.

"What can you possibly want from me today?" Erik asked stiffly.

"And a good evening to you, Erik." Hafiz smiled, coming into the room. He was smartly dressed and as usual wore his astrakhan cap.

"Be quick, what do you want?" Erik did not bother hiding his displeasure at the visit.

"I came to pay a social visit," Hafiz answered, amused. He walked to the fireplace in the parlor and stretched his hands out toward the warmth.

"Well then, if you don't need anything, you can leave. You interrupted our evening practice session," Erik told him curtly.

"Erik!" Christine shook her head at her husband. She stood beside him. "Hafiz, how wonderful to see you! Won't you please take a seat?"

Erik groaned loudly and sat down as well. She gave him an exasperated look and sat next to him. Erik could feel the warmth of her body as she sat closely to him on the divan. He was still irritated with the Persian's appearance, but this appeased him for now.

"How have you been Hafiz?" Christine asked.

"Quite well, thank you. I am sorry to interrupt your session," Hafiz said with a smile and a gleam in his eye. Neither of his hosts seemed too happy to see him although Christine, at least, was making an effort at civility.

"I was giving Christine a singing lesson," Erik cut in quickly. He looked toward Christine, met her eyes briefly, and turned back to Hafiz.

"I will go make us tea. Please excuse me," she said, quickly leaving for the kitchen.

Sitting side by side, they looked as if one had stolen the goat and the other one sold it. *What is going on with these two? Could he be forcing himself on the girl?*

"Not only are you a fool, but you are a meddling one as well. Don't think I cannot read your filthy mind," said Erik, annoyed.

"My dear friend, why do I sense hostility coming from you? Am I not welcome in your home?" Hafiz teased his friend.

"No, and you never were, but your presence is insufferable today!" responded Erik, infuriated. "You come at will as if I should always welcome you. Well, I do not!" His hands fisted, but he kept his temper in check.

"We have an agreement! When I saved your life in Persia, you promised to stop all your crimes and that I could visit you wherever you were and check that you were keeping your word." the Persian reminded him. This was not the first time the assassin had tried to renege on it. On the other hand, it was the first time he had seen Erik so upset without his temper getting the better of him. *Good girl, you're taming the wolf!*

"Yes, yes, an agreement, that is more like a

lifetime jail sentence! And I will remind you, that I was forced into it. You extracted that promise from me at a time when my options were to accept to your agreement of face execution." Erik glared at him.

"An agreement all the same," answered Hafiz. "I never saw my parents again."

Erik looked away and groaned. They were linked for life.

Hafiz needed to remind Erik of his loss, especially now that Erik had that innocent girl living with him. He would need access to the assassin and the girl more often.

"Why did you come today…simply to vex me?" Erik hissed. "You are not welcome!"

"Regardless, I have come," Hafiz answered unruffled.

"Erik, I heard that! Are you being rude to our guest? Erik?" Christine called out from the kitchen.

Under his breath, Erik murmured, "Damn it! Curse you, Daroga!" He turned his face toward the kitchen, changing his voice to a more melodious tone and said, "No, I was not rude. I was teasing Hafiz."

Erik's rage-filled eyes caused Hafiz to double up from laughter. Hafiz's raucous laughter filled the room.

She came in with a tray. "Oh good, you *are* entertaining Hafiz!" She gave her husband a big smile.

"Here, Christine, let me help you with that." Hafiz took the tray from her before Erik could get to it. "You have no idea how entertaining our Erik can be."

"Why, thank you Hafiz," she said, putting out the tray's contents. She placed the teapot and teacups on the side table by Erik. The tray with her pastries went on the center table.

Hafiz could feel Erik's eyes on him. He was tempted to laugh again, but thought of his personal safety and decided against it. The wolf was being domesticated, but it was still a wolf.

"I will join you promptly. Please begin pouring without me," said Christine, leaving them alone again.

In a sudden change of demeanor, Erik leaned back nonchalantly. "Help yourself to any of those," Erik said, pointing to the patisserie on the tray. "My wife makes them for me. Makes fresh ones every day, but only the ones I like of course." He sighed deeply and shook his head. "There is no end to the trouble it causes me to have to acquire the ingredients she requires. But she insists on using only the finest ingredients to make me tarts and such."

It was the exaggerated, affected voice of nonchalance Erik used that perked his attention. He sounded, like a pretentious nobleman, annoyed by the fact that he had to choose among so many pairs of shoes. Hafiz noted that Erik did not refer to Christine by her name, but instead called her 'my wife.' The light shining in Erik's eyes, betrayed the immense pleasure he derived from repeating those simple words.

Christine returned and sat with them, her hair freshly brushed and pinned back with combs. Erik's eyes remained glued to her in reverence. She poured Erik's tea, putting in one and a half teaspoons of sugar and stirring it. She handed him the cup with a smile. Erik took the cup from her. Their fingertips touched and she blushed a little looking away. This simple interplay alarmed Hafiz. Could there be more than simple companionship between the two?

She turned to their guest and poured tea for Hafiz. "Sugar?"

"Yes, four, thank you."

Hafiz noticed Erik frowned slightly at Hafiz's teacup, and then looked away. "Is there something wrong?"

"Ah, no, not at all."

"You are looking at my tea as if there is something wrong. What is it?" the Persian inquired.

"Well, you won't be able to appreciate the pastry as you should."

"I do not see why, but please explain."

"My wife says you should not have so much sugar in your tea if you…"

"Oh Erik, leave him alone…he can have his tea any way he wants it," she rebuked him.

Erik shrugged and drank from his cup unhurriedly, picked up a tiny morsel and put it in his mouth.

Hafiz gaped at Erik. He had never seen him eat before.

He turned to Christine. "As always, my dear, delectable! Thank you." He took her hand and brushed his lips lightly against her knuckles. "I just hate to see your sweets wasted on a tongue that cannot appreciate them."

She smiled up at him and placed her hand on his knee. Erik patted her hand and continued to sip his tea leisurely.

Incredible! He was talking to Erik, the vicious, ruthless executioner, the heartless slayer of those unfortunate enough to have fallen out of favor with the *Shâhanshâh*, about the optimum amount of sugar one should have with tea. If it were not for the mask, he would have thought this was another man, a man without blood on his hands and soul.

"Actually, I did come bearing gifts." Hafiz took a large packet out of his coat and thrust it at Erik. "Your wedding photographs." Erik snatched the envelope from Hafiz's outstretched hand. He tore the top open and spilled the photographs onto the table with the tea service. "You should have given this to me immediately, instead of dallying with your absurdities. It took your photographer long enough" He frowned. "And, it is not a gift since I paid a goodly price for it."

"You demanded that every single photograph be colorized! And I will take that as a thank you. So, you are welcome," said the Persian calmly.

"Thank you, Hafiz," said Christine, shooting Erik a warning look.

"You need not thank me, Christine. It was my pleasure," Hafiz said.

"She does not need to thank you, but I do? I, who have been perturbed by your nonsense." Erik picked up a photograph. "May I see them, Erik?" she asked, reaching out with her hand.

He cleared his throat, picked up all the photographs, and under his breath, his voice husky, he said, "Excuse me." Erik rushed out of the room with the packet of photographs in hand.

"I suppose I will see them later," she said looking at Erik's back.

Hafiz noted the disappointment in her voice and wondered if her disappointment had to do with the wedding. Would the photographs remind her of her lost opportunities with the vicomte? The wedding, though genuine, had come about based on threats and abduction. He did not know the details, but he could guess. He would not be surprised if she were still miserable about her situation.

He moved closer to her on the settee. "By what manner of threat does he keep you down here, Christine?" Hafiz whispered, looking in the direction where Erik had left. "Please be honest."

"What do you mean?" she asked.

"I know you were engaged to the Vicomte de Chagny. Do not tell me you preferred Erik over that young man."

"No, but it is done. I am Erik's wife now."

"Do you need help getting away from him?"

"From Erik?" she asked surprised.

"Yes, has he hurt you?"

"No, why would Erik…"

"I have to speak plainly, before he returns. He promised me he would not touch you as a husband. Has he kept his promise?" In her innocence, he hoped she would fall into his trap and give him the information he sought..

"Erik told you about that?" The color rose on her face. "Why would he tell you? He said he did not want anyone to know about his affliction."

"So he has kept his word." Relief washed over Hafiz. His police skills were still sharp.

"It was supposed to be private," she cried. Her face showed her distress. "But yes, he has even allowed me to keep my own room."

"Forgive him for sharing with me, please, but despite our jousting, we are like brothers. I should not have mentioned so delicate a subject." There was hope to get her out of harm's way if Erik had not unleashed his unnatural passions on her. "Christine, I must know from your lips. Do you still love the vicomte?" he asked her, careful not to sound offensive.

Tears welled up in her eyes and slid down her cheeks. After an almost imperceptible nod, she took out her hankie, mopped her eyes and blew her nose. "Erik must not know I have cried," she said easily.

She *was* beginning to know him.

"Erik treats me with love, and respect," she said with absolute conviction.

"If he ever comes to believe that you have betrayed him, he will hurt you."

"I won't believe that."

"You must." His smile vanished. "I have known Erik for over twenty years and I assure you, he is capable of hurting you badly,"

"Erik loves me," she said squirming.

"He is obsessed with you! And he will not share you."

"He loves me and needs me," she persisted, her eyes wide and childlike.

Hafiz relented. "That perhaps may be true, but do you love *him*?"

"I cannot love two men." She sniffed. "I am not so fickle with my feelings. But I care for Erik."

He did not expect her to be so forthcoming. "Until you are ready to leave, can you find some measure of happiness down here with him?"

"Yes," she said. "I vowed myself to him." How could she understand the meaning of a lifetime with Erik?

"When you need me to rescue you from him, and you will...do not hesitate to let me know, I will help you no matter what," he murmured.

"Erik is my husband now. I doubt I will need to get away from him," she said tersely, looking away from Hafiz.

"Take a care, Christine, if you ever plan to contact the vicomte for any reason."

Her blush betrayed her. If the girl thought she

could have a lover behind Erik's back, she would soon get to know just who her husband really was. She was a sweet little thing, but not very clever. There was not much that she would be able to hide from Erik for any length of time. He prayed she would keep away from Raoul de Chagny, or she would be in grave danger.

She moved a little closer to him. "Erik, gave me a bottle of poison on our wedding night. He said to use it on him if he went mad. Doesn't that prove he wants me safe?"

Her loyalty to Erik was endearing. "No, Christine, it means he knows what he is capable of doing and hopes you will stop him before he does it to you."

She blanched at his bold statement. He had to give her a safety net…she would need it soon.

"Enjoy your life with him while you can, but keep my warning in mind. I will continue to visit from time to time. If you ever need my help, wear red, as much red as you can find, and I will understand without a word from you, remember…*red.*" He would need to visit more often and be on the alert, to help her escape as soon as he saw the signal.

"Hafiz, aren't you his closest friend? A brother, as you proclaim? Then why do you talk like this?" She sounded confused.

"I know him as no other does. I was with him when…" He stopped himself. It was not his place to give away Erik's secrets. He shook his head.

"When what?" she asked.

Silent as ever, Erik returned to the parlor, the photographs in hand. "Should I gather that *I* am the reason for your hushed conversation?" Erik's eyes went from one to the other, observing them. "I assume you asked my wife if I was torturing her. I expected that. And so I stayed away long enough for her to have run away with you. I see you are both here. Hopefully, your itch is satisfied, daroga."

"I did ask, and it seems your wife is perfectly content to stay with you."

Erik shrugged, looking smug. "Your job is done, Hafiz. I approve of your photographer. I am even more in your debt—which should delight you." He handed the photographs to Christine and stood by her.

"Christine will be singing in public again!" he announced to Hafiz, pointing upstairs to the opera house.

"When?" Hafiz grinned, showing brilliant white teeth. That would make it easier to help her escape when the time came.

"When? When I say she is ready, and not a day sooner!" He crossed his arms over his chest.

Christine was engrossed in the photographs. Was this possible? For a woman who had been forced into a wedding, she was acting much more like the blushing bride than the aggrieved victim. "These are beautiful, Erik," she cried. "Come sit next to me. Look at this one..." She patted the divan and her obliging husband sat dutifully by her side, looking at the photographs with her. Neither of them noticed Hafiz get up and walk toward the back door.

"I leave you to enjoy your photographs. Thank you for your delectable patisseries," the Persian said with a small bow.

"Good, show yourself out, just like you showed yourself in. One day I will have a small present for you in that tunnel," cackled Erik. Christine, wholly engrossed in the photographs, nodded politely toward Hafiz.

Just before he walked out the house, he turned back and looked at the couple; she, a petite, beautiful young girl with golden hair, he, a tall, gaunt man with thinning hair, wearing a black half-face mask. They sat side-by-side, shoulders touching, both bent over their wedding photographs, murmuring to each other. They looked like a happy couple. Two things eased his mind. Erik had not touched her and she had her own room. *How long will she be safe?* The Persian pursed his lips and headed home.

Chapter 9

Summer in the Cellars

She saw a drop of sweat emerging from the bottom of his mask; it dangled at the edge of his chin. Erik whisked it away with a gloved finger, then lifted his mask just enough to dab at his face with a handkerchief. The music room, like the rest of the house was warm.

"Erik, why don't you remove it? You must be horribly uncomfortable," she said.

"I will be fine." He reached for a glass of water atop the piano, only to find it empty.

"I'll get you a glass of cold lemonade. I made some this morning," she said as she headed toward the kitchen. She took the lemonade from their icebox and poured him a long glass.

"Thank you," he said, taking the glass from her

and putting the drink to his lips. The edge of the glass met with the bottom of his mask and clinked— he pushed his head back further to be able to drink.

She went to sit in a comfortable chair, tucked her legs under, and opened a copy of Voltaire's *Candide*. Erik had selected the book for her. As a novel, Christine found the political references boring. She tried to understand Erik when he spoke about science or politics, but in reality it was beyond her comprehension. She would much have preferred to sit with the latest copy of the *Moniteur de la Mode*. Christine stretched her arms in cat-like fashion and yawned. She was dressed in nothing but her chemise under a light silk dressing gown tied loosely around her waist. The day was too hot to dress at home. She pitied those upstairs at the opera house. If it was this hot down here, the people upstairs must be sweltering.

Erik's music relaxed her, and she leaned her head back and watched him through barely opened eyes. The book laid ignored on her lap. He wore a white shirt open at the neck, and his neck and chin glistened with perspiration. He adjusted the bench and began playing again, stopping every few notes in a feverish attempt to write down his composition. He continued this way for a while. A few moments later, she noticed that another drop dangled from his chin, threatening to fall onto the music paper. Shaking her head at his stubbornness, she looked back to her book and heard a muffled curse. He was dabbing at his music paper with his handkerchief, making it worse.

"Remove your mask. Why are you torturing yourself?" She got up and went to his side.

"I am fine, just a little warm…"

"I can't sit here and watch this…I shall go to my room so you may have the privacy you need to be comfortable."

"No, wait, do not leave. I compose best when you are near. I do not like to impose this on you," he said, his finger pointing to his face.

"You make me feel like an outsider, like we're not family." *I had never considered him family before, but he is.* He was as much family as Mama Valérius. Erik was her family.

"Family! Well…well, I suppose we are." He gave a deep sigh and unbuckled the straps. He grabbed the edge of the mask. "Are you certain?" he asked.

At her assenting nod, he sucked air into his lungs and with a flip of his wrist, he removed the black piece of leather from his face. He angled his face away from her, and wiping his face with the handkerchief again, bent over his work.

She left the room to get a cool cloth, and returning a few moments later she stood behind him. She pulled his resisting head gently back until the top of it rested against her abdomen. There were ink stains all over his face, but she barely saw them. His yellowed skin was blotched from the heat. She almost gagged but managed to bite her lips. There was almost no fat or muscle under the skin as it stretched over the skull. The tiniest bump kept his nose from being flat against his face, with cavernous nostril openings at the bottom. His piercing eyes stared at her from their crevice behind a brow that was thick and jutting. She breathed deeply and gently covered his face with the cloth.

She was glad to be able relieve some of her husband's discomfort in this heat. If she had to see his awful face to do it, then so be it. A few moments later he removed the cloth and his eyes again searched her face. They were a dark gold at that moment. She also saw a glint of steel, but then it was gone. She found his eyes beautiful, though mostly she loved the devotion with which he looked at her, as if there were no one else in the world worthy of his gaze.

"Thank you," he said, his eyes continued to roam her face and finally settled on her lips, he licked his lips and closed his eyes.

He picked up his mask again and began to place it on his face. She very much wanted him to wear it, but took it from his hands.

"It is too warm, leave it off."

"I cannot, Christine," he said sadly. He took it from her and replaced it on his face, adjusted the buckles and began to play. Her heart went out to her husband. Hiding his face was so ingrained in him that even when there was no one to ridicule him, he still imposed the mask on his face and hid, seeking its safety. She was ashamed of her reaction to his face, even though she had kept it to herself.

She sat by his side as he played part of his new composition for her. He asked for her thoughts and at one point she bravely gave her opinion, suggested a change. He tried it on the piano, nodded his approval of her suggestion and made the change on the music sheet. It took the piece in another direction. "My muse," he murmured. He switched to the violin and played a Haydn minuet for a while.

She had danced to that tune with Raoul, and her thoughts strayed to the latest note she had sent Raoul. He should have received it by now, perhaps even answered it. Christine suggested to Erik that she should visit with Meg. She was surprised when he readily agreed and she almost ran to her room to get dressed, but restrained herself. She gathered her things and slowly walked to her room. She could hear Erik playing and she relived every moment she had spent in Raoul's arms as she got herself ready for her visit with Meg. The last thing she did was peek at Raoul's photograph before she put it at the bottom of her drawer again.

As soon as she was ready, Christine set out on a visit to her friend. She wore a yellow summer visiting dress with a low collar and a jaunty little hat with a tiny yellow-green feather perched on her head. Erik rowed them across the lake and accompanied her to Mme. Giry's door.

As she knocked on the door, he kissed her cheek,

his lips curling just a little. She greeted Meg as she opened the door. As usual, Erik was already gone.

Meg was in a loose house dress, dabbing her face with a handkerchief. "They had to cancel rehearsals today—Sorelli almost passed out from the heat!" She made a face, imitating the swooning ballerina. They both giggled.

"Look, Meg." She pulled out a few wedding photographs from her bag.

"Oh, no! My hat was crooked." Meg looked in mock horror at a picture of the entire wedding group.

"What?"

"My hat...look," Meg said, pointing. "It's not quite right. We will just have to take that picture again."

"Oh Meg!" Christine giggled and lightly punched her friend's arm.

"You were a beautiful bride. Everyone said so. The photograph is lovely. Too bad Erik has to wear that thing on his face. It must be awful what he hides under there."

"It is not awful at all," she lied in his defense. "He's just not a very good looking man. Why, if he were not so shy, he could show his face very easily."

"I'm sure you're right," Meg said without conviction.

"And, how is your relationship progressing with your beau?" she asked her friend.

"Éduard says he is gathering his courage to tell his mother about us," Meg answered sadly. "He must have a lot of courage, because he has been gathering a long time."

Meg looked around and said in Christine's ear, "Comte Philippe handed this to me." Meg took a piece of paper from her drawer and gave Christine a folded note.

Christine felt her hands tremble as she held what must be Raoul's response to her own note. She felt her stomach clench as if she were going to throw up.

"You look ill, Christine!" Concerned, Meg touched her arm.

"I feel terrible. Look at what I hold in my hand!" she cried, waving the note. "A knife to plunge into my husband's heart! He loves me so much, Meg, that sometimes I can't stand it. Poor Erik!" She buried her face in her hands. "Have I sunk so low?" she whimpered, her eyes filling with tears.

"Please, put it away…if my mother should see it…" Meg said nervously.

"Meg, what do I do?"

"Throw it out. Give it back and I'll burn it."

"I can't it's from Raoul. What if…"

"You have a kind husband who dotes on you and you start having an *affaire* with your former fiancé! My dear friend, you are spoiled!"

"I am not having an *affaire*. I…" she began, her eyes filling up.

"Yes, you are, Christine. You send notes to each other behind your husband's back. It is a *liaison*! And look at me, I am betraying the man who for years has given my mother financial stability." She pointed to a pair of tiny ballerina slippers hanging on her dresser mirror. "He bought those for me when I was nine."

"I have put you in a terrible position, I'm sorry."

"Oh, never mind all this sadness. I know what we need…let's get a mineral water from the Bon-Deux café, they always have frigid drinks there!" Meg suggested.

"I can't leave, Erik doesn't know," Christine protested.

"Come on, Christine, it's only around the corner."

"All right, but we'll only get a mineral water, and we'll come right back."

"Let me get Maman, she will want a cold drink too." Meg looked down at herself with a gasp. "No, you get my Maman, while I get dressed."

Before getting Mme. Giry, Christine paused in the doorway and opened Raoul's note.

Dearest Christine,

My health and strength have returned, so that I am again capable of dealing with the fiend who inhabits the bowels of the earth.

When can we meet? Your kisses are still fresh on my lips. Our passion feeds my heart, yet I hunger for more. You have spoilt my lips for anyone else. I do not depend on dear Philippe as I am a naval officer and have my own resources.

I know he makes you write of obligations to him,

but those are not your own thoughts. He hopes to weaken my resolve. The rogue who came between us months ago could never understand the purity of our love or how everything we have shared throughout the years endures.

On my honor, I will set you free from that farce of a marriage.

Forever in your debt,
Your fiancé,
Raoul, Vicomte de Chagny

Christine dabbed at her eyes with the monogrammed handkerchief Erik had bought her and went to get Mme. Giry. If only Raoul had saved her before she got married. It was too late, she had given her solemn vow.

He had doubts about letting her go outside their home on her own. "Are you sure about returning to the lake on your own, Christine? The stairs and tunnels can be confusing. This composition is not so important." A terrible feeling of doom clung to his heart. He no longer felt like working on his music.

"I will be fine. Oh pooh, I know the way back to the lake, you'll pick me up and bring me home," she insisted.

It eased his mind that she had said home, but the awful feeling did not leave his chest. "At what time will you be by the shore?"

"I will be ready to come home by five o'clock."

There it was again, the word 'home.' If she considered it her home, she would return as promised. He felt he should trust her, but his past history with people and his heart told him otherwise.

"I will be there."

He sat at his piano, working on a particularly difficult part of his composition. Lately, he had found inspiration coming to him in great spurts. At times, he even found himself sitting at his desk designing buildings that he knew would never be built. Her mere presence in their home caused his mind to imagine structures that were beyond the capabilities of the available materials. *Perhaps a hundred years from now those very tall buildings he was designing could be built.* His compositions also took on a lighter note, their complexity achieved not by darkness but by light. His music was still sensually rich and mysterious, but the stark darkness that had permeated all of his earlier work was gone. He had even set aside his tortured, *Don Juan Triumphant*, finding nothing to add to that composition.

He took his watch out. It was almost time. He went back to his music, but a few minutes later he was checking his timepiece again. Once more, he attempted to let the music take his mind off a terrible foreboding, but he did not last a full minute this time.

It was five o'clock sharp as the boat approached the shore. He could not see her by the shore. *What if something had happened to her on the way down?* Although they had been through the tunnel and stairs leading to the lake several times together, it was the first time she would come down by herself. There was no possibility she could get lost. She knew the way, he was certain. He rubbed the back of his neck as he watched the water gently lapping against the stones. She was late!

He trudged up the trail leading to the small Giry apartment. He put his ear to the door. Usually he could hear the girls, their peals of laughter through the door. Now there was only silence. He went around a side passage. Not having used it in many years, it was full of spider webs. He could see well in the dark, and soon found the latch that opened a panel inside a cupboard. He went through and into the Giry parlor. It was empty. He crossed the room, and let himself into the rest of the apartment. All the rooms were empty. The air in the room seemed to rush out and he was left gasping for breath.

"Ahhh! No, no." His anguished cry rang through the empty house. He felt a familiar ache in his chest which made him double up.

They betrayed me! From the old hag, to her useless daughter, this folly will cost them dearly! His heart beat wildly in his chest. Christine wouldn't break her vows lightly. Not now, they were married. She seemed peaceful when she was with him. They had shared so much. She said they were family! She would not, could not fake all that just to fool him, and be free of her cage. *I should not have let her see my face this morning. It was my damnable face that drove her away.*

Christine would not be coming back. Erik could barely breathe. The pressure in his chest built and he pressed against it with a splayed hand. His medicine was down in his house. He let himself back into the cupboard, leaning against the back until he could fill his lungs fully again. The chest pains weakened his legs, so he descended slowly toward the cellars, feeling his way along the walls. *So, she has made her escape with two accomplices.* By now, she could be in the arms of the boy, perhaps in his bed.

You fool, Erik! You sleep on the *floor like a maggot and she goes to writhe in his bed!*

His legs trembled. He heard the rumblings of the Voice clearly but what if he had heard wrong? What if it was only of rats in the tunnels, stage hands moving equipment? His jagged breathing made him stop in the darkened stairs in order to orient himself. He had repressed it since he left Persia and now after so many years, it was back in his head.

Fool!

Stop! Please not now. Erik cannot listen to you now.

He would not listen to *that* voice. It stood for death, and corruption. It stood for the most evil things he had ever done. That voice in his head was responsible for the bloodbaths he had been in charge of in Mazandaran. True, he was under the orders of the sovereign Shah, but it had been Erik who had, invented and constructed the torture chambers and most important, it was Erik who had pulled the deadly levers hundreds of times and watched for their effect. He continued down to the fifth cellar, holding onto the walls for support. His chest felt as if it would explode.

Fool for letting her go. You had her, and let her go. How could it be any other way? You forced her to be with you.

Erik is her husband, not the boy! His neck corded as he shouted at the Voice.

But who is her lover now?

No! She is an angel!

Who has ever loved you?

No one! But she can look into my face and not cringe! Who else would do that, but an angel? His chest felt tight, as if a hard lump was wedged between his ribs. I thought she could forget him and learn to love me.

She is not an Angel! She is with you to save the boy. She has sacrificed her life for him.

I love her and she can get used to me in time.

You expect her to forget the boy and love you? Fool!

Not love, how could she, but she can learn to care for me.

He would get her back, regardless of the bodies he had to pile up to get to her. Once through the door of his home, he grabbed for the bottle and took a deep swig of his medicine. He slumped into a chair and waited for the worst of the pain to pass.

You must go and take what is yours.

I will get her back. Blood will flow through the

streets like an overturned bath. They will all pay, the guilty and the innocent alike.

I will be with you.

Yes!

Erik dragged himself to the entrance of the tunnel and screamed as loud as he could manage. "Sebastian, Sebastian!"

Erik heard running footsteps.

"M'sieur, what's wrong?" Sebastian was dressed all in black. His short hair was plastered against his scalp with an overabundance of cheap pomade. He was slightly shorter than Erik and twice as wide. His strong features were overpowered by his soiled appearance. His dark eyes were surrounded by pale, dirty skin.

"She has been stolen," Erik growled. He was not willing to admit to anyone that she had run away to be with the vicomte.

"You wife M'sieur? Stolen?"

"Yes, yes stolen. Who else would I care about?"

"What am I good for M'sieur?" the big man asked.

"I need guns," Erik said.

"Thought you didn't like guns, M'sieur."

"I will have my lasso, but...I am not a fool. That boy will be waiting for me. Get two rifles—the best you can buy. Here, that should cover it." He handed Sebastian a few bills, careful not to touch the filthy hand, even with his gloves on.

"I'll hav'em by tomorrow," the rat-catcher answered.

"By early morning—and ammunition—bring plenty of that," Erik added. "And four sacks of saltpeter. I have everything else we'll need."

He nodded in comprehension. "Who we huntin'?"

"The Vicomte de Chagny and whosoever gets in the way!" he answered.

As soon as his chest ache subsided, he took out a bottle of cognac and poured himself half a glass.

Erik paced back and forth in the parlor, feeling unnaturally cold in his misery. He drank deeply as he walked. Later, he would alert his siren. She had to guard the lake. He felt a pang of guilt. Since his marriage to Christine, he seldom sang to the siren. He had met her by the sea when he was a child and now because she chose him, she only had the small underground lake under the opera house to roam, instead of an ocean. More than once she had pulled under the few souls, who had been intrepid enough to venture into his underground realm in the fifth cellar. So many years together and now with Christine by his side he had ignored her. He had forgotten about her for weeks, favoring the company of that wretched, deceitful wife of his. He took another swig of his medicine and retreated to his bedroom with the bottle of cognac.

Christine waited on the other side of the lake for Erik to pick her up. She knew he would worry because she was late. The three women had gone to the café, and time had gotten away. She enjoyed her outing, but now she was ready to come home. Funny, how she had come to regard the house by the lake as her home. She loved being out in the sun, but now she longed for the soothing, cool darkness. When he arrived, she would hug him and he would hug her back. Christine rang the bell again. She noticed a few roaches crawling along the wall. Ugh!

Quickly she rang again. As her anxiety increased, she noticed more and more insects. Christine closed her eyes against the invaders. She hated every kind of bug. Christine picked up her skirts off the floor and rang again.

"Erik!" she called out. It was so quiet down here that he had to hear her. She had imagined him pacing and worrying. Now she realized he was still probably involved in his music, and hadn't given her a thought all day. He wasn't even aware of her return. She supposed that that was good, since what scared her most about him was his obsession with her. Clearly, that was played out now that he had her. Perhaps the daily contact had withered the novelty of her presence. Still, he wasn't even showing her the common courtesy due a wife. She saw a large rat staring up at her from a corner.

"ERIK!" She rang and rang the bell. *Damn his uncaring soul!*

134

From somewhere in the muddled of his mind, he heard the sound. Erik fought back to consciousness and sat up in the coffin. The stupor of pain and drink had fogged his senses.

Christine...Christine?

Christine! The bell! She came back to me! Somehow, he crawled out of the coffin, lost his balance and fell, sprawling on the floor. The coffin rocked on the dais.

"Christine!"

He had to get to her, but his mind and his body would not cooperate and obey him. He felt numb, his brain was held by a vice that didn't let him think. Half crawling and holding on to the walls, he made his way to the boat. Twice he slipped and nearly fell, but kept going. He slipped onto the seat and began to row the boat across the lake.

"ERIK!" He heard her scream. Erik heard her final shriek just as he made out her moving form. Christine was holding up her skirts and doing a little dance on the far shore. He could see her eyes glued to a rat hiding on the side. She was calling his name, talking to him, but he was still too far away to hear her. The scene was so amusing to him that he threw his head back and laughed. When he reached the shore, she jumped into his arms, complaining and hugging him tight. He had to peel her off and before he could help her get in the boat, she rushed past him and sat on the bench. He regained some control over the boat and his emotions, managing somehow to row them back. She kept staring at him with her wide innocent eyes as if he had just saved her life.

He was anxious to get her across the lake and back into their home. On reaching their shore, he took her off the boat and held her tightly. Still in his arms, Erik nuzzled her neck and dared lay little kisses on her exposed collarbone. Christine moaned and clung to him. It was nearly his undoing. Longing overtook reason. He let his hand wander just above her waist to where her body rounded softly. He backed away from her, realizing where his mouth had been and horrified at what his hand had been about to do.

Erik walked ahead to let her into their home and she waltzed past him looking angry. Perhaps she had guessed his intention and was offended or she was still upset about his delay. What mattered most was that Christine had come back on her own! Tomorrow morning he would have Sebastian store the new rifles and the hefty supply of ammunition away from their house. No doubt, he would also find out why his wife was so upset with him. Erik dropped back into his coffin and with a smile on his lips slept until morning.

Chapter 10

The Tunnel

"Are you content Christine? Living here with me?" He did not give her a chance to answer. "It makes me so happy to have you with me, I would loathe to deny you some level of contentment."

They sat in the library having their afternoon tea. She looked up from her cup, wondering what had prompted this line of questions. He wore a new suit, black like most of his clothing. Like all his garments, it was cut and padded to hide his thinness. The half-mask covered most of his expression, but she could see his mouth was set in a straight line, his hands holding on tightly to the chair armrest. "I am fine, Erik, especially since I can now visit with my friends. I enjoy that very much. I will serve you a second cup, you only had the one," she told him.

"I will have another cup if you sit by me. We can look at our photographs again," he offered.

"Oh yes, I would love that." She sat on a low stool by his side, poured his cup of tea, and handed it to him. "Here's your cup."

"Thank you, Christine. You are joining me in one?" he asked her

"I guess I could have a second cup myself," she answered, and poured a second cup. "But no more than that." She looked at him pointedly.

"I have been meaning to apologize for that. It was unconscionable of me. In my defense, if there is any, I imagined you were thinking of…of him…and it drove me…"

"That is over, Erik. I am your wife. My thoughts are about us."

"I hope so, Christine." His eyes searched her face for sincerity.

She pointed to her friend in the photograph. "Look at Meg, she looked so pretty that day," she said, pointing to the picture

"I remember little Giry as a child. She was so silent, a proper little lady, always following her mother."

"*That* does not surprise me. I did not remember how many people attended our wedding," she said, pointing to the group picture. "All the guests are here except for those friends of yours you won't talk about…and no I'm not asking about them." It surprised her when he broke into raucous laughter.

"Those *friends* as you call them, are automata."

"Is that a type of singer like the *castrato*?"

He barked in laughter again. "After I built the palace in Persia, the Shah had me make…let's call them mannequins, with mechanical part that move."

"Your friends were not real people? But…" She was both fascinated and horrified.

"The Shah's automata were exact replicas of him. If you wound them up they would move their eyes, blink, and move their mouths, even an arm. My two newest ones can turn their heads and even swivel their torso, not all at once you understand, but I digress. The Shah, wanted his enemies to think he was where he was not. What better way, than to have copies of himself distributed throughout the palace?"

"But yours don't look like you."

"Nor would I ever want them to." He faked an exaggerated shudder.

"I built mine for company. I was alone in these cellars for ten years. They are some of the kindest people I have ever known."

"I thought they were your friends." It was the saddest story she had ever heard̄mannequins for company. *Poor Erik!*

"Mm…I wanted them there as fillers to make the room look fuller for our wedding."

"And the man in the shadows standing by them, was he a mannequin too?"

Erik smiled benevolently. "No, he kept winding them up and eventually took them away. They can't walk you know."

"That was the man who came to our house that time. The one you were kind to."

Erik nodded. "He is the Opéra rat-catcher and you will never meet him," he said in a tone that closed the subject.

"Why not?"

"He catches rats! I do not want you near disease. He can be of no service to you."

She sighed, knowing that nothing else would come of further questioning. "It was a wonderful wedding. Meg says they still talk about it upstairs."

"Exactly *who* talks about it?" he asked, whipping around to face her just as a buzzing alarm sounded. "What now for pity's sake?" he exclaimed.

"Could it be Hafiz?" asked Christine.

"In that tunnel? No, that is an internal passage. It has to be a rat that triggered my alarm," he told her.

"Maybe it's that friend of yours. The rat-catcher," she said, tempting him into responding.

Silently he got up, stretching up to his full height. "More likely a rat he failed to catch. I will have to go see," he said. He handed her the photographs and stormed out the front entrance toward the lake.

For the first time since they were married, Erik left the front door leading to the lake open. Christine followed him out the door. She saw him light one of the torches he kept by the side of the lake, and watched his tall, dark form walk up a few steps; eventually fading away into the tunnel's shadow. As he walked in, she could hear him cursing whilst he groped along trying to light other torches along the tunnel walls. She smiled at how easily he became frustrated and annoyed. Christine had just turned back toward the house, when a thunderous crash froze her in her tracks. She turned to see a great blast of dust puff out the tunnel with force, and then silence.

At that moment, Christine felt her heart stop. Her mouth opened, but she could not move. "Erik?" she whispered. "Erik?" she repeated louder, and rushed to the tunnel entrance. It was completely blocked by rocks. As the dust settled, the darkness and silence were entombing. "Erik!" she called again, yelling this time, her mouth dry. She felt light-headed, and had to hold herself up against the wall. *This cannot be happening!* Her legs were trembling so much; she could not move another step. "Erik, please answer!" Images of Erik flooded her mind, his golden eyes following her around their home, Erik in the kitchen squirreling away cookies when he thought she couldn't see him, curled up on the rug in her room. *It can't be.*

She waited to hear his voice booming in the tunnel. *He will come out cursing and damning half the world!* She tried to smile at the thought, but her stomach tightened at the silence, the only sound being the lapping water at the lake's shore. Her heart raced and she gulped in air. Her eyes stole to the small boat by the lake. The gas lamps by the lake flickered creating shadows on the cavernous walls. *If he were...I would be free. I could go to Raoul and marry the man I love. No more cellars. No Erik.* But she found no satisfaction in that half-thought. Her entire body felt cold, and she slid down onto the steps. *Don't be dead, Erik, please!*

She remembered Meg's words from her last visit, she was spoiled! Even now she expected him to save himself, to get out, to come to her. From her very center, she found a kernel of strength that was new to her. "Erik!" she began to shout. "Erik!" Her voice grew stronger. "Erik!" *Maybe if he can hear me, he will find his way out.* "ERIK!" *He will be so upset if I hurt my throat!* Christine walked over some of the rubble the tunnel had spewed and at the blocked entrance began to remove small rocks from the top to let air into the passageway. She wasn't sure how helpful it was, but she continued to remove debris. "ERIK!" she shrieked several times through a small opening she made. She took a nearby torch and placed it near the opening. Swallowing a sob she called to him, "Erik! Come this way."

Sections of the tunnel collapsed as he tucked himself securely between the support beams, for once grateful to be so thin. Even his torch was unscathed. He slipped out to check how much of the tunnel had caved in. He cursed himself for not checking it more carefully. Who knew what structural damage it had sustained during the reign of the Commune? His torch burned brightly. Air was coming in from somewhere. Behind him, the section leading to the lower cellars was blocked. It was impossible, but he thought he heard voices behind the fallen rocks. *Ghosts?* His lip curled. The dust was thick, but he could see that a part of the tunnel near the entrance had also collapsed. *Now, I have to dig my way out through that rubble in my new suit!* Every breath drew dust into his lungs. The closer he walked to the entrance, the thicker the air was with dust. Grit was in his mouth and eyes. He heard his name, Christine's voice. She was calling for him! In his annoyance, he had left the door open and instead of running away she was calling for him. He did not dare call out to her, fearing the vibration from his voice would cause another collapse.

Even through his gritty, tearing eyes, he could see a glow in the direction of the entrance. He had a pair of gloves in his pocket— he did not dare think of the damage to his fingertips without them. He donned the gloves and began to remove the fallen rocks, rolling the away smaller boulders. The tunnel shifted again, and again he dashed under a support beam so the debris would not fall on him. When the tunnel stabilized, he went back to removing rocks and throwing them behind him. His torch was burning down. Sweat beads formed on his face. He took off his jacket.

Sweat poured off his body, soaking his clothes.

He would need to fit between the rubble and the space at the top of the tunnel. Even with gloves on, he could feel the rocks damaging his hands as he dragged himself through. He gritted his teeth and pulled himself over the jagged rocks. He saw a waving light and continued crawling through the crevice toward it. He was almost at the entrance when he felt a tremor in the tunnel behind him. There were no support beams he could get under—he would be crushed. No time for a dignified exit. Erik jumped through the hole, dislodging the remaining loose rocks and allowed himself to roll down the pile of rubble, almost crashing into Christine. He landed on his back, wheezing and coughing.

"Erik!"

He looked up to see her pale face hovering above him, wide eyed. She was all over him, hugging him and laughing all at once.

"Are you all right?" she asked him.

"I'm…fine…Christine…I heard you from…the back of the tunnel," he tried to catch his breath between spasms.

She hugged him again and held him so tight it hurt his tired muscles. "Come, come inside." She pulled him up, and they entered their home again.

Surprisingly, she clung to him as if he would disappear into the tunnel again. She had one arm around his waist, her head on his shoulder. His arms dangled wearily by his side. In this manner, they walked into the kitchen.

She pushed him down and made him sit on a stool while she got hot water, soap, and rags. When she returned, he was still seated on the stool, hunched over and coughing deeply. His dirty, ripped shirt clung to his skeletal frame. She made him hold his hands out in front of him while she removed the tattered gloves from his hands. The sharp rocks had torn his gloves mercilessly, but had saved his hands.

She approached him with a towel and a bowl of water, but he stood up.

"Where are you going?" she asked him.

"I am in a state of undress. I will go seek my clothes and…" He had to stop as a bout of coughing made him breathless. "Clean my mask." He coughed.

"Just sit down, Erik."

A hacking cough overtook him. She patted his back until the spasm ceased. He took the towel and bowl from her and turned away. After removing his mask, he wiped his face with the wet towel, then plunged his head into the bowl, keeping his eyes open to get the grit out, and swished his head around in the water.

"All done." She smiled, holding his cleaned mask. He took it from her and replaced it on his face. "It's still a little damp so why don't you leave it off? You do not need to wear it at home," she pleaded while her heart beat wildly. She wanted him to feel comfortable at home, but feared her own reaction to his face.

"I can't walk around…" He stopped to cough.

"Before we married, didn't you walk around without a mask?"

"Yes, when I was alone and could not offend anyone." He coughed. "Unless I passed in front of a mirror." He grinned slightly at his own joke. "This face of mine is not meant to be seen by anyone." He stopped for another coughing episode. "Not even by its owner."

"So, I am anyone to you?"

"You know what you mean to me." He lifted her chin with his hand and looked into her eyes. "I just cannot just walk around without a mask on, as if I were normal. I am tied to this accursed thing as much as it is tied to me!" he said, shaking his head. *My wife does not want me to wear my mask? So I did die in the tunnel after all!*

Erik spent the late evening working on his composition, stopping to cough or to drink water. She sat next to him, put her arms around his waist and gave him a soft hug.

"You should turn in early and get extra rest." He did not protest, and went to ready himself for sleep. She was waiting for him when he returned dressed for sleep in his kameez and soft trousers.

"Come on," she said, giving him a warm smile. "You must be exhausted, and need proper rest."

He did feel exhausted, and went straight toward his rug.

"Not there...no more of that." Her mouth quivered.

"I'll rest in my room then, good night," he mumbled, hurt, but not completely surprised she no longer wanted him in her bedroom. It had to happen one day. He headed for the door with firm strides, hoping to save a little dignity.

"That is not what I meant," she said, stopping him and taking him by the hand. She walked him toward her bed.

He pulled back when he realized what she wanted. "I can't." He coughed. "I will be fine right there." He pointed to the rug by her bed.

"And you would leave me in bed, all alone, when I feel so nervous about that horrible accident?" she asked in her sweetest voice. "I am still shaking from it."

"It is too much. How could I…" He wondered what had gotten into her that she would make such a suggestion.

"Erik, you are my husband! Come to bed." She pulled and pushed him until he was sitting on her bed. "Lay down, Erik," she insisted. "That cough worries me. Let me take care of you tonight."

It felt wonderful to have her touch him with such concern. He would stay in bed with her, if only one night…perhaps he could remain until she cringed away from him as she was bound to do, and that day even if it were tonight he would crawl away and die.

"I will interrupt your sleep with this…damned cough!" he complained through another coughing fit.

"I know it's bad. You too, might find comfort when you sleep by my side."

Innocent child, what man could sleep in comfort lying by your side? Even a eunuch would resurrect that which was lost to him. And, I am no eunuch! He coughed again.

She had a jar of honey in her hand. "Open," she ordered, tapping his lips with a spoon. He opened his mouth gingerly and she gave him a teaspoon of honey. "This will help you with that cough."

He slipped in beside next to her. The bed felt marvelous, softer than his coffin, similar to a bed he had used in Mazandaran. He lay stiffly next to her, facing the ceiling. He had never slept next to another human being. From the corner of his eye, he noticed she was scrutinizing him.

"It won't do," she finally said.

He had been to heaven, if for a few moments. *She is such a good girl, but it is too much for her.* He prepared to get off the bed and return to his rug if she allowed it or to his room and proceed to close his casket lid.

"You can't sleep with your mask on."

He was too exhausted to fight all the changes she wanted. "I will do as…you wish," he managed to cough out. "But only after the light is out." As was his usual custom, he would be up at dawn long before she had a chance to wake up next to his face. He would not risk his wife dying of such a fright.

"Then good night, Erik," she replied, turning down the gas lamp.

Even now that he was a married man, women

were still a total mystery, and as baffling as ever. Perhaps all that did not matter if he were dead, and he had to be, because his wife wanted him to sleep in her bed, without a mask covering his face. He removed his mask in full knowledge that at any moment now he would hear the nails sealing his coffin.

Chapter 11

Sunday Ride

No one had ever wanted to take care of Erik. When injured, he had licked his own wounds. A few years before he had suffered from a severe bout of bronchitis and had endured the high fevers and chills in his underground home—alone. Once he had walked over a mile in the desert with a knife stuck in his side. As a child he had survived his father's beatings. Erik was no newcomer to pain. Now, he had a wife who wanted to take care of him and he was not even sick! All he had was a slight cough due to inhaling dust. Christine was acting silly, fussing all over him, and though he loved it, he was not sure how to stop it. Mostly, he did not want to hurt her feelings, so he relented and allowed her ministrations. He had even agreed to be without a mask during their music sessions since he did not face her directly, and at bedtime. She made him put his pipe away. He missed his pipe in the afternoons.

She had concocted a mixture of honey, radish juice and lemon into a sickening syrup for his cough. Since the tunnel incident, she had poured more than a pint of her honey syrup down his throat. He was terrified of making any type of noise that she might construe as a cough. Even the smell of plain honey nauseated him now. Yet, he knew that if she stood in front of him with her concerned eyes, and offered him a spoon filled with her syrup, his mouth would open wide, and despite his shivers he would swallow the vile, sticky substance. She always caressed his jaw after he swallowed.

Christine was a rough sleeper. She turned, tossed, pushed, kicked, shoved, and hit as she slumbered, keeping an angelic look on her face through the night. He did not sleep any better for being in her bed, but for the long hours of lying in bed, he was always rewarded by an errant hand on his knee or thigh. Throughout the years, he had heard other men complaining about how their wives were rough sleepers, how these men suffered when their wives would hurt them in the middle of the night. Erik sneered at their weakness. It seemed his Christine was also a rough sleeper, and this was what happened to married men in bed, men just like him—so he delighted in a nightly pummeling by his wife.

After the second jar of her syrup he knew had to put a stop to her fussing. An idea came to him. He walked out of the bedroom yelling, "Christine, get your shawl."

"Whatever for, I'm not cold."

"Get your shawl now!" he repeated himself.

She started to walk toward her room. "Fine, but I am not cold."

"I need fresh air for…for this cough. We are going out!" he commanded.

"Outside?" Her eyes widened with excitement and she rushed to her room. In a moment she was back with a shawl in her hands.

"Are you sure you are up to it?"

"Yes, now allow me to help you," he said, wrapping her shoulders in the woolen shawl.

Erik sat next to her on the Coupé and opened the window to allow fresh air to enter the stuffy carriage. They had not been out on a carriage ride since before they were married. Months before, as his pupil, he had taken her out a few times, but a chance meeting with the vicomte one night had put a quick end to those rides. The boy had recognized Christine and chased after the carriage calling after them. She had been merely his pupil then and he, her voice Maestro. Things were different now, she was his wife. He had the right to take her out wherever he pleased.

The horses clopped along the streets. He saw her

look out the window as they passed places of interest to her, made little comments about a fountain or monument she liked. Her hand lay on the seat between them. He covered it with his, and held his breath. In a sense, they were in public, and so Erik expected her to slide her hand away, if not at first then as soon as possible. He was surprised that not only did she not move her hand away, but rather, she turned it over so that her palm faced his. The feeling was tremendous and he was unable to concentrate on anything else for the rest of the ride. It came to him in a flash that it was Sunday, and he was riding with his wife in a carriage on his way to the park, just as he had always wanted to do, just like any other man.

On their way down the Champ Elysées she called out, "Oh look. Erik! We are nearing the Tuileries. Can we go into the park?" He looked out the window and saw a sea of carriages like theirs heading the same way.

"We can go wherever my wife wishes to go," he answered.

Christine mentioned being disappointed that she knew no one. Although he wore his most lifelike mask, he was glad not to have encountered a known soul. By the time they returned the gas lights along the Champ Elysées were lit up, and the entire avenue was bathed in a romantic glow. Couples sat in the open-air cafés or strolled down the concourse. She placed her head on his shoulder, and he leaned into her.

"Can we visit Mama Valérius next time we're out?" she asked him.

"Of course, if it is your wish."

"You have not coughed once. Maybe we should go out more often. It could be that the fresh air helps clear your lungs." She sighed.

All the time they were riding, she had not once disengaged her hand from his. Only upon their return home did they disengage so he could help her descend the carriage. At once, he placed her hand over his arm to walk into the opera house via the rue Scribe.

Christine had hated the mask he wore during their carriage ride. It had an expressionless face that she found disturbing when he turned toward her. Whenever she looked his way, she felt as if a stranger sat next to her. She held on to his gloved bony hand to assure herself it was he. When his voice emanated from behind the strange face, she relaxed into the tranquil security found in his voice. Regardless, she could hardly wait until he took her out again. Perhaps he really would take her to see Mama Valérius.

In his last note to her, Raoul had set a date for them to meet. They had exchanged several notes since she had married Erik. All her letters said the same thing: she was now married, and could never be with him again. All of his letters said: he would come for her and save her from Erik. What if Raoul charges down here one day with half the Parisian police?

Where would Erik hide? How would she protect him? Christine felt exhausted from keeping secrets.

"Are you all right, my dear?" Erik looked up slightly and watched her. He seemed to frown a little, but kept on playing.

"I am fine. I am just going over my list of things to do. Did you realize we are running out of cleaning soap again?" she rambled, feeling awful about the lie.

For the first time in her life, she had a permanent home. Even Daddy Daaé had not been able to provide that for her after her mother passed away. The closest she had gotten to a home was while they lived with Professor and Mama Valérius. Now she had a home, her own home, with a husband who adored her. A husband she was not in-love with, but whom she cared for. She did not want to lose what she had.

In their home she insisted on cooking meals for him while she considered him ill. Once he released himself from her care, he found that he had to share the kitchen with her. At first, he had been incensed to have her meddling while he was trying to make them a meal, but he learned to enjoy cooking their meals together with her. She kept breakfast and the afternoon Salon du Thé as her exclusive domains.

Christine was convinced that all his ills emerged from malnutrition and told him so. She insisted that as a good wife, part of her care was to feed him. He finally consented to eat in the same room with her, but not at the same table.

"Here's your breakfast." She set the food in front of him on the kitchen counter and sat across the room at the table with a similar plate. He had to lift his mask to eat his breakfast. He filled his mouth with eggs, and chewed on several pieces of ham with unusual hunger.

"If you ate like this more often you would gain a few pounds. You're very thin you know."

"Yes, I have an idea." *What an absolutely atrocious habit that healthy, beautiful people have! Why do they feel an irresistible need to inform others like me, about the state of their bodies, as if the owner of that body were completely oblivious to the state of their health, weight and looks?*

"Here," she said, setting another piece of buttered bread in front of him. He was full but did not want to refuse her kindness. She went back to her seat at the table to finish her own breakfast. He noticed she did not take her eyes off him until he took a bite of his toast, then she smiled and tucked into her meal.

Later in the day, Christine walked into the library to find Erik reading a letter. When he noticed her, he folded it and put it in his coat pocket.

"I didn't know you received correspondence," she said, looking at him sweetly.

"Why should I not receive correspondence? Am I

not like other men who know people who would write to them? I am not a ghost or an angel, but a man of flesh and blood," he barked. "I had a life outside these walls before I entombed myself here, and have known many people throughout my life." She was silent and round eyed as he paced in front of her. "Nor am I a criminal, hunted by the police," Erik spat at her, and began to fold up his letter.

She cringed under the barrage and made herself as small as possible on the divan. "I am sorry, Erik," she managed to say in a shaky voice. "My silly comment was…not intended as you thought."

He noticed how pale she had become, and cursed his temper. "No matter, I apologize for raising my voice, and frightening you."

"I…I *was* frightened a little," she said, in a small voice.

"I will be gone for a few days," he said, seeking to make her feel better. Erik feared her reaction. Would she hoot and dance or would she run to pack, and wait for him at the lake's edge eagerly awaiting her deliverance? He braced himself for her glee.

"Where are we going?" she asked smiling, color returning to her cheeks.

Poor girl, she still does not understand that she will be free of me for a few days. "I apologize yet again, my dear, but I need to travel alone."

"Oh." She looked disappointed.

"You will remain with Mme. Giry. I will make the arrangements."

"How long will you be gone?"

"Two or three days at most."

"May I know where my husband is traveling to?" she asked stiffly. She looked dejected, which was to him a further surprise.

"Near Rouen, to visit an old acquaintance."

"I see." She pursed her lips. "Will you be leaving immediately?"

"Tomorrow," he informed her tenuously.

"I would like to pack right away," she said in a thickened voice, and ran toward her bedroom, slamming the door behind her. Her reaction thoroughly confused him.

Erik shook his head as he walked to the liquor cabinet and poured himself a large brandy. He glugged it down until the glass was empty. He sat with a second glass, admiring its golden hues; it was one of his favorites, an amontillado. *Damn it!* Why could she not ever do anything he thought she would do? He took out the letter again and reread it.

Dear Erik,

It would please me if you spent a few days with me, in this your home. We must share conversations that a letter would render wordy. Allow me to say my piece, and then you can make your own accounts. I will send a carriage for you on Thursday morning. It will be stationed outside rue scribe entrance to the Opéra at midday.

Your father,

LR

He turned it over in his hand, admiring the fine linen paper. A small watermark in the corner showed an intricate LR. *Even the ink is of high quality*! He placed it in his pocket once more. It was the third letter he had received from the man.

It was well past midday on Sunday when Erik stepped out onto the rue Scribe. His cape snapped in the wind, alerting the coachman of his presence. The full-face black mask covered his face. He blinked hard at the bright light. The sun shone brightly on a nearly cloudless sky. Just to the side of the street the black Landau waited for him. Erik noticed the emblazoned coat of arms on the side and snorted. As he neared the carriage two men in pale blue and silver livery bowed, one opened the carriage door. His luggage disappeared into the carriage and a footman lit the inside lamp for him. A hand appeared to help him up. He batted the hand away and swung himself onto the seat. The interior was burgundy velvet and leather. *So, this is how he lives! He will miss it in the next life.* As the carriage lurched forward, he put his hand under his cloak and assured himself of the lasso's presence. *Not unreasonable, it only took him forty-two years to recognize me as his son. It will take thirty-nine seconds for me to sever the relationship, not unreasonable either.* The Opera Ghost grinned as he reclined and slowly sank into the plush comfort.

Chapter 12

New Prospects

He was impressed, not by the opulence, for he had seen greater in both Persia and Constantinople, but by the fact that it belonged to the man who had sired him.

Years ago, after he returned from his travels to the Far East, he had gone to see his mother, Cecile Ménard Bernay. His informant had told him that a few years before her husband, Pascal Bernay, had thrown her out in favor of a young, curvy barmaid. Cecile now lived in a small attic room she shared with several other servants. He sent her word and she agreed to meet him after dark around the back of the house by the servants' entrance. She was older, her slower movements a testament to the fact that she was worn-out. Her drab brown hair showed streaks of gray. The beautiful woman he remembered had been replaced by a used up hag. Cecile had been as bad a mother to him as there could be, but it bothered him to see her this way. She stared at his mask as he approached her, then for the first time ever she looked straight into his eyes and did not shudder as she often had in the past. He handed her a wad of money and she quickly tucked it away in her skirt pocket.

"It's enough money for you to leave here. No need for you to live like this. I'll give you more next month."

"You done well fo' yerself. No thanks to me."

He didn't need to answer. She continued to scrutinize him.

"All grown. I thaut you was dead."

"And you cared?" There was no answer.

"No," she said finally. "But din't wish it neither."

He had been about to turn away when he felt a light pull on his sleeve. It was the one of the few times that he remembered her willingly touching him. With a hand gesture, she motioned him to sit on a rough wooden bench.

"None of us done right by you. Specially him— his Da. He din't do right by no one but hisself. Not even by his own boy."

She told Erik of his origins. She had been pregnant when she married Pascal Bernay, the man he had called father for so long. His father had been the marquis' son on the estate where she was born then worked in. The marquis had taken her as a mistress when she was fifteen and blossomed out. A few years later he selected her to bed his son because she was beautiful and experienced. Erik was terribly embarrassed hearing the story, and hoped she would not go into details. Apparently, his mother had also been uncomfortable and glossed over most of the story, looking away from embarrassment rather than disgust of him.

Erik did not have a high regard for the concept of fatherhood. Pascal Bernay, his mother's husband—his father, as he had always known him, had hated him. He understood now—but would not forgive the man's cruelty towards him—after he heard his mother's story. Pascal had known that the child was not his and accepted payments from the marquis for his care. As a child, he had treated him like a stranger, and beaten him like a dog. He was the first to use the word 'beast' to refer to him. For Erik the words *'father'* and *'pain'* were inexorably linked together. As soon as Erik knew he would never return home, he had divested himself of his father's last name and became Emmerich Ménard and eventually just Erik.

"Louis was an innocent sweet boy back then. A dreamer. Nottin' about him was tainted. He wanned to give me a high place, he did. And his Da knocked me back down to wheras I belong."

"How can you *not* blame him?" He felt for her the anger that life had beaten out of her.

"He was a babe and we ruin him," she insisted

"Do you need me to help you move out?"

"Got my bed and my bag is all."

"I'll find you a place and take your things. Leave the bed, I'll get you one."

"Can't, his Da gave me that bed. The bastard. It's a Louis-Philippe from the château stores, he said. You was born on it. Is the only thing of value I got."

He was not the first bastard sired and abandoned by an aristocrat. That was not why he fingered his lasso as he stood in the foyer. When his mother first told him the man's name, he was taken aback. He was known as one of the "Darlings" of Parisian society, although his home was near Rouen. For years, his amorous exploits had been at the center of the society page in the Époque. His mother said he had been nothing like that when she knew him. Erik smiled, thinning his lips.

After hearing her fantastical story, he had more questions than answers and sought to know more about his real father. Luckily for Erik, it was not difficult to find him. The man frequented the Opéra when in Paris—which was often—and like many other aristocrats, he was a fixture in the dance foyer and he could be found frequenting the dressing rooms after hours as well. It had been a shock to see the man so close when Erik peeked from behind a trap door. They shared the same height, build, chin, lips and dark hair. It disturbed him to think he might have looked like that, had fate dealt him another hand. The man possessed ruggedly handsome features, not pretty like the vicomte, but manly, with a faded scar over the left eyebrow that told of past scrapes. Erik was fascinated, and yet repulsed by the man's attitude toward women. He had so many to choose from he treated them like cargo—nothing too valuable, and easily replaceable with the next shipping. Would he have been like that had he had that face, money and title? After a few years of watching him, Erik purposely ignored the rumors about the man and eventually lost track and interest in him.

About a year before his mother's death, he had visited her again to give her the annuity he bestowed on her since his return to France. When he finally told her that he had seen her former lover at the opera house, she was very pleased. A little brightness shone in her tired eyes. She had insisted that he contact him. She had even suggested that the nobleman would welcome him as his son. When Cecile began to cough up blood, her insistence that the man would welcome him if only he knew who Erik was, increased. Her wrinkled, knobby hands pressed a small locket into his hand. It had her portrait as a way to introduce himself to the nobleman. He did not laugh out of respect, but thought her naiveté amusing. She actually believed a member of the nobility, a marquis—which was to say, almost a duke—would welcome a by-blow; a deformed son born from one of his discarded servants. A son he had not looked for in over four decades.

What bothered Erik most was that his callousness with women had extended to his mother. Had he kicked her out when she told him of her pregnancy? Did he use her right up until the end, pushing her away when she was too heavy with child to satisfy his appetite? What chance did she have to claim anything from an influential aristocrat? How many sous did he pay her for her services?

He was not the first bastard sired and abandoned by an aristocrat. That was not why he fingered his lasso as he stood in the foyer. The man had abandoned his pregnant mother and never bothered with his offspring except to throw a few sous at Pascal Bernay, to keep his dirty little secret. His hand tightened over the lasso in his cape. He was standing in a foyer large enough to serve as the entire living quarters of most Parisian households. He looked around him, at the rich wallpaper and carved wood moldings. At the far end, he saw a tall, slim man walking toward him. His gait was relaxed, a broad grin crinkled his handsome face. This was the face he had seen so many years ago, chasing after the ballet rats and singers in the opera house. He was grizzled now, but he still did not look old enough to be his father. At last, he had his opportunity to even the score for her.

With the wave of the hand, the man dismissed both the butler and footman standing nearby. The two servants looked at each other with concern, but instantly obeyed. The man came closer until finally they were alone in the grand foyer. He approached Erik, his eyes shamelessly traveling over him from head to foot, and then lingering on the mask. *Throw it now. End his magnificent life!* He would have to kill the coachmen outside, perhaps one or two servants. *Simple.* Making it out of the grounds unscathed would be tricky, but not impossible. *Do it Erik, now!*

"Emmerich!" The smooth voice called to him. "You came!" The man stood five to six feet from him. Erik held the tightly coiled lasso. *Optimum distance!* He clutched the catgut and locked eyes with the man. *His eyes are just like mine!* How had he missed that before? His hand loosened slightly around the lasso.

The man covered the distance between them and held his hand out. "I have been a nervous wreck all day, thinking you might not come."

Erik kept his hands in his pockets while eyeing the icon of Parisian gallantry.

"By God!" The man stared at the mask.

Erik's eyes narrowed dangerously.

"I...I am your father." The extended hand lowered, but the smile remained on his both lips and eyes.

"How the hell would you know?" Erik retorted.

"I imagine your mask is not a fashion statement. You wear it because...because of your face. That is why I know I am your father," the man stated simply.

Erik looked at him in confusion. "Explain yourself!"

"It will take a long..."

"I have time to listen...you, on the other hand, should begin talking."

Erik noted that the man's eyebrows shot up, catching his implied threat. *I will give him a few more minutes, just to satisfy my curiosity.*

"Let us begin again…I am Louis de Reuxville."

Erik interrupted him with a wave of the hand. "I know exactly who you are and I care little for all that! What makes you think that you are…?"

"I *am* your father. I know without a doubt, just like I know what is under your mask," Louis said, looking straight into his eyes. "I have not seen it, but I can conjecture you have your grandfather's face."

Louis, the twelfth Marquis du Bourdeny had almost given up hope of finding his son, but as soon as he heard the story that there was a masked man in the opera house, he was enervated to investigate and question some of the workers. For months, Louis stayed on the track of the Opera Ghost. He listened to rumors and was most intrigued by one story in particular. A stagehand named Joseph Buquet, who stored and took care of the opera sets in the lower cellar levels, claimed to have personally seen the Opera Ghost's face while in the third cellar—his description was of a skull-like head without a nose. That could not have described Louis' father better. Recently, at the Chagny's home, Raoul's description of his fiancé's abductor gave Louis the final clue that the 'monster' Raoul described under the opera house was the son he had sought for so long.

He hired an investigator to gather information about the infamous Opéra Ghost. This investigation had yielded some, if inaccurate information. The report said that the man who lived under the opera house was an uncouth heathen, a beast. It saddened him to hear that, but he did everything he could to contact the man. Finally, his inquiries led him to a Mme. Giry, whom he gave his letter and begged her to deliver and read its contents to the Opera Ghost. The woman smiled at him strangely, but took the coins and agreed to his request. The man he had expected to arrive at his door should have been an uncivilized being. He was ready to hire the best tutors for his son. Louis was shocked, to say the least, when a well-dressed man met him. His son was well-spoken, obviously, a cultured man with a classless accent. A dangerous man as well, if his son had inherited any of his grandfather's character. How had he come to live in a filthy, watery cellar under an opera house? Did he keep a cot down there? How did he keep himself looking as gentleman like as he appeared? Positively remarkable; except for the mask, under which he was certain lay his father's face. He was baffled and had more questions than he would dare ask without first establishing a solid relationship between them. *How could Cecile have instructed her child when she was barely literate herself? Just as important ‾where had he been all these years?*

"Please come to the library, we can talk there privately." He allowed Erik to pass ahead of him.

Erik looked around the hallway while keeping his eyes on him. "I am not sure I have much to say to you."

"I can imagine your opinion of me; the aristocrat who has his fun with the servant, and then turned her out to the street," he sighed.

"Do you deny it?" his son asked with such lack of emotion that it made him swallow dry before he could answer.

"Absolutely! And in the strongest terms," countered Louis, his eyes not wavering from Erik's.

A footman rushed to open the door as they reached the library, but Louis waved him away. "Come inside, Emmerich."

"For you, it's Erik. But I will take a seat, and brandy. And then you will explain to me why you had me come here. I suggest you do not waste my time."

"Come in, I have some of the best brandy in France." He swept in front of Erik.

They entered a room paneled in black walnut. The table in the corner was strewn with open books and other papers. The desk was in the same condition. The overstuffed leather chairs were well worn and inviting. A small fire and hot embers glowed in the fireplace.

Erik stretched out in one of the chairs, managing to look as coiled as a cobra.

Louis offered him a snifter. Erik took it and turned the warm glass in his hands

"It's an Armagnac," offered Louis hesitantly.

From the look Erik gave him, he gathered that not only had he known that, but found the comment amusing rather than offensive.

His son's eyes were fixed on the honey-colored liquid in the snifter. "Nine years." He sniffed, then put the glass to his lips, tasting the liquid. "Maybe ten. It is good, but not the best in France. I expect, it is not *your* best."

Louis laughed and bowed his head in respect. He was intrigued— not only had his son guessed the correct age of the liquor, but he sounded like he had tasted better. Getting to know his son was going to be interesting. He offered Erik a cigarillo, which was promptly refused with a shake of the head.

"I only smoke my own blend," Erik said dryly.

"You did not seem surprised when I said I was your father," Louis said, lighting up his cigarillo.

"It was not news."

"You knew about me?" He could hardly contain his excitement.

"Yes."

"How?"

"My poor mother," Erik said, bitterness seeping into his voice.

"When did she tell you?"

"Some time ago."

"Where is she now?" Louis asked.

"Dead," answered Erik. His father paled. "Eight years now."

Louis squeezed his eyes shut and shook his head.

"I feared that." He took a seat behind the desk.

"I had just visited with her. She was ill." The younger man watched him intently.

"Eight years…where have you been since then? Why did you not come to me if you knew?"

Erik sat tapping his fingers on the armrest. "I will be posing the questions," Erik said sharply.

"Yes, of course."

"How did you know of my association with Mme. Giry?"

"I have spent a small fortune looking for you, as did my father before me. Madame was one of many stones overturned." Louis now understood Mme. Giry's amused smile.

When he got the first letter from his father inviting him to visit, Erik wondered why the man seeking him out now. *What does he want from me? Does he wish to hire me to do 'special work' for him?* As the Shah had expected from him in Persia? *Perhaps he wishes to offer me money for my silence regarding my birth? The opera house managers pay me 20,000 francs for the sake of peace at the Opéra. I should be able to get 40,000 francs to keep this idiot from having to affront the scandal of having a disfigured bastard for a son.* I might just let him live for that amount if he pays on time.

"Don't hate him, he was just a boy," his mother had said. "Look for him, Erik. Heard his Da is dead. He'd welcome you. Give him this here," she had handed him a small silver locket. "He'll remember, cain't have changed that much. Is all I can give you." Her tired eyes looked far away.

Erik will not hate him, mother, but I will take all he owes you and what I am owed. He had made some rough calculations a few years ago. *It is a tidy sum he owes for ignoring us.* The marquis' brandy was good, but he had better in his own cellar.

Erik dangled the silver locket. The older man's breath caught and he stared at it as if transfixed by the shiny object. Carelessly, he threw it to him. Louis caught the small oval with unsure hands. He turned the pendant over and scratched at it. A secret compartment opened. Erik's mouth slackened— he had carried the locket with him for over eight years now, and had never discovered this compartment. Frankly, he had not even thought to look. The older man looked up, and cocked his head. He extracted a tiny piece of folded paper and a few strands of hair. He gingerly touched the plaited strands of dark colored hair, and replaced them. He unfolded the note and read it.

He closed his eyes, put it to his nose, and inhaled deeply. His lip curled slightly. He opened the locket again and stared at it. He turned the picture to Erik; an amateur miniature portrait of a young Cecile.

"I have seen it," Erik said, annoyed.

With a flick of his nail, Louis flipped the oval and again, he showed it to Erik. It was another miniature this one, exquisitely painted—it was a very young boy. He handed the locket to Erik.

"Who is this?" he asked, but knew what the man would say.

"I was fifteen when it was painted."

"What does the note say?"

He passed the note to Erik.

This is your son. He is Emmerich!

"How did you know that compartment was there?"

"I gave Cecile that locket…it was my grandmother's," he answered with a tight-lipped smile.

Every part of his conversation with his mother made sense now. "You *were* a boy…at the time. And that's your hair." Erik returned the note to Louis.

"I had hair to spare then." With a finger, Louis pointed to a portrait on the wall. "The miniature was painted four years before that one there. I painted hers—as you see, that was not where my talent lay. I had just turned fifteen the first time he sent her into my room." Louis recounted as he refolded the note putting it into his pocket.

"He?"

"My father."

"Wanted to make me a man, but I fell in love. How could I not…she was at least ten years older, the most beautiful woman I had ever seen. The thing is…I believed she had come to love me too."

"Why did you make her leave?"

"I had no such power. Not even to leave myself.

My father sent her away. Did she say anything else?"

"She was sent to Lyons de la Fôret, where I was born," Erik informed him. "She worked in the manor."

"I learned that many years later." Louis pointed to Erik's mask. "May I see?"

"It is not your business," he growled at Louis.

"Forgive my manners."

"Did you hate him? Your father."

Louis shook his head. "Despite everything, I loved my father the best I could. He always wanted what he thought was best for me. It is not his fault that he did not have a clue what that was. He was more or less a prisoner here because of his face, so he made me *a man of the world* after his dreams, and desires. He lived through my misadventures; I wanted to please him, so I outdid myself. All I ever wanted was to lead a quiet life, have a family. In the end, we were both very frustrated and unhappy."

"How did your mother handle the…mask?"

"She loved him." He lifted his shoulders in a lazy shrug in answer.

Chapter 13

Madame Coquette

Christine sat having dinner with Mme. Giry and Meg. She had been abandoned by her husband and cast to the winds. She would have to live on charity until he returned—if he returned. She had a little saved up from her performances and still had that money. It was not much, but it would have to do for now, she could talk to the managers about singing again. She knew she had displeased Erik when she made the comment about the letter he received. Who had written to him that he would need to rush off like that? And was that comment so offensive that he would abandon her?

"Thank you for having me, Mme. Giry."

"You know you are always welcome here."

"These are going to be the best three days ever,"

interrupted Meg.

The old woman nodded, smiling, and began to gather the dinner plates.

"You barely touched your dinner, Christine."

"I'll bet she misses her husband," Meg teased.

"Let me help with the dishes." Christine's heart constricted at her friend's comment. She rose from the table and began to pick up dishes. "I can help in other ways too."

Mme. Giry took the plates out of her hands. "No, your husband would not like that. He does not want you to lift a finger except to enjoy yourself. You know how strict he is."

"He wants me to enjoy myself?"

"Yes, he does, he left a very generous sum. More than enough for your shopping needs, rides, restaurants, tea houses, whatever you want to do. So start wanting."

Settling back on her well-worn couch, Danielle Giry picked at a bit of food lodged between her few remaining teeth as she eyed the young girl across from her. Mme. Giry did not have a clue as to how Christine Daaé had managed to get herself mixed up with the Opera Ghost, much less how she ended up marrying the man.

For years now, the Ghost had offered her his support by paying her well for small services. She did not care if he was a disfigured lunatic or a real ghost impersonating a man—he thanked her generously and she took everything he gave her. Now, she had herself a sweet deal, caring for the Ghost's young wife. A little effort and kindness would pay off. As always she would follow his instructions to the letter. And he left very specific instructions that his wife was never to be left alone. A widow without a pension and a child has to take advantage of every opportunity life offered.

After Meg went to practice, Christine approached Mme. Giry with a solemn look.

"You look upset, dear."

"There is a slight problem I...needed advice on."

"What is it?

"I promised Erik I wouldn't tell—but I'm desperate and need advice." She wrung her hands. "My marriage is...um...not yet...consummated." The girl blushed.

"Why not?" Months had passed since that wedding. How could this be?

"I did not want to."

"You need to explain yourself dear."

"Raoul, the Vicomte de Chagny and I knew each other since childhood. When we grew up he acted like he was interested in me, in that way, but he never declared himself and it never came to anything. After he heard me sing, I don't know what happened. Everything was different this time and we fell deeply in love. I...I was already betrothed to Erik and I kept my promise to marry him. But, I wanted to remain faithful to Raoul."

"Married to one man and faithful to another." Danielle shook her head and wrinkled her forehead, trying to understand what was inside the girl's head. "Do you still insist on following this path?"

"Oh no, I see my error now. But, that won't help my bigger problem."

"Which is?"

"Erik, says he has an affliction."

"An affliction?" Danielle asked with a frown.

"Um…he…he says he can't…um…um…make love, because of…he is incapacitated, he called it."

"Mmm, I wonder. Did you let him know you were not interested in making love with him?"

Christine just nodded looking to her feet.

"The mask was it?"

Poor man. What else could he do, but to tell her that nonsense story? The way she had seen the Ghost looking at his wife, she doubted he would not pounce on the girl wholeheartedly if she but winked his way. If that man was incapacitated she would be happy to eat both feathers on her bonnet.

Christine's behavior was shameful. To keep her husband waiting for his marriage rights, because he was ugly was just not right. Well, the girl would learn.

"He may have a problem in the nether regions or is he satisfying his needs elsewhere. Every man needs a release, dear girl." Christine gaped at her words. "And if his wife won't satisfy him or makes him beg for it, there are plenty of ladies out there ready to play Madame Coquette."

"Oh no! He received a note, but he wouldn't tell me where he was going," Christine moaned.

The girl had to be talking about the letters that posh fellow paid her to deliver to the Ghost and *read* to him. She smiled at the irony.

"Oh, my dear, how could he tell you?"

"You mean…it's possible…he might…this trip might be for…a release? He has gone to a Madame Coquette?"

Mme. Giry laughed at the girl's naiveté. "I would not doubt it. When the wife is not amenable to pleasure, men take frequent little…side trips," Danielle answered. "Perhaps that explains the generous sum he left for your entertainment—guilt money," she whispered.

"It was a lot?"

Mme. Giry nodded slowly, giving her a sad look. "You will see tomorrow."

"I do not want to use that guilt money. And he will not buy me with it."

"Make up your mind then. Do you want your husband for you alone or do you want to share him with Madame Coquette?"

"I don't want to share. I couldn't. I don't know if I can forgive him for going to some other woman."

"Nonsense girl, it is all your fault. The only way to fix it is to be the wife he deserves. When he comes home to you. You must want to be a willing participant in the marriage bed."

"Yes, I am set on it!"

"I think you need a hint or two..." Mme. Giry said, moving in close to Christine, and calmly began to explain her plan.

Erik's book had peaked her interest in the physical side of matrimony. They never talked about it, but Christine still thought about the book. It made her feel like doing something. She wasn't sure what, but she wanted Erik's hands on her. Now, that he was sleeping in her bed, they had grown much closer and she was certain she wanted the physical side of marriage. She was willing to overlook Erik's mask, but that was only one of the problems standing in her way to becoming his wife fully. Christine had not planned it but asking for Mme. Giry's advice had been a fruitful idea.

By the time Mme. Giry finished explaining things to her, she was beyond embarrassment, not sure if asking for advice had been such a good idea. She kept her eyes on the floor, her lips pressed tightly together and listened intently, as the older woman shared her wisdom.

To Christine the older woman looked so dry and devoid of womanhood, it was hard enough to place her as Meg's mother, never mind as a woman knowledgeable of men. Christine had never thought of Madame Giry as a fountain of that sort of wisdom.

"Unlike you, my dear, I was never pretty, so I had to have my womanly ways, if you get my meaning," she said, accentuating her words by wrinkling her forehead, accordion style. She leaned in again and continued whispering to Christine.

Christine felt heat travel up and down her body. Her chin dipped further down with each detail. She took mental notes of every word Madame said to her.

She didn't know how to bring it up but finally, she blurted out about finding Erik's book and looking through it.

"If he's reading saucy books, I doubt there's any affliction!" said the older woman. "Sounds like he didn't want to be humiliated by your refusal. Now, he just needs a push to get him going. He needs to know you want him. Good thing you read it too, so you know what to do."

"I…I can't do those things."

"Not yet, but you *will* do what I tell you. That is unless you want Madame Coquette to take your place in his bed."

Christine thought of Erik lying in bed with another woman. Sharing a joke, laughing with her, kissing her. She felt a tightness in the pit of her stomach that travelled to her chest making it beat fast. It made her want to throw up and at the same time hit Erik over the head jealousy. *I have been so stupid! Mme. Giry is right, I drove him into her arms.*

Mme. Giry got up with determination and walked to Christine's trunk. "Let's see what you will wear when he returns." She passed over her cotton night rails, cotton bloomers, and loose chemises.

"Nothing here will do. Tomorrow we go shopping." Mme. Giry drew herself up to her full height. "I have not done this in fifteen years, not since Jules died. But this is something I could never forget. You see in my Jules' bed, I was Madame Coquette! Dried him up like an old prune. Left nothing for any other woman. You will need to be Madame Coquette for your husband if you want to keep him home."

The three women stood outside an elegant boutique in St-Germain-des-Pres. Christine wore a green afternoon frock with a matching hat, and Meg was dressed in lilac. Mme. Giry wore a new dress in her usual black, her favorite bonnet with its declining feathers completed the look.

"Ah, Mme. Jolïete's boutique. Girls, this is the place," Mme. Giry said, pushing the door open.

Mme. Giry led the small party into the middle of the small store. Her drab bonnet placed just so, high on her head, her shrunken cheeks surrounding a closed-lip smile. A slim, well-dressed older woman in cocoa and gold, greeted them. She was many years past her prime, but she took care of herself.

"Well, it took you long enough to find my new store Danielle Giry. How long has it been?" The two women kissed.

"How's business?"

"Not as much as I'd like. Are you finally discarding your black?" Mme. Jolïete joked.

Mme. Giry smirked. "It is not for me, you sassy woman... It's for this young thing." She pointed to Christine. "A newlywed in my charge. Mme. Christine Ménard."

Mme. Joliete eyed her new customer. "At her age, and with her looks, she will not be wearing my creations for long." Both women whooped.

"Oh," escaped from Christine's lips as her face heated up. Meg snorted and elbowed her friend showing her own rosy cheeks.

"She is willing but the groom needs coaxing."

"With a wife this beautiful...he needs coaxing?" She raised a plucked eyebrow and gestured with a loose wrist. "He is efféminé?"

"Oh no, it's not that! Just needs coaxing." said Mme. Giry.

"And the other beauty?"

"That's Meg, my daughter. She is courting with a young comte, but I have higher plans for her." Mme. Giry puffed out.

To which Christine elbowed Meg and the ballerina cringed.

"We never looked like these two beauties, did we Danielle?"

"We didn't need to," she snorted, her bonnet feathers rallied to a valiant wave.

"Come, I will show you my *infallible collection*."

Mme. Joliete showed the small party to the back of the store.

Chapter 14

Rendezvous

Since Erik arrived at the château, no one had stared at him. Strangers always stared, that had been a given all his life. It was almost like being in a dream, and all the servants acted as if his wearing a mask was normal. He tried to catch them sneaking a peek at him but failed. As he passed them in the halls, they greeted him and dipped their heads reverently.

Although he missed Christine terribly, he was enjoying his escape from the cellars. It reminded him of his old traveling days. He could imagine how much she would enjoy all this luxury. Despite that, he would not tell her of his connection with Louis, not until he could be sure of her feelings for him.

On his lone explorations of the property, he came upon a room with a piano. He fingered the name board; *Ignaz Bösendorfer made in the workshops of Joseph Brodmann.* His own piano in the cellars was a newer Brodmann on which the cellar's humidity had taken a severe toll. He sat at the hand-carved piano and began to play scales. The sound was marvelous, his fingers caressed the ivory keys, and he forgot where he was as he basked in the glory of music. The dark, dense chords rang throughout the house.

Erik turned to see his father standing just outside the door with his mouth literally hanging open. "It's really not becoming, to stand there like that." He turned to face the man. His hands still tingled with pleasure.

"How did you learn?" the older man asked.

"Old Lady Calceger, at the manor where mother worked, had a grandson my age, Karl. He was a stupid boy and had a hard time learning his lessons, so to motivate her grandchild, I was allowed to sit in on his lessons. She believed that competition would light a fire under his intellectual soul, not realizing he was working with wet kindling. His tutors soon began paying more attention to me than to him. It suited Karl just fine—I used to do his assignments, and it pleased his grandmother to think he was improving. Karl hated the piano. There was no greater torture for him, than to have to sit and practice. His piano tutor spent all his time teaching me. I would sit and practice the piano for hours. At first the old woman thought it was her grandchild playing, but she soon caught on. She loved my music so much, she just let me play. When she was in the parlor downstairs with visitors, she liked to tell them it was Karl playing. I played, and he sat on the floor by to the piano, playing with his tin soldiers."

Erik turned back to the instrument as Louis lowered himself onto one of the nearby chairs. Quietly, his father motioned to Favreau, the butler, to join him and together the two men listened to Erik playing on the piano as if mesmerized. Erik enjoyed the audience, he had not played for anyone, with the exception of Christine in years.

Louis heard the melodious sounds and rushed to the music room. The door was slightly agape and Favreau was listening by the door. He stared at his son through the opening. "As talented as your father was, my lord," Favreau, the old butler, said sadly. Louis nodded. He had not entered this room since before his father's death. He kept the piano tuned, but he hated the room and had never wanted to enter it again since childhood. Louis remembered sitting at the that piano, playing and singing children's tunes for his mother, instead of the more complicated pieces his father wanted him to learn. Mother laughed and clapped at his antics. His father had entered the piano room, brushed past him and began ripping up music sheets while he ranted. He had been terrified, thinking he would be beaten. Louis ran to hide in the stables. The music sheets were replaced; the incident was never mentioned again. Louis never sat at the piano again and eventually, the music master stopped coming.

He was stunned to see that his son was a virtuoso on the piano. After they left the music room, Louis tried to finesse the question he had wanted to ask all day. "Is your wife the same Christine that Raoul de Chagny claims as his fiancée?"

"One and the same. We married a few months ago. I admit it was under less than desirable circumstances, but entirely legal non-the-less."

"I would not doubt that. Does she love you?"

Erik shrugged.

"Do you love her?"

Erik's voice thickened as he spoke one simple word. "Yes."

After a moment Erik asked, "Do I have brothers and sisters?" Louis let his son change the subject.

"No. That was the reason your grandfather finally confessed what he'd done. I married and became a widower two years later, there was no issue from the union. So there are no other heirs. Your grandfather and I went to Lyons de la Fôret, where he had paid a Pascal Bernay to marry the pregnant Cecile. The man had been paid regularly for your care. Not surprisingly, he failed to report that both you and Cecile had left years before. I don't know what happened to Bernay, but your grandfather was greatly displeased. That's when the search for you began in earnest…my father died two years later, believing that due to his meddling, our lineage would end with me. You are my sole heir."

"I am not your heir! There is nothing that I want from you. It is enough that your reaction to me had been…welcoming."

"This is your birthright!"

Erik turned and walked away.

"Emmerich! Emmerich!"

It was unheard of that anyone would walk away from the Marquis du Bourdeny when he was speaking to them. He had the power and resources to destroy almost any man in France. And here was his son who wanted and probably needed nothing from him—walking away in the middle of a conversation. Louis snorted and trailed after the younger man.

He could hear the steps behind him in the hallway. The man would not take a hint. He turned suddenly forcing Louis to make a short stop.

"Since when has a by-blow had a birthright?" Erik demanded in a booming voice.

He saw the older man blanch. "By-blow? Is that what you think? Cecile told you that?"

"No, she didn't say much, but what else could it be?" Erik barked bitterly.

"Come with me."

Erik followed Louis into a small office. Louis went behind a desk behind a desk, while Erik remained on his feet. It was the same picture as in the library, ledgers and papers were strewed everywhere.

Louis looked in one of the desk drawers and pulled out a sheath of papers and untied the string. He handed Erik a yellowed document from the bottom.

"You're not a by-blow," Louis' voice trembled. "Didn't she tell you?"

Erik unfolded the document and had a shock almost greater than when Christine agreed to marry him. He held in his hand a marriage certificate for a Louis de Reuxville and Cecile Ménard. "Impossible…impossible!"

Louis shook his head. "It's not. After a few months of knowing Cecile, I got it into my head that if we got married and kept it quiet, our union would have to be recognized when I gained my majority. I was only fifteen, but my pin money was more than enough to have my poor forgery of my father's signature overlooked, on the consent papers. We were wed at a small chapel in Bonsecours. For the next few weeks we lived in terror that he would find out. And we were right, he somehow found out anyway. He immediately had the marriage annulled, and sent her away. At the time I was told she had run away with a man from the village and believed it. No one, not even my mother, was ever allowed to mention my *faute*. I was sent off to school in Paris for the next few years."

"No, I do not accept this. She never said

anything." But she had in her own way. *Small wonder, that she had been so sure he would accept me. Did she use me, as her revenge for the way she had been treated denying the old marquis his heir?* "Anyway, it was annulled before my birth."

"A marriage may be annulled, but if there is issue, and there was…well, the child is irrefutably legitimate. You are not a by-blow Erik. You *are* my very legitimate heir."

"Damnation. You sent for me. I did not come here seeking fortune, just information. I have no need of your money or property."

"Yes, I know your resources are adequate." Louis cleared his throat. "If you recall, I had *you* investigated."

"I am an extortionist."

"I know, but 20,000 francs a month? Doesn't it seem somewhat…exorbitant?"

Erik laughed. "My expertise in casting has made them thousands, and the notoriety of my presence even more. It is a fair sum!" He did not mention to Louis that he had planned to stiff *him* for 40,000 francs.

Erik no longer felt the antagonism that had driven him to meet his father so he could dispose of the man, but he could not say he had any warm feelings for the man who stood before him. Legitimate father or not, he was a stranger to him. Now that he had his answers he could as easily walk away from the man and never turn back. Louis, was rolling out the carpet to him, opening the doors to his home and life. He had more to think about now than himself, there was—Christine. He would take advantage of the opportunities offered to him, but in his own time. Foremost, Christine was not to know yet. *If she ever loves me, it has to be for myself, not because I am some noble's legitimate jack-in-the-box.* There were many things he had to think about.

He had the means now, to somewhat level the playing field with the boy, but he did not want to not yet. He did not want her like that. The field would remain as it was, the boy with his looks and title on one side and he—deformed and talented—on the other. He knew perfectly well that he had the advantage, if only because she was married to him. His dear, pious Christine would not easily break her vows, even if her heart still pined for the boy.

Christine! How he missed her. He was ready to go home to his wife. If Mme. Giry had kept her part of the bargain and kept Christine happy, he would reward her. If she had failed, she might find herself on the lookout for another job.

"30, rue du Bourg-Tibourg," Mme. Giry said to the coachman. "Salon de Thé Mariage Frères." Mme. Giry insisted on renting a Barouche carriage. "He does not want you in a Hansom cab," she had said.

The carriage left them in front of the tea parlor. The three women were dressed in new afternoon gowns. They stood in front of the building's wood paneled façade, feeling awed by the understated elegance. They looked at each other and excited, they entered the most luxurious tea parlor in Paris with their heads held high. Meg wore a light green dress with a pleated skirt and low-neckline, which accentuated her compact bust. Christine's coral dress also had a fashionable front pleated skirt and showed off her small waist. Danielle Giry, as always, wore black, and had added fresh feathers to her bonnet. She knew she did not look like a lady, but in her new dress she could reasonably pass herself off as a chaperone. With so many years of practice working with the privileged classes as concierge at the Opéra, Danielle went into her natural role of escort/caretaker to the rich. She pushed the two girls ahead of her. The white tablecloths and pale walls contrasted sharply with the dark wooden furniture. Soft, dappled light entered through the tall windows. Lush palms, hibiscus, bromeliads and other tropical plants contributed to give the teahouse an air of romance.

They each chose a different tea, but Mme. Giry could not bring herself to venture further that a strong black tea laced with cream, like her usual morning café au lait. Meg chose a Darjeeling with a hint of hibiscus flower; Christine chose a white tea with peppermint, she said, because it reminded her of her afternoon teas with Erik. A solicitous waiter in starched white uniform brought in the three steaming teapots. A short, bald gentleman passing their table, leisurely ogled Meg's face, then her low cut décolletage. Mme. Giry cleared her throat and met his eyes with a look that brooked no nonsense. He dipped his head and kept walking. The three women made a concentrated study of the patisserie cart. Finally, each one selected the dessert of her choice.

"Impertinent," declared Mme. Giry.

"Are you sure we can afford to have tea here, Maman?"

"Christine's husband insisted that we should go only to the best places…I will not go against his wishes," Danielle Giry said as she leisurely poured herself another cup of tea and freely poured the thick cream. She had never been near *Mariage Frères* and she intended to draw out her time as much as possible. Her acquaintance with the ghost was truly paying off, and now that he was in love and married, his generosity knew no bounds; he wanted his wife to have the best in their company. So long as Christine was happy, he would keep on providing. Mme. Giry would make sure Christine was happy, well cared for, and as a bonus, ready to be a wife to him. This was a long way off from being the keeper of Box Five at the opera house.

"This is the tea we have at home, I guess Erik comes here to get it…"

"Oh my, Maman," Meg interrupted, her eyes betraying the reason for her pallor. Mme. Giry followed her daughter's eyes.

Two tables away to Christine's back, Raoul and Philippe de Chagny joined the bald man who had been so interested in her daughter's bosom. Danielle Giry felt cold beads of perspiration on her face. If Christine met the vicomte, the Ghost would not like it at all. Meg ducked her face and shoveled a piece of cake into her mouth. The Chagny brothers' bald companion tipped his head in Meg's direction and smiled. Meg looked away with a tiny frown on her brow and glued her eyes to her teacup. Mme. Giry saw him grin. They were stuck, they could not escape, and they could not hide. The three men stood between them and the door. To her dismay, Mme. Giry saw the bald man tap Philippe on the arm, and said something to his companions and nodded in their direction. A cold drop of sweat made its way down Danielle Giry's back. She dried her forehead and the tip of her nose with a handkerchief then stuck out her chin.

The old woman turned to her charge and whispered, "Christine, prepare yourself, Raoul de Chagny is sitting behind you, two tables away." At Christine's gasp, she covered the young girl's hand. "Don't turn around, just stay still, he might not see us." What would she do if the girl took it into her head to run away with the vicomte?

Raoul! Christine held her breath. She fought the instinct to turn around and make her presence known to him. *Dear Raoul. He must be recovered if he is here.*

Their pre-arranged meeting was still two days away. How she longed to turn around and just take a look at him. It had been months since she had last seen him. She suddenly missed him terribly.

She heard a chair crash. "Christine, Christine!" His voice shattered the hushed atmosphere of the teahouse. Every eye in the teahouse turned their way as he approached her table.

Raoul's beautiful face floating above her own caught her by surprise. He was much thinner, and his pallid complexion made him seem ethereal, but it also spoke of an incomplete recovery. "Raoul, I… I…"

"You…here? Am I in a dream?" He pulled her off her seat and held her at arm's length. "Are you all right? Is he here? Or have you escaped his clutches? Is he hiding? I don't see the fiend!" he said looking around wildly.

Had Erik been there, she was sure Raoul would have attacked him, and from the way Raoul's brother was scouring the room, he would have joined in for the kill. She felt her stomach lurch. "He is not here, Raoul. Please sit down, everyone is staring at us"

"Let them. My love!" He drew her into his arms, holding her tightly against his chest. She allowed the embrace, thinking that not to do so would cause more of a stir. He smelled of freshness and expensive cologne, it was a delicious scent. Mme. Giry cleared her throat loudly, and Christine pushed slightly away from Raoul.

"Tell me, he hasn't hurt you!"

"Erik would never hurt me. I have always told you that."

"I know, he forced you to write those notes, never mind…now nothing will separate us. I will take you with me this day." His eyes glowed.

"I can't do that, Raoul. I am married to him," she said pulling away from him.

Philippe was beside them, whispering, and pulling gently on his brother's arm. "Raoul, Raoul, we are in public!"

"Girls, we must leave. Now!" Mme. Giry announced.

"She can't leave, I won't allow it. Christine, I cannot allow you go back to that monster! That marriage is false," Raoul cried loudly.

"I'm so sorry, you don't understand. But I will meet you as agreed. We will talk calmly then." Confused by her feelings and in a panic, she disengaged herself from Raoul. Mme. Giry pulled her away and with Meg in tow, and they ran toward the front entrance of the tea house.

Raoul lunged for Christine, but the other two women cut in front of him, blocking his way.

Philippe perceived Raoul's intention to continue the pursuit and grabbed his brother's arm. "Let her go," Philippe ordered him.

"I can't…she will go back to him," he said, struggling against his brother.

"Then it is her choice," said Philippe.

"No, it is not. She still fears for my life. Her sacrifice is too great," Raoul pleaded fervently.

"Perhaps it is, but this isn't the time or place to deal with that. We do not need a scandal over an opera singer...and a married one at that!" countered his brother.

The clopping of the carriage horses grew fainter.

"If you had only let me follow her. He might have been in the carriage and I could have done away with him then. Now she's gone," Raoul said dejectedly.

Philippe's friend, who had been standing and watching the whole fiasco in astonishment, helped him return Raoul to the table with a minimum of fuss.

"I don't feel well, I want to go home," whined Raoul. He sat in a slouch as if the stuffing had been taken out of him.

"You feel fine and we will all stay." He would not allow his brother to revert to that childish ploy. Philippe breathed deeply. "Let us finish our drinks before we end up in tomorrow's morning paper. Castelot, please wave down a server and order us more tea. I have my flask and we'll put something stronger in the tea than sugar. If you two don't need it, I do," said the comte.

"There, one is bearing down on us. Then one of you will have to explain in detail what in blazes is going on here. And in particular, who was that dark haired beauty?" asked Castelot, flagging down an attendant.

This business with the chorus girl was becoming a dangerous headache. He wished his brother had never laid eyes on the girl. His own affaire with Sorelli had always been kept as just that, a deliciously private matter. She understood the limits of their relationship, and so he could afford to be generous with his time and money.

Louis' valet packed his bags for the trip to Paris with Erik. They had spent the last three days in each other's company. Both days they had been up until the early hours of the morning talking. His son had wanted to know about his mother. Erik eventually began to ask him about his life. Louis tried to be as honest as memory served him. Evasive answers would only lead to distrust, and there was enough of that without his adding anything to it.

When he asked Erik about his own life, he hit a wall, and Erik gave him a very patchy recount of his life. He did talk about his wife, Christine. On this subject, he lingered and remembered every nuance and detail of her songs, walk, and smiles. Erik reeked of love. Louis was disappointed that his son had chosen a chorus girl from the opera house for his wife. To make it worse, aside from her involvement with Raoul, he recalled some sort of recent scandal attached to her name. For now, he had no choice but to welcome her. Given time, that situation might be amendable, when Erik met proper ladies from their circle. In Paris, he would legally recognize Erik as his son and heir. Louis grabbed the nearest bottle and two glasses. "We are off then, with a little something for comfort," he added, his eyes twinkling. He put his arm lightly over Erik's shoulders, felt him stiffen and move away slightly. *Too soon.*

They were not long into the trip when Erik started driving Louis to distraction. Before they left Rouen, Erik got off the carriage to visit several stores to purchase gloves for Christine. Louis got off at the second stop and bought her a fine perfume in a delicate hand-blown bottle. He did not get off at the subsequent stops. As soon as they entered Paris, Erik got off to buy her a rose, and then he got off again to buy a ribbon for the rose. Considering all the women he had ever known, Louis could not recall one woman for whom he would have descended a coach eight times. Erik had bought her scarves, gloves, a hat, and jewelry. Louis almost envied his son the feelings that that kind of love must bring.

His son thought nothing of entering a women's undergarment shop and buying things for his wife. Louis thought that Erik and Christine must be very close. How did he know her size, what she needed, or liked. When he asked, Erik looked at him, perplexed, saying, "She's my wife; of course, I know everything about her." His last purchase was a burgundy velvet cape trimmed in silver fox fur around the hood. "She needs a good cape for the coming winter."

Louis moved a little further into a corner of the carriage to make room for the latest purchases, and with a laugh poured himself another drink. He changed his mind about envying Erik's devotion.

The three women re-entered the opera house through the side doors, full of parcels. Mme. Giry went ahead with her own bags and the package laden coachman.

Mariele, the cleaner, intercepted the two girls. "Well, well, is it Noël?" Mariele asked, her voice dripping with sarcasm. Christine had not seen her since the unpleasant exchange at her wedding.

"No, just Christine's husband buying her a few things," Meg answered her.

"Thas a lot of packages. New rocks on your ears too?"

Christine did not want to talk to Mariele after her comments at her wedding.

"Poor Christine she will just have to make room for all her new clothes and jewelry. But maybe not— she has a room just for that," answered Meg as they pushed past Mariele.

"You gots a strong belly is all I say. Watch he don' plant a lil' monster in that belly. " she called after Christine.

Christine looked over her shoulder and cringed at Mariele's sly smile. "Don't egg her on. She gives me the creeps," she whispered to Meg.

After their supper, the girls went over every detail of the mishap at the teahouse.

Christine slumped on the parlor couch. "I have to meet Raoul in two days, and when I do he will want me to go with him. How will I convince him that I won't leave Erik?"

"Now that you have seen him again, how do you feel about the vicomte?" Meg asked.

Christine sat up. "I'm not sure of anything, but I do know I did not want to go with Raoul today."

"You're in-love with Erik!" Meg whooped. "You married the right man."

Christine smiled. "I think I have loved Erik for a long time now, but am I in-love with him?" She rubbed her chin. "I want to make him happy. He has led such an unhappy life. When I hear his stories of how his parents treated him well…it makes me seethe. He is learning to be happy. I want that for him. I don't know if you can understand me, but I love being home with him. I am ready to have a full marriage and be a real wife to him. Erik deserves that."

"Poor man, he hasn't a chance now."

"Who?"

"Raoul, of course, because I think your love for Erik is deep-rooted, much more than what you ever felt for Raoul."

"It will be very hard but, I must make Raoul understand that what we had is over."

A knock at the door put an end to their

conversation. Meg opened the door. Christine turned to find the doorway filled with her masked husband.

"Erik!"

Before Erik could greet anyone or move, she ran to him and threw her arms around him. She kissed his jaw, and he drew her to him. She could smell his peculiar Erik smell and was glad he did not smell of expensive cologne.

"Has my wife been well cared for?" he asked, his voice booming in the tiny room.

"She's been a superb pupil," Mme. Giry said, with a wink to Christine.

Erik looked down at her with slightly narrowed eyes. "Get your things ready, we're going home!" he ordered. She had never heard sweeter words.

As she gathered up her things, Mme. Giry whispered in her ear, "Not tonight, Christine, he has traveled all day and is tired. Have patience, and don't waste your resources."

Christine nodded. She turned toward Erik. "I have a little more than what I brought up," she said turning her palms up.

"You do not disappoint. I would not have expected less from you, my dear. Just take what you will need immediately, and I will come up for the rest of your belongings," he told her and sat down.

Mme. Giry offered him a drink from a little cabinet in the corner.

"I will help her," Meg volunteered.

"Don't look so glum Erik, I won't be that long," Christine said.

He leaned toward her. "Yes, you will, my dear. I know that about you," he said, looking amused and taking a seat. He leaned back while waiting for Mme. Giry to pour him a drink. A little chagrined about his observation, Christine went to pack.

Chapter 15

Homecoming

They walked down to the cellars slowly, taking no shortcuts. They strolled, holding each other close around the waist, he kissed the top of her head, and she cuddled up closer. Midway down, he presented her with a red rose which appeared out of thin air. She clapped, and kissed his jaw. When they docked the boat at the house by the lake, he hugged her to him again, close, feeling every inch of her body become a part of him—he felt whole again. She lay quietly within his embrace, feeling tiny in his arms. Once inside, Christine made tea for them, and he produced a box of marzipan in the shape of roses.

"They taste like roses!" she exclaimed, biting one.

"I believe they are flavored with rose water," he informed her.

She sat on his lap, and although he stiffened at first, her warmth made him relax. Her head rested on his shoulder. He loved having her sit on his lap, and wrapped his arms loosely around her.

"I met my father." He wanted to make it sound casual.

"Is that who sent you that letter?" she said, giving him a broad smile and an unexpected hug.

"Yes." He nodded. "This man is my real father. I stayed in his house, and we talked."

"Is he pleasant?"

"I suppose he is. Says he had been looking for me, and he wants to give me his name."

"What name is that?"

"Just a name."

"Shouldn't I know, since it will be my name also?"

He sighed softly. "de Reux…ah…Reuxville."

She sat up a little. "It sounds important."

"Humph." He had expected that reaction from her. He had to be more careful with the information he gave her. He wanted the cat to stay in the bag for a while yet. "We'll both keep using Ménard for now."

"Where does he work? What does he do?" Her eyes widened in anticipation as she waited for his answer.

"He…makes his living from the land and keeps horses." He felt guilty not adding that Louis owned the lands, the horses, and that "making a living" for him probably meant going over books someone else kept in order to keep track of his earnings.

"He is a farmer then? At his age, it must be difficult for him to work."

"Well…" He didn't want to wholly lie to her, so he diverted the subject. "He is here in Paris…for a few days."

"That's wonderful. When do I meet him? He must be…" she said.

He interrupted her. "A man…that is all. And no, meeting him will not be possible…at this time," he said cautiously.

"Why not? What is he like? When are you seeing him again? What does he look like?" she asked in rapid succession. She stopped when she noticed his warning look.

He could see how excited she was, but if he intended to keep a tab on the whole matter of who his father really was, he would have to divert her attention. "He looks like anyone else's father. Did you expect him to have my face?" he snapped, grimacing at her.

Ignoring his testy answer, she continued, "I asked because I wanted to have an idea of what you will look like when you're old."

He was going to retort when he realized what her answer implied. She was looking into the future and he was a part of it. Despite himself, a slow grin spread on his lips.

"I *am* old!" he teased her. He was twice her age. If he started to recount everything he had been through, she would see him as old as France itself.

Christine giggled. "You're not old, Erik, how silly. Mme. Giry is old, and look at how energetic she is."

"Mme. Giry and I are of an age. What do you care if I will be energetic or not?"

She blushed prettily, and pressed her head onto his shoulder.

Why would that make her blush? Did she think she would have to be his nurse? As if he would allow that!

They sat in comfortable silence for a while, her head resting on his shoulder. She smelled as if she had been walking under the sun. She always smelled of light and life. She picked her head up from his shoulder and lightly brushed his jaw with her lips. A tremor ran the length on him. He had not seen her for three days and Erik wanted more, but he had never initiated a kiss himself. *What if she turns away?* She held her face close to his, her mouth slightly open, and he recognized it was an invitation. His heart pounded, nearly coming out of his chest. Erik held his breath. *Please God, let me be reading her intentions correctly.* He had dealt with rejection all his life, but this was too close to his heart. He knew he would not take it well. He pressed his lips gently to hers. She returned the pressure and immediately, he felt her lips soften and part. His heart beat faster if that was possible. *If I do this, and I am wrong…don't let her die!*

His tongue slid gingerly along the opening, trembling. Still unsure, he let himself slide in further between her lips. *I am kissing Christine!* He felt he would explode and wanted to stop, to run away and lie down in his coffin, where he had the security of death. He continued and explored just inside her lips, suddenly meeting the hard shield of her teeth. *She has set up a barrier to stop me*! Before he finished the thought or pulled back, she parted her teeth and leaned against him. He could hear his heartbeat drumming in his ears now. She was not stopping him, so he ventured further into the warm crevice. The union with her tongue sent an electric jolt through his body. He nearly jumped off his seat, but was held down by having her in his lap. Erik could have never imagined the moist warmth of her mouth. *How fresh she tastes, like the juice from a freshly cut pear.* The impact of that encounter almost made him pull back, but he held on to explore the soft textures of her mouth. The hairs at the back of his neck stood as she responded to his invasion by sucking on his tongue. If he had not been sitting, he would have toppled over. This was more than he could take. Erik moaned and shuddered. He had no idea what else to do, so he pulled back, and looked into her eyes in wonderment, his breathing was jagged. She had a dreamy look on her face. *She enjoyed doing that with me.* Then her face washed out as tears filled his eyes. Erik's head fell on the back of the chair and he felt nothing more.

Christine liked the power she had over him. One of her kisses would leave him gasping for air, and she loved how he trembled in her arms. She was nothing next to him—he could out think her any day, sing better than her at her best, his acting skills were superb, and there was no area of learning that she could think of over which he did not have a command. *But, with kissing, I can make him mine.* This seduction business would not be so complicated; it just had to be timed right as Mme. Giry taught her.

As a young girl, she had kissed a boy at a fair during the last year she performed with her father; her first kiss. The boy had curly black hair with bright blue eyes, and he looked after the tigers. His bravery with the beasts impressed her. The boy took her behind the animal tent and pressed his lips hard against hers. When it was over, she ran back to her father and was glad when they left the next day.

When Erik kissed her, he smoldered just under the surface. It made her want to forget her modesty, run to her trunk and start to pull out and wear what Mme. Giry called her *resources*. He had been so moved by their first kiss that he almost passed out and cried. She held him and wiped away the tears that spilled over his mask. She prayed he was not as incapacitated as he'd said, and if he was, Christine Daaé Ménard would find a way to be his cure.

"Erik, are you all right?"

His mouth opened and no words came out. He wanted to tell her that he was better than ever, that it was just the emotion from his first kiss, but he was incapable of speech.

She hugged him hard and stroked his tears away from the bottom of the mask and he kissed her hands.

"I am…fine," he managed, sounding a little strangled.

It irked him that she knew how to kiss so deliciously. How did she know just where to delve her tongue to drive him beyond his limit? The boy! He should have never allowed her to leave his home after she unmasked him. Christine had promised to return to his home and did so on her own. Then, the boy sought her out, pressed his attentions on her and confused her. Erik had given her a gold band to wear as a reminder that she belonged to him. It was the boy's fault that Christine had thought to escape from him by staying away from the cellars and his trapdoors. He had followed them to the opera house rooftop, silent as a shadow, observing, listening to her tell the boy about Erik's ugliness̄ finally, dying when the boy's lips touched hers. That kiss should have been his. What else had he taught her? Were there other times when she had gone against his wishes and met with the boy outside the opera house? He pulled back from her embrace coldly.

"Erik?" She looked surprised.

He got up and set her on her feet. "Go finish one of your books. That should keep you duly occupied. I need to finish my composition," he said as he walked away.

He sat in the library alone, a tall glass half filled with drink, and an unlit pipe hanging from his mouth. The liquor had no taste or color, and it burned going down. Still vivid in Erik's mind, were the kisses he had seen her share with the young vicomte on the opera house rooftop under Apollo's lyre. Their lips had met and lingered, pressed together. The vicomte's hands had travelled the length of her body, from shoulders to thighs. She had sighed with his kisses and caresses, holding the beautiful blond head close to hers. The boy had kissed her repeatedly until his lips were sated. While *he* was forced to watch, his own lips parched with unfulfilled desire, feeling uglier and more disfigured with each kiss the couple shared. *Why did you betray me, Christine? You had promised.* Was that her nature to lie and betray, to break promises? He had never told her, but he had been sick after that night. The rage had provoked violent retching and for two days afterward he burned with a high fever. He hated her that night, freely giving away kisses that belonged to him. Now she was 'experienced', as Louis had described his mother.

He did his best to cover up his weakness for her, to control her, but in the end he was no more than an unimportant gnat in her world. With a sweep of her hand, his world would disintegrate and with her smile he would be whole again. He, who had held the Paris Opéra in the palm of *his* hand, was content to be a weed in her garden, praying every day that she would not pluck and discard him. Was she aware of the power she had over him? Did she know one of her kisses could bring him to his knees?

The effect of their kisses lasted well past bedtime. Erik was unable to sleep knowing her to be so near. Once she was asleep, he removed his mask and he moved closer to her, almost touching her. He positioned himself so that her warm breath would caress his cheeks and lips. He inhaled her breath, and contented himself when she kneed his thighs a couple of times and he gasped when she elbowed his chest.

I am a fool; tonight she bestowed her kisses on me, allowed me to kiss her, touch her, and I spoiled it all. I could not blame her if she never lets me near her again. Nothing else but the two of them should matter. He had experienced ecstasy tonight, and because of his own foolishness, those sensations might have to last him a lifetime.

Chapter 16

Letters and Scents

Last night, Erik had suddenly pulled away from their kiss, his eyes flaming with anger. Christine wasn't sure what had gone wrong. He stood up suddenly, nearly dropping her from his lap. Their kisses had been so delicious, she had thought they were finally on the right path. Was he upset because she did not try to stop him, or did he expect her to do more? *Mme. Giry was right; he was tired and grumpy from his trip and maybe he remembered his problem and was angry about his own limitations.*

He stayed in the library for hours and she gave him the time he needed to sort out what was bothering him. He came to bed late and did not take his mask off until he thought she was asleep. She felt him get very close to her, but he never touched her and eventually sleep did overtake her.

Next morning, she heard Erik moving about outside the kitchen. He was growing hungry, and impatient as the time for her to call him in for breakfast neared. She had made him croissants, poached eggs in a special sauce, and hot chocolate. The smells mingled and created an aroma that murmured 'home'. However, Christine's attention was not fully on her cooking that morning.

The note from Raoul burned in her waistband, so she put her hand over it, as if to stop the heat from searing her through her clothes. Then, she thought of the picture hidden in her dresser. It had been her constant companion when she first married Erik. She had not looked at it for weeks now, but it was still there amongst her things. Tomorrow she would return it to Raoul.

She had read the note while she was in Meg's room, but she needed to read it again. Christine needed to check the hour he had appointed for their meeting tomorrow. It was difficult to have privacy now that Erik slept in her bed. She took the note out of her waistband and unfolded the fine paper.

Dearest Christine,

Our time for happiness draws near, my love. We will meet again at the Giry apartment on the tenth of the month at midday. I will take you away then, and deal with your abductor, if he dares to challenge me. Your sacrifice will not go unrewarded, nor will the scoundrel's

evil deed against you, go unpunished. No doubt, my
bullet will find its mark. I will take you away and make
you my beloved wife and my lover in a true marriage.
    Your faithful and loving fiancé,
    Raoul, Vicomte de Chagny

"What are you reading, my love?" Erik asked as he entered the kitchen before she called him in.

She had been so engrossed in her own thoughts that she had not heard Erik approach from behind. The note was open in her hand, Raoul's signature evident at the bottom.

"Erik! You're in the kitchen before breakfast is served—you know that is not allowed."

"I just came in to get a drink of water," he said, sniffing the air. "Smells good! I'll have you know, my dear wife, that my stomach is making ungodly noises." As if to underline his words, his stomach growled.

She turned the note over and patted his stomach with the other hand. "Why didn't you ask me? I will get you something refreshing to ward off the growlies, juice perhaps?" She began to shoo him out the door. "In a few minutes your stomach choir will be silenced when it's filled with my goodies." She stuffed the note into her skirt pocket.

"What was that paper anyway?" he inquired, slowly walking back toward her.

Her heart was now thumping in her chest. She managed to control her voice, and casually answered,

"It's a secret recipe, so never mind me and my pieces of paper. All you have to do is have an appetite when I'm done here. And this," she patted her pocket, "is a little invention of my own to see if I can tickle my husband's taste buds tonight."

"You wrote a recipe for me?" He looked at her incredulously. "For me?"

"Yes, now go, and let me finish my work. I'll bring you a drink." She kissed his jaw and she shooed him out the kitchen. *Meg was right about me. If he knew, he could parade me through the streets to be spat upon.*

Erik walked out of the kitchen, a smile plastered on his thin lips; his hand caressing his jaw his drink of water forgotten.

Tomorrow was the tenth, the day she would sever all ties to Raoul de Chagny. From his response when they kissed last night, she surmised it would not be very difficult to convince Erik to try to consummate their marriage. She had to find a way to help him, if that was what he needed. Still, she could not calmly lie on a marriage bed while her mind was occupied on dissolving the last ties to her former relationship. *How can I give myself to my husband, when another man claims me in his heart?* Erik deserved to have her wholly—body, mind, and soul.

After breakfast, she saw he had changed his mask to one that left his lips more exposed as well as the yellowed skin around his mouth and chin. *I have to get used to his face!* "Why do you wear that, if we are alone?" she asked him, hoping he would leave it on.

"You know why, so let us not get into that."

He grabbed her by the wrist and pulled her into her bedroom. To her amazement, the bed was full of all sizes of packages. Her heart leapt; presents! Not even for Noël had she seen so many boxes and parcels. He was looking at her with a smile on his lips; his eyes were bright amber with excitement.

"Oh Erik," she went to hug him, but he shoved a box in front of her. She began to remove the tissue carefully, but the anticipation was too great, and she ended up tearing right through the wrappings to reveal her gift. He laughed at her and she shrugged pulling out her prize. It was a new hat. It would go perfectly with her new blue carriage dress. "I can wear it when we visit Mama Valérius or when we take a carriage ride on our own." She kissed his lips lightly, and he thrust another package in her hands. This one contained white kid gloves so soft they glided on her cheek. She gave him another kiss, this one a little longer than the last one.

Erik handed her a few books tied with string. He took out his ivory-hilt dagger and cut the string for her. He saw her admiring the dagger and volunteered that it he had acquired it in India. One of the books was *Delphine,* a novel by Germaine de Staël. He reminded her that they would continue her education the very next day. The other book was Bascherelle's *L'art de briller en société*. Why would she need to know how to shine in society? She reluctantly thanked him with a peck. He laughed again.

Next, he handed her another box, from which she pulled out a pink frosted glass perfume bottle. "A gift from my father," he said soberly. She dabbed on the perfume and made him smell her arm and neck, which he did, depositing a tiny kiss on each.

"When will you see him again?" she asked him.

"Later today."

"Thank him for me. Tell him it was…very successful."

His eyes dazzled with merriment. "Yes, I will thank him as well." He smiled and Christine giggled.

She opened up a few more presents and put them aside, always rewarding her benefactor with one of her kisses for each. Finally, she opened the largest box and pulled out a velvet, burgundy cape. She put it on her shoulders and twirled around the room in it. Christine walked up to Erik and wrapped him in the cape with her, making a cocoon around them. He claimed her lips lightly and pulled her close to him.

He took a small black box out of his pocket and handed it to her. She opened it only to find it empty. He laughed at the puzzled look on her face. From behind each of her ears, a cobalt blue sapphire earring appeared in his hand.

"Oh, Erik." She laughed. "They are so beautiful, please put them on me right now."

He helped her put the earrings on and saw as a tear slipped down her cheek. "We can change them if they make you sad."

"No, no, I love them but…" She felt embarrassed. She had been to several stores while he was gone. She and Meg had bought several outfits and matching accessories for themselves, but she had not bought anything for him. "Oh Erik, I have no gift for you." She lowered her head in shame. He lifted her chin with a bony finger and shook his head. "How very silly my little girl is. Have you not kissed me, Christine?" She nodded. "Where could that miracle be purchased?"

She laid back on the bed, still wearing her cape, pushed all her gifts to the side and patted the bed next to her.

Christine stretched out on the bed on her new cape, wearing the glittering sapphire earrings and surrounded by all the gifts he had just given her. She patted a spot on the bed and opened her arms to him. His first thought was to resist, but he found that he could not do so. He slid into the bed and her arms snaked around his neck as he lowered himself to lie on top of her. He pressed his lips on hers, and as if by magic, she opened her lips to permit him entrance. Finding the position too arousing, he shifted to his side. *She will feel my reaction to her and I cannot allow that after the lie I told her!* He entered her mouth and was rewarded by the silken feel of her tongue. *I think she likes me to kiss her. Perhaps, she will let me kiss her every day!* He drew her closer to him.

A box corner dug into his ribs, making him shift again, moving his hips closer to her. Christine's hands went to his face, and she removed his mask. He froze, and his breath caught in his throat as he felt her claim his upper lip, which the mask had denied her fully. Erik could not believe that she would kiss him without his mask, but he did not dwell on this marvel, rather he forced himself to enjoy her kiss. In turn, he forbade all thoughts to enter his head. He deepened the kiss and allowed an errant hand to brush the tops of her soft mounds. Heart pounding, he held his breath. His finger quivered at her cleavage, poised to make the audacious descent. He intended to raid the store before she had another look at his face. One finger audaciously descended. He swallowed her gasp as she tensed for the encounter. They heard the alarm sound at the same time.

"No! No! It is he," he yelled, sitting up on the bed. "That is it, I will kill him and pay my debt to God!" Erik thundered. "This is too much!"

He jumped off the bed and went to his room. He found a pistol and ran to the back door, with Christine on his heels.

"No, no. Stop that Erik!" she cried. "That is not a good joke."

With his arm straight out, he pointed the gun at Hafiz's head as he entered the back door. Hafiz's mouth dropped open, his face frozen in a mixture of horror and fear.

"What do you want here?" Erik barked.

The Persian did not answer, his eyes glued to Erik's face.

"You will not take a hint, so it is away with you!" Erik cocked the gun.

Christine reached his side, saying, "Erik, that is not amusing. Put that gun away before someone accidentally gets hurt."

From Hafiz's panicked, wide-eyed stare and open mouth, Erik realized the fear was not due to the gun. The Persian did not move a muscle as beads of sweat sprouted over his face. He doubted the man was even aware of the gun in his face.

"I see that you are staring at me, Persian! Well, get used to it. My wife does not like me to wear a mask at home. If you do not like it, you can leave, which would please me to no end," Erik said in a shaky voice.

He had not intended for the Persian to see him barefaced, but in the excitement of being in bed with Christine and the untimely interruption, he forgot to return the mask to his face. Although his stomach knotted, he refused to allow the Persian to see his distress. He remained barefaced under Hafiz's horrified stare. He wanted to kill Hafiz for humiliating him this way in front of Christine. This should have been Christine's reaction to him when she took off his mask a few moments before. Hafiz's reaction made her kiss even more of a miracle. Aside from Christine, no one else had seen him for years with the exception of that busybody Joseph

Buquet and that no longer mattered.

"I hope you can understand, Hafiz. My husband should be comfortable in his own home. He has no need to hide from anyone." She reached up and placed a kiss on his sunken cheek. He could not believe she would touch her lips to his naked face in front of a normal person.

"Would you like tea?" she asked Hafiz.

Unable to verbalize his desire, Hafiz jerked his head up and down in silence.

Erik still pointed the gun at the Persian's head. "Erik, put that gun away now," she said to him, shaking her head. "Pardon, Hafiz, he carries his jokes too far."

Still eyeing the shocked Persian, he lowered the gun. "I should kill you anyway, and be done with it, but my wife would not like it." Erik wanted to run and hide his shame, but he forced himself to walk slowly toward the bedroom tears nearly overflowing. "Coward," he called back, knowing Hafiz was still beyond hearing.

Hafiz slumped in the nearest chair and mopped his face with a large handkerchief. He was much more upset over seeing Erik's grotesque head bobbing above his skeletal body as he ran toward him, than he had been about having a gun pointed at his face. As if that were not enough to drive him nearly insane, he saw Christine touch her delicate mouth to the monster's head. Her lips pursed and kissed the dead flesh. He had seen Erik's face once before in Persia; he had hoped then that the event would not be repeated in his lifetime. To his great relief Erik returned with his usual mask back in place.

"I do this for you, because you are weak," Erik said, pointing to his mask, "but my wife will not be happy."

Sure enough, as if he were a witness to a comedy of follies, Christine came in on cue and frowned when she saw Erik's masked face. She put the tea tray on the table.

"Hafiz, I did not have time to make my pastries today." She stole a look at Erik and blushed. He returned the look with a mischievous smirk. "But we do have some cookies," she offered, pointing to the cookie tin on the tray.

"What cookies?" Erik questioned her.

"The only ones we have."

"He cannot have any of my cookies!"

"I'll make more tomorrow," she retorted.

"And they will be mine as well!"

"Erik, stop this nonsense."

"Mark my words, he is not getting my cookies!" His voice boomed throughout the home.

"Erik, we have a guest!" She looked horrified at his rudeness.

"Our guest can have all the tea he can slurp, but he cannot have my cookies. If he wants something sweet, he can add extra sugar to his tea, which he does anyway, but he will *not* touch my cookies," Erik continued.

"Stop it, of course he will have a cookie." She took the tin and opened it in front of Hafiz.

He was tempted, but Hafiz kept his hands away from the cookies, fearing Erik's reaction.

"Did you not make them especially for me?" Erik stood up and inquired in a strangely calm voice.

"You know I did," she answered, smiling into his eyes.

"Then they are for me alone!" he howled. Erik grabbed the tin box from the table, slammed the lid on, and walked away with it to his room.

"Just this once, Erik, please. Don't be rude," she pleaded after him.

Christine turned to their guest, "I am so embarrassed, Hafiz. I don't know what to say."

For the first time since his arrival, Hafiz relaxed and began to laugh. He noticed her blush deepened. Erik returned from his room empty-handed.

"What in heaven's name is so special about those cookies?" Hafiz asked him.

"My wife makes them for me and me alone. They are not for anyone else." Erik sat back on the divan.

She stood, hands on hips, shaking her head at him. "I am utterly mortified by your behavior, Erik!"

He turned to her. "And the answer is still no." He narrowed his eyes and spat, "No, I will not share them!"

She served Hafiz and herself a cup. Erik sat still, waiting for Christine to serve him tea.

"Well, Christine, did you forget something?" he finally said, tapping at his empty teacup.

"Why, I thought we were no longer following social conventions in this house," she said sweetly. "You may serve yourself, my dear husband."

Without looking at Hafiz, Erik swallowed dryly and poured himself a cup. He didn't say another word, but color rose from his neck to his chin, making his skin a deep orange. Hafiz managed to hide his grin in his cup.

He enjoyed his tea and drank slowly as he watched the couple. Christine gave Erik dirty looks, and Erik pointedly ignored them, all the while sitting pressed together in a corner of the divan.

"I actually have a missive for you, Erik. It's from your father." Hafiz had never thought of Erik growing up in a family.

Erik snatched the letter from Hafiz's hand. "I see the surprise on your face, Daroga. You may lower those scraggly eyebrows of yours. Did you think I was born from a lone egg in a forest?"

"Do you know Erik's father?" she asked Hafiz in amazement.

"No, I was upstairs and Mme. Giry gave me this letter to give to Erik."

"Ha! For once you have not a clue as to what I am up to," Erik cackled.

Hafiz ogled him in growing fear. Could Erik be

demanding money from some hapless old man who feared exposure as the father of a monster?

Erik wore his flesh-colored mask when he met his father that afternoon. "You sign here, and you, my lord, can…sign here." The nervous clerk pointed to the documents. He tried not to be obvious, but kept eyeing Erik's face as if something were amiss. Erik met his eyes every time the clerk gave him an inquisitive look and the man quickly looked away. Though it looked like skin, the lack of facial expression made his face look strange. He had added stage makeup to the edges of the mask, and from far away it looked like an ordinary face. The mask was never meant for such close-quarter inspection as this, and though the clerk did not catch on that he was looking at a mask, he looked uncomfortable, probably due to the lack of expression in Erik's face.

"Congratulations, my Lord, and congratulations Monsieur de Reuxville." Both men briefly nodded in unison.

Father and son walked out of the clerk's office as quickly as they could. Autumn was upon them, and the air outside was brisk. A light drizzle fell. Both men picked up their collars and donned their hats; Erik, a wide brimmed fedora and Louis a top hat. They descended the steps of the Palais de Justice. Without saying another word, they climbed into the waiting carriage. Louis knew better than to embrace Erik, so he comforted himself by tapping his son on the shoulder. "Well, it's done. I, for one, will sleep easier. I am sure your mother will rest easier as well."

Erik turned to Louis. "I arranged with the managers for you to occupy Box Five tonight. *Orfeo ed Euridice* is playing, but unfortunately, it is with La Carlotta. You should hear my Christine sing. Her voice is incomparable!"

"Thank you, I will certainly come tonight. Will Christine be singing soon?" Louis shuddered inwardly at the thought of his daughter-in-law taking the stage, but kept a bland look on his face.

"She is not ready yet, but yes, soon."

The carriage moved away from the *Île de la Cité*.

"Will we be able to have dinner together tonight?" Louis inquired.

"No, my wife is cooking for me."

"Perhaps tomorrow," he said, disappointed. "I will be here for the next few days and we have more official business to conclude." Louis wanted to mention that he wouldn't mind a last minute invitation to dinner giving him a chance to check over his daughter-in-law, but he held back.

"I will meet you tomorrow as agreed, but the dinner will have to wait."

They passed another carriage, and Louis tipped his hat as Erik moved back into the shadows. "That was Éduard the Comte de Meux. Pleasant lad, injured by damned Prussians. His mother is a shrew. I do not know the young lady traveling with him."

"Margaret Giry."

"The ballet rat? I've seen her...a saucy little number that one. His mother will never approve of the girl—even as a flirt."

"I have known her since she was a child and have always found her to be a hardworking, serious girl. Actually, I am surprised you are not more familiar with her, since you have used her mother's services to get your letters to me. Yes, she is the daughter of the excellent, Mme. Giry. I might add that Mlle. Giry is my wife's closest friend," Erik said dryly.

Louis cleared his throat at Erik's censure. "I see...well..." Too late to take back the 'saucy' comment. "I hope I will be able to meet my daughter-in-law soon. You can bring her home to Rouen whenever you like."

"Yes," Erik answered dryly.

After his insensitive comment, Erik must now think him an awful snob, no one he would want to invite to his underground home. Louis sighed at his own asininity. He would have to be more careful with his comments in the future. Even if Erik were reticent about establishing a closer relationship with him, Louis would continue to pursue the matter. Erik was all the immediate family Louis had left and he would not be brushed off.

Chapter 17

A Wine to be Savored

He had not dreamt last night, so there could be no confusion. It was morning, and although his eyes remained closed, he was sure of this particular oddity: Christine was kissing him, and he was not wearing his mask. Surely, the effects of the wine had not lasted this long.

"*Bonjour* Erik. Come on, we have a big day ahead of us." She bounded off the bed. By the time his eyes fluttered open, she was on her way to the bathroom. He licked his lips to savor her gift.

Last night when they had gone to bed, she had been affable. They had talked until late, drinking wine, and kissing. How he loved kissing her. Since his trip to Rouen, she actually seemed to be eager for him to kiss her. His hand grabbed his mask from the side table. He held the mask in his hand, turning it over, but did not put it on immediately. His fingertips trailed over his face. Yes, the usual skin stretched over his skull, the bump that stood for a nose, the full horror was still there. He had hoped that his former life had been a dream and that he had woken up an ordinary man. He sighed, but had reason to smile because that meant that Christine had kissed him— deformed as he was.

The last two days, she had him so fired up that even a brush of her fingertips on his hand was enough to start him down the path of deep longing. All the self-restraint he had forced on himself in his forty-two years of life was gone. He wanted her badly, and it was becoming impossible to hide it. That tiny kiss she had just given him would make him keep his back to her during breakfast in an attempt not to embarrass himself. He had to remember what she had told him about not wanting to have intimacy with him and his own lie; that he was incapable of said contact. What if she had changed her mind? Would she be very upset that he had lied to her? Her actions over the past few days indicated that she might just be having a change of heart about that issue. If that was the case, he was willing to be proclaimed a liar to the world if need be, so long as he could claim her. He chose a loose pair of trousers to wear.

The night before, when he came to bed she was still awake. She was lying in bed in a thin night rail rather than the warmer one she often wore. The garment went up to her neck, but the material revealed the shape of her breasts and thighs too clearly for his comfort.

"Erik?"

"Yes?"

"I'm a little thirsty."

"Would you like a glass of water?"

"Actually, I was thirsty for a little wine."

"Wine! You seldom drink wine. Ah…but, I'll bring some for you."

"Would you join me?" she asked, before he was out the door.

"Yes, I will join my wife in a glass if her thirst demands it." He returned with two glasses of wine and a bottle. "This is a Château Latour, a particularly fine year, 1868," he said. "It is a Bordeaux. Sip gently, my love. This is a wine to be savored."

He took up his glass and swirled the liquid. He put the glass flush to his mask nasal opening, and inhaled deeply. She just took a sip.

"Do not drink from yours yet," she said to him, getting closer. "Taste it from my lips."

He had looked at her as if she offered him a banquet, and he, a starving mongrel, was ready to lap up what she offered. "Christine…"

He kissed her tenderly, flicking his tongue on her lips. She opened slightly, but he did not enter, leaving her as hungry as he was.

"You did not taste much," she had reprimanded him, looking peeved.

"The night is long Christine, and a good Bordeaux should never be rushed." They drank, talked for a while and kissed several times, until, looking a little woozy, she turned over and buried her head in the crook of his shoulder, his arms wrapped around her tightly. The last thing he recalled was the soothing comfort of feeling her fall asleep in his arms.

After breakfast, he readied himself for another meeting with Louis. The man had insisted on not only recognizing Erik, but on naming him his heir. Today they would go to an attorney to draw up the papers. This was a prospect that Erik had originally refused, but rethinking the matter, he saw as an opportunity that held possibilities for both him and Christine. If his father had money, land and whatever else, why let it go to some snobbish relative?

Just before he picked up his oars and sat on the boat, she had pressed herself to him, and they shared a long, deep kiss at the edge of the lake. She whispered something in his ear about a surprise for that night. He no longer felt like going anywhere. He felt warm all over, his longing provoked again by her proximity. Somehow, he managed to leave her, to go meet the man that claimed him as his son.

She had meant to ask Erik about that strange rumbling she heard every once in a while—this morning while he slept she had heard it again. It sounded like it was coming from inside the walls. His leaving had distracted her, and she forgot. She would bring it up when he returned.

Tonight, I am going to be his wife fully. If he needs help, I will do what Mme. Giry advised. She felt the heat rise in her cheeks at her memory of the older woman's advice.

At the boutique, Mme. Giry had held up a filmy peach night rail with tiny roses of a deeper hue on the low-cut neckline. "Ah yes, this will do it!" The old woman had grinned mischievously and wrinkled her forehead like a paper fan as she leaned into her. "You will wear this. He will not be able to resist you for long. Remember to forget your dressing gown outside the bathroom. Then you can come out like this…" Mme. Giry swished her hips provocatively. Christine could not believe it, with a few movements, Mme. Giry transformed herself into a tantalizing woman.

This is just like a dress rehearsal for the opera! She giggled to herself. She was turning and twirling around in front of the mirror when she felt eyes watching her. Startled, she spun. Erik stood in the doorway, his eyes opened as wide as his mask allowed.

She was unable to move. "What are you doing here?"

"I…I left my…" his voice caught. He continued to stare, his mouth hanging open. "Dear God…you are…you are so…" he muttered, but was unable to find the rest of the words to finish the sentence. His eyes roamed her body, falling finally on her chest. The yearning and need in his eyes frightened her.

She made a dash for the bathroom. *So much for a surprise!*

Tonight, nothing and no one would stop her from giving herself to her husband. She had been practicing and was able to kiss him without the mask. Christine was sure she would be able to forget about his face if he kissed her deeply and heated up her blood like he had been doing lately. If his hands went where they had almost gone the other night, she did not think she would care if he had a rotting pumpkin on his head. *And in the last instance I can keep my eyes closed until he turns the lights off.*

He closed her bedroom door behind him and gulped in air, and dropped onto a chair in the parlor stunned. In her cotton night rails, he had thought her the most alluring creature. The vision he had just seen was incomprehensible. He had no defenses against it. *That had to be the surprise she had for tonight! Oh God! Nine hours until nightfall.* If his trip were not so essential to their future, he would demand that 'surprise' right now. He had never imagined that a woman could look so seductive. She made the harem girls look brutish. How could he even think, that she would consider doing with him, the things he desperately wanted to do with her.

Safe reasoning flew out of his head, letting dangerous hope in. *Do not spoil everything now, Erik! You are not like others; this thing you want is not meant for you.* He tried to control his thoughts before they destroyed his resolve. *What would happen if I go back into that bedroom now and…?*

What in heaven's name had he returned for? He was still trying to calm down. He wrote music in his head and concentrated on not forgetting the notes. Suddenly remembering what he had returned for, he retrieved the documents he needed from his bedroom and left quickly before he changed his mind.

Why did she have the garment on now? Was she planning to wear the gown all day? How could he go about doing the business he and Louis planned to do, when Christine's image in that gown would be burning in his mind? He hoped he could get enough blood back up to his head to sound intelligible. If not, he didn't care, because he had a wife that was waiting for him in a peach night rail that he would gladly strip from her on his return. He tried to swallow, but his mouth was dry. Erik pushed off on his boat once again, grateful for the cool mist coming off the lake.

Chapter 18

With Eyes Wide Open

She wore a dress Erik had bought for her. It was gray and pink plaid with white lace around the collar and sleeves. It looked modest and demure. Her makeup was minimal, and she wore no scent or jewelry except for her wedding ring. She took the smaller boat and rowed herself across the lake. On the other side, she realized that she had forgotten to take Raoul's picture from her dresser drawer to return it to him—too late. Then she climbed the stairs and walked to the Giry home. Erik would not have liked her rowing herself across the lake on her own, but he would not be back for hours. She would be back home long before he returned.

Meg opened the door for Christine with a bleak face. "Maman is doing something for the managers, but she could return at any time. You can't take long. Eduard will be visiting in fifteen minutes."

"I will be brief. Is he here?"

"He's been around since an hour ago," she whispered. "Are you sure about this? I will send him away if you want me to."

She nodded quickly, before she could change her mind. "Give us a few minutes alone," she said.

"Alright, I will be in the kitchen. Just shout and I'll come in with a broom. You have no idea how strong ballet dancers are." Meg grinned, making a fist with a delicate hand. She smiled back and pushed past Meg, entering the parlor.

Raoul stood in the middle of the room. He had looked like a pale, frightened boy at *Mariage Frénes*. Today, he looked like the young officer in the picture. He was dressed in a superbly cut dark brown suit. Handsome as ever. His eyes were a deeper blue than she remembered, graced by long, curling lashes. He was so very handsome it astounded her. "Oh!" she said running into his arms.

"Christine, I have you again. Never will I let you go, never," he said, burying his face into her hair to hide his tears.

"Raoul, how I have missed you," she said, comforted by his arms.

"How did you escape him? Never mind, tell me later. Let us leave this place quickly," he urged, holding her tighter to him.

"Are you all right, Mlle. Daaé?" Philippe entered

the room and asked her with a stern face. He stood just behind his younger brother. "You will be fine now. Do not worry. Your plight is over."

She nodded, feeling dazed.

"Come; let us be gone now, before that monster comes after you," Raoul insisted.

Monster? His words brought her back to reality. "Raoul, I am married!"

"It is not a valid marriage," the young vicomte responded.

"Erik and I…we married before God. I took a vow."

"He forced you to marry him to save me. I heard his threats." He pulled her to him, running his fingers through her hair, kissing her forehead and her cheeks.

How easy it would be to walk away with Raoul. She would have everything she could think of, a handsome husband who adored her, a title, riches, fine gowns, and balls to attend. She had dreamed of having all of these things once. Did she still want them? *All I have to do is leave with Raoul. I can erase the past few months.* A vivid picture of Erik removing his mask, trusting in her. his deformed face rushed into her mind, his hopeful, grateful eyes. Erik would be alone in the cellars again. Who would keep him company while he composed and make sure he ate properly?

"Did you not get my letters, Raoul? I explained it all. I…I just came to say good-bye properly."

"We can certainly respect that. We will leave you then Mademoiselle, if you feel you are safe. Come

Raoul, "Philippe said a little too quickly.

"No, no Philippe," Raoul said to his brother. Turning back to her, he grabbed her arm. "Good-bye? I will not let you go again," he said. "Is he still threatening to hurt me? Let him try. I am ready for him."

"I am married to him."

"I tell you my love, that that marriage is not valid."

"It is to me!"

Raoul turned to his brother. "He has her spellbound, we must take her away..."

"Take me away?" Against my will?" She could not believe her ears. "How dare you?"

"Christine, he has turned you against me!" He looked at her as though she had just slapped his face.

"This is not a good idea Raoul. We should go. Perhaps you can meet her again at another time— when you are both calmer."

"God only knows what unspeakable things he has done to her. What new tortures he has devised to drain her mind of her love for me. I know what evil he is capable of."

"I am not out of my mind and my husband does not torture me." She glared at him furiously.

"Fine, do I get a goodbye hug?" His eyes were huge and watery in his pale face.

She went into his arms readily and hugged him. "Good-bye Raoul."

Raoul wrapped his arms around her and before

she realized it, he pulled her with him, half lifting her up off the floor and headed for the door.

"Raoul, stop, stop I do not want this…" She struggled against him to get on her feet again.

"Call the carriage Philippe, I have her."

"We cannot force her, Raoul. For God's sake, put the girl down!" demanded his brother not moving from his spot.

"If this is goodbye, I'll leave you with something to remember me by," his voice roughened. Raoul set her down, grabbed the back of her head and enveloped her lips with his. She felt sadder than ever for their lost love and allowed him that last bittersweet kiss. She saw Philippe avert his eyes and leave the room. He ended the kiss and she tried to push against him, but obstinately he held on to her.

"Let me go now," she cried as he walked her back into a wall.

"If you won't leave him, I'll make sure he throws you out."

"Erik would never…"

He shoved her against the wall and twisted her head to the side to expose her neck. He sucked softly on her neck. She struggled against him as he claimed another spot and repeated the same action with greater intensity. Despite her anger, his mouth was producing a delectable ache in her. Raoul's hand covered her breast, massaging it, before his fingers began to stroke and pinch, teasing her. She tried to pull his hand off, but it clung to her.

"Raoul, stop this, you have no right to touch me," she begged him, as the heat spread through her body. The kisses to her neck grew in intensity and she had to fight her own desire to hold his head in place and beg him not to stop. "You…you must stop this, please!" She pressed against his chest and shoulders in an attempt to push him away. His kisses turned into soft bites along her column. The sensation went straight to her center, nearly collapsing her legs. She lost the will to push him away. Her complaints dwindled into a whimper of pleasure that escaped her lips before she could stop it. He forced her head to the other side and attached his mouth to her neck again. Raoul was tapping into the pent-up desire she had suppressed for Erik's touch during the past weeks. It infuriated her that Raoul knew exactly how to make her body betray her.

"Erik will see my marks and he will know you will always belong to me," he rasped triumphantly.. She wasn't sure what he meant, but this enraged man could not be her sweet Raoul. She did not want to belong to this man.

"Let me go and leave," she managed to gasp.

He lowered his head to her and kissed her mouth. She pulled away and he pressed on the juncture in her jaw, keeping her mouth open. He entered her mouth and explored it at leisure, capturing her tongue. He was absorbing her, taking her into him. She pushed against him, but to no avail, her hands pressed against an immutable wall. His fingers were untiring and had not stopped tormenting her breast. She didn't want him to know the staggering results of his incessant touch. He removed his hand from her jaw only to lower it, bunching up her skirt. Raoul slid his hands over her bottom and pressed himself against her.

She pulled away from him. "Raoul, get off me! Erik will…"

"Erik, Erik…how hate that name. I will wipe that word from your lips." Then, he was at her mouth again, swallowing her protests. Frightened by his forcefulness, she struggled harder, pushing and hitting against Raoul's chest; it served to inflame his passion and he shifted his body against her, roughly grinding himself into her. She could feel his arousal moving against her belly. His ragged breathing filled the room and added to the pulsing need her abused breast demanded.

Her eyes grew wide as Erik appeared through a trapdoor she had thought was a solid wall. Silently, he stepped into the Giry parlor. Her husband stood still as a statue watching them. Thank God, Erik! At any moment he would jump on Raoul and rip him away from her. She didn't want Erik to kill him, but Raoul was about to learn a very painful lesson. Raoul had his back to the door and continued the kiss, unaware of Erik's presence. She met Erik's eyes as Raoul ravaged her mouth. She could feel her skirts almost to her waist. Her body turned to ice when she saw Erik's eyes follow Raoul's hands; one on her breast and the other buried under her skirt. All the pleasure she had felt before was gone. In its place was shame at her body's treachery and the desperate need to get away from Raoul's touch. There was almost no space between them, but she managed to spread her hands on Raoul's chest so she could push him off; it did not help. Why didn't Erik intervene? She was desperate and called out to Erik. "Erik, Help me." Raoul took her tongue into his mouth at that moment and only a croak came out. Erik's eyes locked with hers; the hurt and disappointment she saw in his eyes made her feel ill. Couldn't he see she was struggling? How could he just stand there, instead of helping her? *Does he think I want this?*

With a bored look on his face, Philippe returned to the room at that moment, and she saw him freeze as he took in the entire scene—her skirts bunched about her waist, his brother pressing himself against her, his hands on her body and Erik watching them silently from a few feet away. She called out to enlist Philippe's help, but only a languid moan escaped her. Color rose in the comte's face as he glanced at her with the same distaste shown a rotten piece of meat. Her shame deepened. The comte opened his mouth twice without a word coming out and was finally curtailed from speaking by his younger brother's wail.

Raoul broke the kiss suddenly and turned to his brother. "I knew it. She's still a virgin!" he whooped, letting her skirts drop. "That so-called marriage has not even been consummated," Raoul called to Philippe. "We have to take her..."

Chapter 19

Gentlemen's Rules

"Gentlemen!" Erik's voice rumbled. He took a step toward them, breaking free from whatever had held him bound. He bowed sarcastically with a snarl, grazing his lips, but keeping his eyes on her. There was cold steel in his eyes, where a golden glow had blazed that morning. He was dressed in his usual black; tall and lean, he looked resplendent. The black mask added an air of danger.

"Erik!" cried Raoul, quickly disentangled himself from her and did a turnaround toward Erik.

"Erik, I…" she pushed away from the wall to go to him. Erik's eyes went to her mouth. Her lips felt hot and she knew they must be reddened by Raoul's savage kisses. She wiped the moisture from them and the look of loathing in his eyes stopped her from approaching him.

Raoul drew his service revolver, pointing it straight at Erik.

"No!" Her pulse raced, and her eyes went to her husband's hands. Erik was unarmed. A stranger came into the room from behind Erik. Although he seemed somehow familiar to her, Christine did not know him. He was an older man, handsome, and obviously a gentleman. The older man's eyes grew very wide at the sight of Raoul and Philippe. He noticed Raoul aiming a gun at Erik and surprise turned to terror in his eyes.

"What is going on here?" the stranger demanded.

"Raoul! Stop, he is not armed," Christine cried.

"Was I armed when I fell into his trap? Who has the upper hand now, Erik?" Raoul aimed and fired, making contact with Erik's side. Erik grimaced and veered sideways without uttering a sound.

She heard her own scream. "Oh God, you shot him. Stop, stop," she choked out, and pushed down on Raoul's arm, but she could not budge it.

"I still have enough lead left to make her a widow," Raoul shouted.

"Hand me the gun, Raoul! Have you gone mad?" the stranger said. Raoul looked toward him and Erik whipped a rope across Raoul's face, making Raoul move back a few steps. Philippe produced his parlor pistol and advanced on Erik from the side. Christine moved quickly and stepped in front of Erik. Just as quickly he pushed her away from him.

"No Erik, don't push me away, they won't dare shoot if I am here," she told him shakily.

"I demand you put down that gun, Raoul," the stranger said.

Raoul aimed again. Erik pushed her further away from him, but Christine followed his movements and stayed as close to him as she could. Philippe closed in on Erik's flank, as did the stranger. *Two against one!* Her whole body shook with fear. She felt as if her movements were slowing down. *God, help us!*

"Get out of the way Christine, I have this cretin cornered."

The stranger stood in front of Erik and moved toward Raoul, swiftly pushed down the gun barrel and held down Raoul's arm with one hand, while he managed to lower Philippe's arm with the other. "No, he is not armed!" His tone did not brook argument.

"As you can see, Monsieur, I am no more than a rabid dog to all of them," Erik addressed the older man. She moved in closer to Erik.

"Gentlemen's rules will never apply to me." With those words, a profuse cloud of smoke enveloped all of them. Christine felt Erik's arm tighten firmly around her waist and he lifted her off the ground. She closed her eyes as they moved through the cloud of smoke. Erik was in charge and she would be fine. When she opened her eyes, they were no longer in the Giry apartment. They were in a small enclosed space and the smoke left behind. Erik's hand covered her mouth tightly. She clung to him. *Thank you, God. He is safe. I will repay your favor by loving him always. Never, never will I do something stupid like this again.* Her foolishness had nearly cost his life. Through the partition, she could clearly hear all three men talking at once.

"Don't let him get away," shouted Raoul.

"I can't see through the smoke enough to take aim," said Philippe.

"Don't shoot, Philippe, he is holding Christine as a shield," cried Raoul

"You shouldn't have stopped me, Louis," cried Philippe. "That's the phantom that nearly killed Raoul."

"What? Let you shoot an unarmed man?" the stranger asked. "Since when do you behave with such dishonor?"

"He has taken her again!" cried Raoul desperately.

"Mercy! How could he just vanish?" said Philippe.

"It did not seem that the young lady wanted to stay. Did she not run to his side?" the stranger asked.

"She does his bidding and has no will," Raoul insisted.

"Then, she is no worse off than before," Philippe consoled his brother.

"Damn him straight to hell! I had her," Raoul countered, his voice sounded heavy with grief. "I had her and he took her from me again."

Christine heard steps enter the room. A deep

masculine voice asked, "Why are the three of you in Mlle. Giry's apartment?" The voice had to be from Meg's beau, Eduard.

"Where's Christine?" She heard Meg ask.

"Mlle. Giry, both Christine Daaé and that phantom have disappeared...again." Philippe informed her. "We tried to save her, but he escaped with her."

"Escaped? You mean he took his wife home?" Meg clarified in annoyance.

"Chagny, you were shooting at a man who was taking his wife home with him?" asked Éduard, his voice dripping with disdain. "Lost control over your mistress?"

"Good God, no!" Philippe stammered, "That...that's not how it was."

Raoul insisted on continuing to tap on the walls. "They have to be here. There's a trick wall in this room, just like the mirror in Christine's room,"

"I'll have you all leave Mlle. Giry's apartment immediately, and find the tricks in your own walls at leisure," commanded Éduard sounding piqued.

"Come. Let's leave mademoiselle's home," said the stranger. "Philippe, I must talk with you privately. This very moment."

"Only a demon can disappear at will," Raoul commented on the way out.

"If he is a demon indeed, then you should have come armed with a priest and holy water, not guns," retorted Éduard. "Better yet, not have come here at all but met him in a…more honorable way."

The voices, continuing to argue and footsteps faded, then—silence. Christine heard Meg's voice. "Christine? Can you hear me? They are gone. You are both safe. I hope you can hear me, my friend." Erik still held his hand over her mouth and she could not answer, but nodded in the dark and sent Meg a blessing.

After they emerged into the corridor leading down to the cellars, Erik let go his hold on Christine's mouth. He shoved her ahead as he followed. She almost tripped but kept going without saying a word. She wasn't sure how to handle Erik's leaving her to her own devices and not helping her when he saw Raoul mauling her. It should have been obvious to him that she was struggling with all her might. Was it possible that he thought she wanted Raoul to kiss and touch her? By the time they walked into their home, Christine wanted to speak her piece, but knew his temper was running high. He was wounded and that had to be her priority.

In the parlor, she turned back toward him, looking down at the red stain on his shirt. "You are hurt, let me…"

He pushed her hands away, as if they were contaminated. "It is nothing!"

"But it must be cleaned."

He spun to face her, his eyes blazing like molten

steel. "Why must it be cleaned, Christine? Is it so that I do not get a fever? We would not want poor Erik to die because that would make you a widow, and then you could go to your lover. Is it more fun to cuckold Erik to his face, make a fool of the disfigured monster, and keep your lover on the side?"

"It was not what it looked like," she answered. "I will explain everything to you, but first let me see to your wound, you are bleeding."

"Was I to wear the *cornes* proudly?" He delineated invisible horns on his head.

He threw off his jacket and ripped the shirt from around the wound. From a small table, he picked up his ivory-hilt dagger and unsheathed it. He put the blade to the lamp's flame, keeping his back to her. His backbone protruded under the shirt as he bent over the fire, each vertebra jutting out, somehow making him look reptilian.

The dagger's blade glowed as red as the blood pouring from his side. "Look, Christine," he sneered. "Look! This is how to cure an animal like me." Erik pressed the blade to his side without taking his eyes from hers. His face betrayed no acknowledgement of pain.

She heard a sizzle. "No, Erik, nooo!" The smell of his burned flesh reached her nostrils. Her hand flew to her mouth, gagging. A gurgle caught in her throat. Her legs gave out under her and she slumped into a chair. "Oh God, Erik." She held her head in her hands, keeping her eyes tightly closed.

"That is how I have taken care of myself all my life. Not with your stupid salves, potions, and silly tonics that dulled my senses and fooled me into thinking you cared for me. No one has ever cared for Erik, no one. Certainly not my mother, not my pathetic excuse for a father, and especially not you," he cackled, filling the cavern with the sound.

He wiped the dagger on his trousers and sheathed it. "Were you worried it might leave a scar?" He laughed again. "With this face by your pillow you really should not worry about scars."

Her eyes were glued to the gnarled, freshly charred flesh at his side showing between the tatters' of his ripped shirt. He paced in front of her several times and finally stopped in front of her. "What a grand gesture, you made, placing yourself in front of me!" He clapped his hands. "Congratulations, you actually looked the picture of a caring wife...but we know better don't we, Christine?" His voice was distorted with anger.

"Let me explain. I didn't want Raoul to..."

His hand shot out, seized her chin, and brought his masked face down, close to hers. "I saw what you are. I know what you are," he spat at her.

"Why didn't you help me?"

"Help you? Should I have held you down for him. Or was I supposed to pleasure your other breast?"

"Erik! Let me explain...," she cried.

"You think if you bat your lashes at me again, I will believe anything that spills out of your lying mouth. It is over. You must take me for a total fool. Your obedient servant—is—no—more!" he roared.

He knelt in front of her, a breath away from her face. Still, she did not fear him angry as he was. Once she explained he would understand.

"This morning, when I saw you in that night rail I believed you when you said you bought it for our wedding night. But it was to entice him while I was gone..."

"It was for you. I…"

"You were waiting for the vicomte, but realized I might return again and went to him."

"That's not true…" She shook her head.

"Do you remember when you said you did not want to be intimate with me? You thought I was too…too repulsive to touch you. I agreed just so I could bask in your company, so you could throw me a crumb of kindness when it pleased you."

"I am so very sorry I ever said that…you know things have changed between us," she sobbed.

"Indeed, they have changed, my dear. I have a confession; I lied to you about being incapacitated. My pride you see. It seems to me you are more than willing to bestow your favors on anyone. Ah, but of course, my accursed face…well then, maybe I will need to be persuasive in my demands." He laughed his horrible laugh.

"You do not need to force me. I willingly give myself to you."

"What sweet words you speak now that you are

cornered. Why did you not speak them last night, when you were in my arms?

"I was waiting for tonight," she answered

"Tonight was for your lover."

"No, I was going to make tonight our wedding night."

"Ah, so you made love with him, just so you could practice and then teach Erik. Very kind of you." He grabbed her wrists. "How many times have you met with him since we married? Huh? Every time you visited with your allies upstairs?" he demanded.

"I have been foolish, but please, just let me explain everything."

"So many things are clear now. The day you were late coming down...of course, you were with him," he bellowed and let her go. He began to pace in front of her again.

"No. How could you even say that?"

"You must have had such fun while I was gone to Rouen. Did the boy come down here to bed you? Did you writhe with him in your bed, my mother's bed?" His face contorted in anger and pain.

"If you will listen to me, we can start over, I want to be your wife."

"You expect me to touch you after he has had his hands all over you?" A flush crept across her cheeks. "You have the nerve to blush? Where were his hands when he can claim you a virgin?"

"He only said that to convince his brother to take me."

"I saw his hands under your skirts!"

"On my bottom."

"Of course, in not too intimate a spot. After all you were in public."

"Couldn't you see that he was forcing me? You saw me struggling to get away. I couldn't get away from him!" she countered. "How do you think I felt when you didn't help?"

"Did you gouge his eyes, pummel his head, scratch at his beautiful face, rip his hair out? No? I did see you against the wall, accepting his tongue down your throat and so lost in the throes of passion as he touched you that you could not stop, although *you* apparently saw *me*. You even had the nerve to hold my eyes as he..." This fists balled so hard that the knuckles turned white. "That is what—I—saw."

Her chest caved in. "You did not see me struggling to get away from him?"

"Poor Christine, you still think to fool poor Erik."

"You are not thinking straight. If I wanted him, I would have left with him."

"You play the role of the ingénue well. I admit it, I thought you innocent! I believed your blushes when you took my book. You were just getting ideas on what to do with your vicomte. Did you have a special practice session planned for tonight?"

She buried her face in her hands as a sob escaped her.

"I would have been happy with a lifetime of your

company. I did not wish to impose my decayed body on you."

"Erik, listen to me," she tried again. "Let us sit down…"

"And now, a goodly number of your own will pay for a harlot's sin."

"What do you mean?" she asked in alarm.

"Your accomplices must be punished."

"Meg didn't know. I snuck into her apartment."

"You admit setting up the assignation?"

"To say goodbye."

"You are more earnest in your 'goodbyes' than your 'good mornings'." He laughed.

"I want to go to my room."

"And you think that will protect you from Erik? No door, or wall protected hundreds before you from Erik," he snickered.

"Please, I want to go to my room now," she pleaded pushing past him.

"So…you want to go to your room so very desperately? Why?" he asked, grabbing her wrist, he pulled her behind him dragging her toward her bedroom. "Let us go see why you might want to go there, my dear unfaithful wife."

Chapter 20

Descent

The attorney had been called away and unable to complete the paperwork, Erik and Louis returned to the opera house immediately. His father had finally waggled a dinner invitation from him for tomorrow and convinced him to let him meet Christine first. When they did not find Christine in the house, Erik used the trapdoor in the Giry apartment to collect her from the only other place she could be. It had not even occurred to him that she had run away. He had laughed thinking of how he would pull her ears for crossing the lake alone. When he emerged from behind the trapdoor, he saw a couple entwined in a loving embrace and oblivious to his presence. He assumed he was seeing Meg with a beau and almost retreated. An escaped blond lock froze him to the spot. He was so stunned to realize that the woman in the passionate embrace was Christine that he forgot he had his lasso in his pocket.

He stood at the trap door blocking his father from seeing his Christine against a wall, making passionate love with the vicomte. His chest tightened. The vicomte had her skirts up to her waist, her legs and undergarments exposed. The boy's hand fondled her under the fabric of a dress Erik had bought for her, his other hand played freely with the breast he had barely dared to brush. The worst part of the nightmare was when Christine saw him, held his gaze and without shame groaned in delight as the vicomte satisfied her. Philippe Chagny had entered the room as long moans of pleasure escaped her. Even *he* had blushed and looked away. Having achieved his goal, the boy pulled away from her and crowed to his brother, 'She's still a virgin.' This while his hand was still tangled in her skirt. There was only one explanation for his sudden discovery. His hand had been in the one place where that secret lay. Erik had suddenly animated, wanting to kill and hoping to die.

He shook his head to clear the memory and pulled her by the arm. In a few determined strides, he crossed over to her bedroom with her in tow. She pulled back, snorting as he walked up to her dresser and opened a drawer of neatly folded chemises. Erik began to run his hand through the garments.

"You have no right," she said from behind him her voice quavering. "Why do you go through my things? Please, let me rest."

Leaving the first drawer a shambles, he opened another drawer and began rifling through her corsets. He touched every nook and cranny, finding nothing but her undergarments. He wasn't even sure what he was looking for, but he was pleased to have found nothing that shouldn't be there. He felt her pull on his arms, but chose to ignore her, continuing his maddening quest.

"Please Erik, let me rest now. I feel tired. You would not want me falling ill would you? We can talk later," she said, obviously attempting to distract him away from the dresser.

Holding his breath, he opened the last drawer. He wasn't entirely sure he wanted to know what she could be hiding, if anything, but her persistence that he should not search her things compelled him to continue the search.

She pulled on his arms with all the strength she had. "These are my things. Stop, Erik...oh please, stop!" she pleaded desperately.

Her night rails were folded and neatly stacked. He dug through them roughly, sending them flying through the air. Papers floated down from between the folds of fabric. His heart stopped. He took a shallow breath, while bending down to pick up one of the sheets of paper. Fearfully, he licked his dry lips and unfolded the paper.

"No Erik!"

She tried to snatch the sheet from his hands, but

he easily placed it beyond her reach as he read the note. She made a choking sound. He read the short note and turned to her. The tightness in his chest and throat increased. His arm hung heavily by his side as it held the letter.

"My recipe, Christine?" he cried mournfully. "This is the special meal you were going to make for *me*?" His voice was cold, and laced with undisguised hurt. His eyes overflowed behind the mask and spilled over. He did not remove the mask to wipe his face.

"I…I…Oh Erik," she wouldn't meet his eyes. She scrambled on the floor to pick up the rest of her papers.

His eyes settled on a piece of cardboard lying on the floor; his heart somersaulted as he bent and touched it. He untangled it from one of her nightgowns. As he held the blank rectangle in his hands, he knew it was a picture turned upside down. Harboring hope that it might be her father or her precious Mamma Valérius in the picture. With trembling hands and in one breath, he flipped the photograph over.

"I meant to return it," she whimpered. Then she lost her composure and her head fell to her chest, and she cried, "I'm sorry…I am so sorry, Erik." On all fours, she desperately gathered her remaining notes and a small book close to her.

Erik got on his knees so he could face her. He held Raoul's picture up to her. "He really is a handsome boy, isn't he? Look at the picture,

Christine," he said, putting the picture closer to her turned face. "Look!" he yelled into her face. He grabbed a handful of her hair and forced her to face the image he had in his other hand. "I said look at your lover's picture! The Vicomte de Chagny," he shouted. "Is this what you look at after you kiss me so that my hideousness does not make you sick?" His tears rolled onto his chest from beneath the mask.

"Why did you let me kiss you, Christine, why? I was better off before those kisses. You made me hope. I had never done that before and you—made—me—hope!" His chest was exploding and felt a wave of dizziness. "Tell me you have never looked at this picture and wished you were with him."

She hesitated then lowered her eyes and covered her face sobbing.

The boy was in a naval uniform. His face appeared so sweet and beautiful that it could have been a girl's, the lips plump, the eyes bright and hopeful. Only the wisp of a pale mustache gave away his gender. Though handsome, the man who had shot him upstairs, grimaced and snarled, baring little semblance to the sweeting in the picture.

Erik snatched the other pieces of paper as well as a small book from her hands. She tried to stop him, but he was too strong and took everything. She remained on the floor on her knees holding her middle. He opened and read another of the boy's notes. Deliberately, he refolded the notes with the picture and book, tucked them in his jacket's pocket.

A sob choked in his throat.

"Did you think you could do away with Erik so easily? How duplicitous of you both. You would have stood a better chance using the poison I gave you." He shook Raoul's notes at her.

Erik picked up the peach night rail she had worn that morning. He caressed the fabric gingerly, and brought it up to his mask, lifted it a little, and inhaled deeply. "It was all for him," he mumbled under his breath. His only solace was that the boy's discovery of Christine's virginity meant that *he* had not been her lover.

"You looked so very beautiful this morning... foolishly, I thought you were wearing it for me," he snarled bitterly. "I...I thought someone had finally learned to care for Erik...loved me for myself," his voice was lifeless. She saw such inconsolable sorrow in his eyes, more than she had seen in all her life, and her own tears flowed freely. He got up, and she saw him stagger a little. He reeled in place, and he held onto her dresser while holding her special night rail. Crumpling the soft fabric into a ball, he brusquely threw it at her face.

"Change!" he shouted.

Christine wanted to tell him that she cared. She wanted to grab him and make him listen to her declaration of love, but she feared his reaction at that moment. Her lies, indecision and deception had created this cold man who had taken the place of her Erik.

"Change into your whore gown," he bellowed. Still on her knees, she closed her eyes.

He had every right in the world to be livid. She had met with Raoul behind his back. She had written and received notes from her former fiancé, again behind his back, and then the scene he had walked into in the Giry apartment. How could he believe that she was not betraying him?

"Put it on or I will put it on for you and I promise you, I will not make it pleasant," he hissed and stumbled out.

She picked up the nightgown and heard the door to her bedroom slam. Any other husband would have beaten her already. He had found her in another man's arms, kissing her, touching her. Found another man's picture among her things, found notes from that man threatening his life and promising to take her away. If all he did were to beat her, every man in France would consider him weak. She took her new dress off and donned the peach night rail—the night rail that was meant to seduce him on their wedding night. She felt she did not deserve to cry for herself, and so she swallowed her new tears.

She wasn't sure how much time had passed, but much later he pushed open the door to her room and came in without a word. Before, he had always knocked and asked if he could enter. She no longer deserved that respect. He had changed and wore a clean shirt. With his finger, he motioned for her to stand in a corner of the room. She obeyed him.

Erik removed the pillows, sheets and blankets off the bed. Then, he took the Louis-Philippe bed apart and removed it, leaving the stripped mattress on the floor. Methodically, he went through her wardrobe and dresser removing all the dresses, shoes and undergarments she owned. The last item he removed was the burgundy cape he had given her the day before. He left her door open and she saw him pile all the garments by the fireplace. *Surely, he wouldn't do something like that* He used the wood from his mother's bed to build up the fire and took up a seat in front of it, his back to Christine.

"What are you going to do with my things?" she called from inside the door to her room.

"*Your* things, Christine?" he answered her without bothering to turn around. "Do you have a bill of sale for any of these items?"

"They *are* mine. You gave them to me." He did not acknowledge her last words and she did not dare leave her room and recover her belongings.

One by one he flung in items from the pile into the fire. He sat in front of the fire, watching the flames devour everything he had bought her. She called out to him to stop, begged and cajoled, but he did not bother to answer and continued his task. She watched everything in the pile gradually disappear into the fire and turn to ashes. Her heart broke, but she did not cry.

He returned and took the one remaining item in the wardrobe; her wedding dress. She clung to it, crying too hard to make intelligible noises. He nearly dragged her with it, but finally tore it from her grasp. The lavender glass buttons rolled on the floor, scattering everywhere. He picked her up and threw her on the mattress. He stood by the fire and pitched in the dress, now torn by the struggle. The roaring fire licked at it, then quickly consumed the beautiful confection. When he brought out the packet of wedding photographs, she charged out of her room toward him and tried to wrestle them from him, screaming at him to stop, although she knew how useless it was. He pushed her aside and hurled their pictures into the fire and held her in place, making her watch as the photographs burned. The flames danced in multi-colors and popped as the pictures bubbled and the edges curled in. She collapsed against him, but he pulled her away, forcing her back to her room. From her door, she watched him add the beautiful mask he had worn at their wedding to the fire. Tears rolled down her cheeks freely as she curled up on her mattress.

Later in the evening, he returned to her room and demanded the undergarments she was wearing. Christine did not believe he meant it and tried to close the door on him. After arguing with him for a few moments, she handed them to him and he added these items to the embers. Erik stood by the fire until every item had burned down to ashes. When there was nothing but ash and dull-red embers, he turned to face her. She could not see his eyes, no fire, no steel, just two black endless holes behind his mask. It was as if the mask had a void instead of holes for eyes. He faced in her direction for a long time, his mouth grimly set, his fists balled up at his sides.

An hour passed before she saw him again; he brushed past her with several tools in a bucket. He went to her bathroom, and after much banging emerged with several pipes in his hands. He returned and with a last clang, left an empty bucket by the door. He did not look at her, just walked out and locked the door behind him. She rushed into her bathroom and found the sink and bathtub were missing the water pipes and her toilet was no longer functional. In horror, she realized the purpose of the bucket he had left behind.

She was asleep on the mattress when he pushed in a tray with food and relocked the door. She had not expected that kindness from him. Why didn't he just let her starve? She drank some tea and nibbled at the cold meat, wondering if it could be her last meal before her execution. Then she heard the sound, it was low at first, then swelled to fill the entire house, making the walls of her room quiver. He was sobbing. Now and then, a long wail would interrupt the sobs. The heart-wrenching sounds continued for hours. She put her hands to her ears, but it still slipped through.

She could not rest or sleep while his sobs tore at her heart. *I'm sorry, Erik. So sorry.* Eventually, the sound stopped, and she fell asleep.

When morning came, the offensive bucket was removed and a clean one left in its place. She had fought for hours not to use the bucket, but had to relent after her meal. She did not even have a towel to cover it. It was mortifying to think of Erik seeing and handling her body's waste. She heard him walking outside her door. *He must be making up his mind what to do with me.* The footsteps went back and forth in front of her door, exactly the same number of steps in each direction—twenty-eight in all. She could hear him talking to himself, but she could not make out the words. At times, it sounded like a chant, at other times it sounded more like an argument. At some point during the day another tray was shoved in, the first one taken away by Erik while she napped. Abruptly, she heard a keening sound, broken by uncontrollable sobs. This lasted for an hour, then silence. Before nightfall, dark circles formed under her eyes.

"That is an incredulous story, Louis," said Philippe as he gulped his whiskey. "But how can you be so certain he's not a charlatan?"

"First of all, it was I who contacted him. Also, remember I had him investigated at length. And, when I offered him his birthright he refused it outright. And most crucial, you remember my father, don't you?"

"Of course, anyone who ever met him would." The comte involuntarily shuddered.

"Why do you think he wore a mask?"

"I never thought much about it. I heard he'd been wounded in some war. I put the mask down to an old man's eccentricity…he had plenty of those you must admit. But, no, you can't mean…the Phantom's…Erik's face…Good Lord!" Philippe took a long gulp this time.

"Father's face had a deformity unlike anything you could imagine. I saw it twice. Once by accident, while he wiped away tears during my mother's funeral, and the last time he was on his death bed."

"Your mother always looked like she adored him."

"She did, unequivocally. What you told me you saw in the ballet rat's apartment, still has me cringing when I think of that girl married to my son."

"Are they really married then? Erik and Christine, I mean."

"They had a proper wedding. He made sure of that. He showed me some pictures and I had the paperwork checked. It's all legal. She will be able to call herself Christine de Reuxville before long."

"A proper wedding you say. No offense, but I'm relieved for Raoul's sake. That boy never gave me a day's worry growing up. Then, he meets the Daaé girl and he becomes his own man with no experience with that kind of woman to back him up. He won't let himself be guided anymore. Defiant to the bone. He had planned to run away with her in spite of my objections. That was why the Phantom…um…Erik, ended up kidnapping her. She had promised herself to Erik first and our Raoul interfered." Philippe smoothed his full, well-trimmed mustache.

"She's pretty enough, beautiful in fact, but quite unsuitable." Louis smirked and crinkles appeared at the side of his amber eyes.

"He won't take it well. Not with the obsession he has for that singer."

"He is young…" offered Louis.

"Did that ever help you mend a broken heart?"

Louis put his drink down and lit a cigarillo. He took a drag and puffed out a plume of smoke. "My heart broke only twice…and it mended, both times…because I was young, I'd never risk it again though…too old to take such risks with my heart now," he smiled rakishly, taking a long drag and a sip of his drink.

"I'll be damned," exclaimed Philippe, with a look of wonder on his handsome face.

"Why?"

"I've never cared enough for a woman to have a broken heart…sad actually," said Philippe pensively. "Who knows, maybe Raoul is the luckier one."

"I doubt Raoul would agree with you."

"Will the girl be all right? I mean if Erik thinks she meant to go away with Raoul…" Philippe said.

"I hadn't thought of that…I must check that she is safe," said Louis, and drank deeply, almost draining his glass. "I don't want Erik involved in a crime of passion.

"Will he allow you into his home? You know what happened to Raoul," Philippe reminded him.

"I need to try," answered a resolute Louis.

Three days passed. She did not see him or hear from him. Erik delivered and removed a tray of food three times a day. The offensive bucket was changed twice a day. She tried to talk to him as he paced outside her door, but he never answered. His sobs and lamentations filled the days and nights. There was no music, and this worried her above all. As the days passed, Christine realized that he would not harm her. Instead, she did not want to imagine the tortures he was inflicting upon himself. The thought of his pain hurt her more than a beating would have. She remembered the straps on his wall. She shuddered. *Erik! I'm not worth it.* When the next tray appeared, she attempted to keep the door open, begged him to let her out, to listen to her. He said nothing, just gently pried her fingers off and closed the door, locking it as always.

She had nothing to do. She had no books to read, no paper with which to write—nothing to do but think. That was exactly what Christine did not want to do. She did not want to think of her deceit.

Before Erik had come through the trapdoor, she had willingly gone into Raoul's arms twice and allowed him to hug and kiss her. The thought of running away with Raoul had even crossed her mind, despite knowing how much Erik loved her and how she had learned to love him in return. She deserved everything that was happening to her. Christine mourned for all she had taken for granted, and now lost. Instead of loathing Erik for locking her up and taking away all her comforts, she loathed herself for deceiving him. She remembered their meals together, sitting side by side, looking through their wedding pictures—now ashes, Erik's reticent glances when he was unmasked as he played music and she sang. She longed for him, for his voice, his touches, his face.

He gave her a drink with each meal, but there was no extra for washing. She had no water to clean herself with. The rank smell coming from her body bothered her more than the dirt of her skin or stained night rail. Another comfort she had taken for granted. Her beautiful tiled bathroom was now a cold mausoleum to her past life of luxury. Her most basic needs were met by a bucket sitting by the door of her room. At night, she tucked her gown around her and curled up on the mattress. Christine consoled herself by remembering that sometimes, she had made do with less when she and her father, Daddy Daaé, left Uppsala and traveled from fair to fair playing music and singing. Wherever they were, in a barn or under the stars, just before falling asleep she always tucked her hand in his and Daddy Daaé had kissed her forehead as her eyes closed. Now lying alone on the mattress she had shared with Erik, she wrapped her arms around herself and cried herself to sleep.

Christine heard the bottom of the boat scrape as it arrived on the shore, then she heard agitated voices. She could only recognize Erik's voice. The other belonged to a man, but she could not identify it. Erik cracked her door open and threw in his own dressing gown.

He whiffed the air. "You smell like a harlot, cover yourself with this and come out," he ordered. She gasped at his words. Christine knew she smelled and had hoped Erik would not notice, a dressing gown would not hide it. "If you gave me water to wash, I wouldn't smell and that bucket in the room doesn't help." she retorted, feeling humiliated.

"Come out now," Erik ordered.

The stranger that had stayed Raoul and Philippe's guns stood in the middle of their parlor. The man had a stern look to his face. He was dressed in a plain suit and stood almost as tall as Erik. Why had Erik brought this man to their home? It unnerved her not to be able to ask Erik.

Erik backed away from her into the shadows as she emerged from her bedroom for the first time in over a week. The stranger approached her and asked, "Are you all right, Christine?"

"Yes." She was struck by a familiarity which she had noticed about him the day of the incident upstairs, and yet she knew she had not laid eyes on him before that day.

"Are you eating well?" His eyes looked through the open door of her bedroom landing on the mattress and then the empty tray by the door.

"I am fine, Monsieur. Thank you. My husband takes excellent care of me, as always." She lowered her voice a little. "But, would you do me a favor?"

"If I can," he said, still without a smile, scrutinizing her as he had done with the room. He gawked at her hair, uncombed for a week, his eyes lowered to her neck, narrowing a little. His face remained impassive.

"Can you make sure that my husband is well? I do not want him to be hurt," her anguish for Erik obvious over.

The older man's mouth quivered in a hint of a smile and nodded. "I assure you, my presence will not harm him."

"Enough talk! Go back inside," Erik told her gruffly.

"Erik!" the stranger said, in a scolding tone.

"You saw what you came to see. She lives and is not damaged. The show is over," he told the man.

She obeyed, and the door to her room was closed and locked again. *What was it about that man that seemed so familiar?* Why would he care to check on her and most important, why would Erik allow it?

She heard them arguing, but it was too low for her to make out what they said. After a while, she heard the scrapping of the boat's bottom as Erik and his guest left.

Next morning, Erik let her out of the bedroom and asked her into the library. She feared he would mention her odor again, but there was nothing she could do about it. When she saw him in the lamp light, she was appalled at his disheveled appearance. His hair was sticking up. He was thinner, much thinner than he had been for a long time. He wore a matte black porcelain mask instead of his usual leather one. It covered his face from his hairline to under his chin. It was roughly constructed with a flat appearance lacking both a nose and lips. She hated it the moment she saw it.

"How long have you had that on? It must be hurting your skin."

"There are things that hurt more." The mask had a tiny mouth opening that muffled his voice. He could never sing in that mask.

"Erik, can we talk now?"

He stared at her neck, his head suddenly, jerking to the side. He approached her and roughly pulled her head to the side, leaving her neck exposed. "You have purple marks on your neck. Have you hurt yourself?"

"No," she said, her chin dipping down.

"Where did they come from? You did not have

them before," he asked, lifting her chin even as she resisted.

"Please don't shame me further." Her chin trembled.

"I ask you again, what happened with your neck?" he inquired, poking harshly at a discoloration with his finger.

"Ow, ow, ow." She felt a dull ache as he poked them all in turn.

"I will not have you hurting yourself."

"I have not hurt myself," she murmured, feeling the heat from her ears spread to her face.

"I do not understand. You had no marks when I brought you home."

"I did, I saw them in my mirror. They were pink and have darkened." She felt the heat in her face heighten. Her guilt also intensified as she recalled the pleasure she had felt as Raoul kissed and nipped her neck.

He said nothing and just stood still for a while. "You mean...you mean to say, he...?"

She nodded, cut him off, before he said the words, hiding her face in her hands.

His knees sagged and she saw him slide into a chair as if the strength in his legs had suddenly given out. He was silent, then slowly shook his head and stared at her neck again. "Damn him to hell! He bit my wife like a common whore," he growled. "That mongrel marked you as a message for me. A challenge!"

She covered her face with her hands, her sobs trapped in her throat. "I'm sorry," she managed to say.

"Sorry?" he grunted. "I doubt that. Erik should make you strip to see where else he branded you."

Looking away from her, he said, in an ice-cold voice, "Erik had not realized you had nothing to read in your room. Please select some books and return immediately to your room. I will provide you with paper, ink and pen later. You will stand behind the door when I bring your meals. Do not show yourself to Erik while you have those obscene marks on you." He strode out of the library. She was glad he wasn't there to see the results of the scorching heat she felt on her face.

She could barely see through her tears and chose a few books at random, returning to hide away in her room. After a while, she heard him lock her door. Again, he paced in front of her room. She could barely read, thinking of the condition in which she had seen him. She had been right; he was starving himself, punishing himself for her foolishness.

The heavier mask was hurting his face. The flattened features of the horrible mask made him look inhuman. In the library she had wanted to rip it off his face and smash it on the floor. It hid his pain from her perfectly, except that she knew him and he could not hide from her. She could see his swollen, red-rimmed eyes through the mask's eyeholes. Tears burned her eyes, but she did not allow them to spill.

Oh Erik, what have I done to us? Will you ever be able to forgive me?

Erik's head felt as if it would explode. One more thought, one more memory, and he would burst like over-ripe fruit. He could barely feel his legs now. He had been walking almost continuously for over a week, stopping only to prepare her meals, collapsing at the end of the day for a short rest in his coffin. Soon he would lay there permanently and sleep—no more walking, no more thinking.

He dared not stop walking. It was back, that awful voice, suggesting he do terrible mischief. The wicked things it wanted him to do! He would not give in to it and so it punished him relentlessly, by filling up his head with thoughts and memories of Christine in the vicomte's arms. He, in turn, did his best to control the Voice by not feeding his body, exhausting himself and keeping his body weak. While he walked, Erik was in control, he could count his steps and not let in the thoughts. He had to protect her, even if she was unfaithful and did not love him. Despite her wayward behavior, Christine had to be protected at all costs. He walked and walked all day, until he collapsed from exhaustion and had no strength to do the wicked things the Voice demanded.

The Voice had always been with him. As a young man, it had told him how to protect himself, when others made his life hell. It was only in Persia that he had given it full rein. It had been liberating to just give in to the Voice. It gave him ideas on how to build the torture chambers and how to test them. All that violence had not been Erik's fault, but Hafiz did not understand this. Erik did not like bloodshed; he loved music, art, he loved learning about all the sciences, architecture, and philosophy, he loved poetry. It was the Voice that delighted in lifeless, dismembered bodies, puddles of blood and lasting pain. How the Voice relished inducing pain!

The incident with the boy had all been Erik's fault. Months ago, when Christine had been about to elope with the vicomte to lead a wonderful life, he had interrupted her plans by kidnapping her. The boy's brother was against the union, but he would have understood and forgiven them once they were married and a babe came. She would have had everything she could imagine and then more. His action had put a stop to her dreams, depriving her of the man she loved and saddled her with a deformed miscreant.

Despite so many years of rejection, he had dared to hope for love. He had hoped for the impossible. It was not Christine's fault that she had a tender heart and gifted him with a few days of happiness, shared a few kisses with him that had probably made her sick afterwards. She was only a silly, kind child.

The boy had left passion marks on her neck. He had counted five dark brown-purplish stains on his wife's neck. Five amorous kisses she had allowed on her neck even before he came up. They were well formed. The boy had taken his time while she bared her neck to his ardor. He might as well have branded her with his seal. To add to his own shame, his father must have seen the marks on her neck when he visited to check on her but had been too kind and polite to mention it. The man had not questioned *him* about it so he must have assumed that it was the boy.

A whorehouse wouldn't take her as she is. What would she bring you on the streets but a few sous? She's marked and has no value. Satisfy your urges on her as the boy did, then throw her out to the gutter with her kind.

No!

The Voice blamed Christine for Erik's broken heart.

An eye for an eye, a tooth for a tooth, and a heart for a heart.

The awful Voice wanted to destroy her. So, he had to stay vigilant. While he was Erik, nothing and no one would hurt his only love. Christine did not deserve such punishment. She had been naughty, kissing the boy like that, letting him touch her and mark her body. Perhaps, if he taught her a lesson, he could appease the Voice. And eventually, he would answer the challenge issued by the vicomte.

Chapter 21

The Torture Chamber

He sat in the library staring at the far wall, his body stock-still, no book graced his lap. As he heard the first scream, he gritted his teeth, then the second and third each more shrill than the last, making him dig his fingers deeper into the armrest. He wanted to move and run to her, but would not budge. She had to be punished for her own sake. He heard her yell his name repeatedly, and heard the door handle rattling. Sweat was dripping down his face under the thick porcelain mask. She called to him and begged for his help. It went against his nature not to run to her aid. The banging began soon after, followed by more screeching, still he sat, growing paler, unmoving. *Christine!* He heard items crashing in the room, his own flesh frozen and wet. How well he knew her. It had been so easy to use her nature against her.

Let her learn a lesson! What would she do without Erik?

That morning he had given her a wet cloth to freshen herself. Christine thanked him profusely and smiled. She had wiped her face, chest, neck and arms with it then returned the cloth, thanking him again. "Smells good, like fresh grass," she had said. He returned with another damp cloth and left her to give her privacy. It was part of the lesson she had to learn.

He had not eaten for over a week now. Before Christine came to live with him, he had gone without food for three to four days because he was too busy composing or he simply did not desire to eat, water had been enough. Christine got his body used to eating at least four small meals a day. He was going through food withdrawal pains. Plain water was no longer a sufficient substitute. For the first time in his life, he was thoroughly famished. His stomach growled as it clamored for Christine's breakfast, tea and cakes.

Never had he felt so weak and despondent. His clothing hung on his weakened body, like a Sunday suit, on a long dead cadaver. He heard her hollering and held on to the chair armrest tightly until his knuckles paled. Sweat covered his body; it ran down his face and back. He took a drink of his medicine beside him. His stream of tears blinded him. *My love, this is for you, to keep you safe!* His sobs began then, racking his thin body. He held on, digging his bony fingers into the fabric. *This is to save you, my darling girl. You need to learn your lesson and then the Voice will stop asking for your blood. Trust in me ̄just a little more suffering and I will end it.*

Even as he sat, preoccupied by the goings on in her room, he could not forget the vision of Christine in the boy's arms. His mind went over the vivid memories of Christine in the vicomte's arms, his lips on hers, her skirts bunched to her waist, the boy's hands moving buried under her skirt, playing with her, earning her secrets. Then to twist the knife further, he had found the damned picture she kept of the beautiful boy and the notes he had written her. Her journal confirmed her love for the vicomte, her sacrifice for his sake. He had read the journal over and over again, alongside the boy's notes. The words never changed. They wanted him dead.

They planned to destroy you.

Kings have conspired against me and failed, and now this whippet of a boy thought he could win against Erik!

And who helped you beat them all, Erik? Who has always been on your side?

You. Always you!

Then rejoice in her suffering.

He wished he could enjoy her fear, her suffering, but he loved her.

Earlier that morning, Erik had relented and given her a chance to refresh herself. She felt heavenly. He was relenting, perhaps soon, he would listen to her and then he would understand. Then in the afternoon, he had locked the door to her bathroom, saying he would be back later to clean. He returned with two large cleaning buckets and left them in the room. She wondered why he would need to clean when she had not been able to use the bathroom. The buckets were covered with cloths and she assumed they contained cleaning solution or water. He walked away with a cryptic warning to her about the sting of curiosity and strict instructions not to go near the buckets.

She heard a noise in one of the buckets and her curiosity got the best of her, so she lifted the cloth just a little, but it was enough to find that a brown grasshopper had hopped up onto her arm. She screamed and the cloth fell off. The bucket was choked with hundreds of grasshoppers in green, brown and fawn; the creatures erupted, jumping, flying or crawling out at once. Some landed on her mattress and others on her hair. She began to scream and run around the room, knocking them off. "Erik!" In her madness to get away from them, she accidentally kicked the second bucket over. Scorpions, as big as her hand, slowly crawled out. She ran around the room pounding the walls and yelling for him, "Erik, help me. Don't let them sting me."

Christine ran to the door and tried to open it, she banged on the door until her hands ached. Then she kicked the door until her feet ached. A fat scorpion crawled over her foot. Her hair stood on end, and she screamed, shaking it off. She saw the scorpions crawling behind and under the mattress. Grasshoppers jumped from one part of the room to the other, some landed on her. The infernal cacophony did not let up; fogging her mind. *If only I had a sheet to cover myself.* The mattress was invaded, so carefully she climbed atop the dresser and stood there. A few scorpions had crawled under the dresser. If she had shoes she could crush them, but she had nothing she could use to defend herself. Tears slid down her face, blurring her vision. "*Erik, help me!*"

Several grasshoppers jumped on the dresser and one landed on her exposed chest, quickly hiding between her breasts. She ripped the neckline of her nightgown in her desperation to get the creature out. *Erik's punishing me for betraying him, but I know he loves me. There has to be some pity left in his heart.* Her bathroom was locked so there was no chance to hide in there. She depended wholly on Erik's mercy.

"Erik! Erik!" she called to him as loud as she could; a grasshopper flew into her mouth and in panic, she bit into it. The bitter insides oozed into her mouth. She howled and nearly lost her balance trying to spit it out. The grasshoppers were landing on her faster than she could swat them off. Exhausted, she hunched on her dresser making herself as small as possible. Grasshoppers of all sizes continued to land on her, and a few got tangled in her hair; she pulled a smaller one out of her nostril. They had crawled under her night rail. She shuddered as she felt them inching their way to her bottom. She could feel the tiny legs as they walked on her bare skin. She wondered if the scorpions had made their way to her as well.

"Erik, help me!" she whimpered. Every once in a while, one of the grasshoppers nipped or licked at her, she could not tell, but it felt different than when they just walked. She rolled herself tighter, almost into a ball and closed her eyes to the plague, with her hands covering her face and ears, she waited for the man she loved to rescue her. It was all she could do as the creatures covered the rest of her body. *Erik will come. He won't let me die like this.*

The screaming had stopped and it terrified him. *Enough!* Erik ran to her room and entered. At first, he did not see her, for a moment he feared her escaped and he faltered. Then, she began to unfurl from what looked like a mass of grasshoppers crawling over each other on top of the dresser. The creatures covered every inch of her body. Only her face, which she was covering with her hands, was spared. The sight horrified him. The Voice had to be satisfied with this! The cloth with grass extract he had given her to clean herself with, had been too much. She jumped from the dresser into his arms, many of the creatures still clinging to her, nearly knocking him off balance. Erik stumbled, but managed to regain his balance by bracing himself. It was a struggle to get the creatures off her body and hair while she insisted on clinging to him.

"Make them go away, make them go away, I beg you!" Her muffled voice begged as he worked to remove them. Her own hands were nearly paralyzed but she managed to help him by getting the ones under the night rail.

Finally free of all the insects, Erik carried her in his arms as she sunk her head in his neck. Warmth spread through him, dissipating the hurt and anger. Trembling in his arms, his wife made him want to wrap himself around her and protect her.

You are so weak, Erik, one touch from her and you forget that she plotted with the boy to kill you.

How could he chastise her, when she was making him feel like this? He sat with her in his chair. She whimpered and he held him tighter, making all space between them disappear. She sat on his lap as he rubbed her back, soothing her. He relished the sensation of being close to her once more.

"I was bad, I know I was," she hiccuped. "I...I know you had to...punish me, but please don't make me go in that room again. P...please, let me stay with you." She broke into soft sobs.

It broke his heart to see her so humble. He preferred his feisty Christine, but the Voice did not. He looked at her neck and saw that the marks were slowly dissipating. Only two were still an ugly brown.

He caressed the damaged area on her neck and kissed her dirty, bedraggled hair—more brown than blond.

"There were scorpions!" she cried, looking half drowned in his arms.

"Calm down, it was only a joke to remind you of how we came to be married. They are harmless," he said, holding her tightly against him.

"Please, get rid of them. I never want to go back in that room again." She buried her head further into his neck and grabbed onto his shoulders.

"Christine, you either let me go so I can get rid of them or we sit here and watch them escape under the door."

She disentangled herself from him, allowed him to place her on the chair, and wrapped her arms around her knees.

"Stay here and I will take care of your room. Then I will bring you a calming tea."

He opened the door to her room saying, "So there you are, my little friends. I guess you wanted to keep my naughty wife company."

After capturing every single insect and scrapping off the ones she had managed to squash, Erik brought one of the scorpions to her. "Here's one of the little critters..."

She was out of the seat and backing away. "Keep that thing away from me."

"It looks like a scorpion but it is not. Actually, it is a Thelyphonida, a whip scorpion. Look at the tail—no stinger, no venom."

"I don't care, keep it away. It's horrible!"

He laughed and returned to her room. "So sorry dear fellow, I think my wife finds you even uglier than me," he cackled.

She drank the tea he provided for her and sat on his lap for hours. He rocked her in his arms until the trembling stopped and she fell asleep. Much later he returned her to her room, placing her carefully on the mattress. He covered her with his blanket.

"Are you sure they are all gone?" she asked, half asleep, hugging the blanket around her.

"So which one did you prefer this time, my dear? The scorpion or the grasshopper?"

"Neither, and I hope this is not a trick question or another one of your jokes!"

"It is not. But tell me which would you choose now?"

"The scorpions I think. They never really did anything to me except walk around and look scary."

"Despite that they are such ugly creatures..." He sighed. "The scorpion is always a good choice!"

Chapter 22

Whose Blood?

*S*he must have felt disgusted when she allowed you to kiss her.

She enjoyed my kisses.

Then why did she go kiss the boy? You saw her, pressing her body to his, delighting in his touches. She should be punished for that.

I already punished her.

She must have looked at his picture before she could get in bed with you.

At least, I tasted that pleasure.

Someone has to be punished! She, for betraying you, or you, for allowing it.

Then let it be me. You will not hurt her!

The voice was incessant and it drowned out his own thoughts. He knew the voice wanted blood, and that eventually it would wear him out in order to get it, it always had. If he could not stop it, then he would appease it and be the sacrificial lamb.

Erik entered her room. She tried to smile at him, but backed away when Erik threw a belt at her feet and knelt with his back to her. "Strike me!" he commanded.

"What?" she asked, startled.

"You will strike me," he repeated.

"I will do no such thing. I will not hurt you."

"You will not hurt me?" He laughed. "Haven't you done a jolly good job of that already?"

"I'm so sorry, but you will not let me explain."

"Explain what? How he knows you're a virgin? If you don't want others to be hurt, you will do as I demand!" He finished unbuttoning his shirt and threw the leather strap back to her.

"Strike me!"

"Erik, please, I cannot."

"I will bring you the boy's heart still beating. Isn't that what you always wanted—his heart?"

"If you are referring to Raoul, I don't want him or his heart."

"Then, I will bring the other part of him which seems to interest you." He got up and began to button-up his shirt again.

"Erik, their home is protected. They have guards. You will be hurt badly or killed."

"Don't you think I can outsmart your boy?" His voice was growing colder.

"One on one, yes, but not in his own abode with his brother there. Please, I don't want *you* to be hurt. Please!" she begged him.

"Too late. You had your chance," he turned away from her heading for the door.

"I'll do it!" she cried, running after him and grabbing his sleeve. "Only, swear to me, you will not go to the Chagny home."

"I swear that if you strike me hard enough, I will not go near the boy."

"Or his house…swear to that, Erik."

"Here, do it," he said, handing her the belt.

"Swear it, Erik!"

With a sigh, he whispered, "I swear it."

He wore a thin shirt which would not provide much protection. Erik knelt in front of her with his back to her. Christine was alarmed at how his ribs and backbone showed through the shirt. He had grown thinner. She took the belt and tapped him lightly near his shoulder, which seemed to have a little more flesh.

"Do not play with me! I said strike me." He snatched the strap from her hand and brought it down on his back with a heavy thud. "Like this," he roared.

She felt lightheaded, like she might pass out. Nevertheless, she had to hold on. Who knew what he might do if she fell unconscious.

He threw the strap to her. "Do it, now."

The mask made reading his face impossible, and there was no reasoning in what she could see of his eyes.

"Strike me!" he commanded again.

"Oh, Erik…you will be the death of me!"

"Do it, or your lover dies," he whispered over his shoulder, turning his face just enough so he could meet her eyes. In his state of mind, he would go to the Chagny manor and be killed. The blind fury caused by her betrayal blazed menacingly in his eyes. *I have to do it, for his sake.* She wanted to swallow but her mouth was too dry. The strap felt barbaric in her hands.

He knelt in front of her, his back to her, hands on his knees. Christine struck him, in fear for his life and in anger, because it was her sin not his—she should be the one punished. She struck his back once hard, then again and again. She raised and lowered her arm. His back recoiled and bowed alternately.

"Harder, yes, like that…yes, harder, harder." His voice was loud, but muffled by the porcelain mask. He dug his fingers into his knees.

"Hurt *me*. Do it for him! Strike *me* and save your lover. Harder. Make me bleed for you!" She lost count of the number of times she struck him, but throughout he kept egging her on, pushing her beyond her limit. Her hair pasted onto her sweaty forehead, blinding her, so that she could not see the damage she was causing him. Blood from his back splattered her night rail. Her arm continued its mission and she raised it and let it fall relentlessly. His head hung from a rubber neck. He barely held himself up with splayed hands on the floor as he swayed. His elbows shook, almost collapsing with each blow.

"Uhm, uhm, uhhm," low guttural grunts escaped him.

Hearing his grunts and ragged breathing, she came to her senses. His body convulsed before her, gasping, finally collapsing on the floor in a heap. Her husband lay on the floor in front of her. His shirt was in shreds and his back zigzagged in bright red welts. Suddenly terrified, she threw herself on him, turning him over, holding him close to her. "Erik!" His eyes were closed, his breathing, shallow and irregular. She held him to her across her chest, so nothing touched his lacerated back and pulled him onto her mattress on the floor. The coppery smell of the blood nearly made her sick.

"Erik, Erik, forgive me!" She held him in her weary arms. Nearly unconscious, he moaned softly.

"Good...girl...too weak...to hurt you...now," he choked out against her chest. She removed the heavy mask. His face was worse than she had ever seen it, a fine red rash covered it, and it was swollen along the brow, the mask had scrapped some of the skin, off his minuscule nose. What rattled her most, was that he did not fight her removing the mask from his face.

It was the first time she had walked into the kitchen in days; it was filthy. The plates from her meals were left on the table with whatever she had not consumed. Flies buzzed about and small maggots squired on the plates like living barley. Christine looked away before it made her sick and she served him a glass of water.

She gave him the water and he sipped a little. Christine poured the rest of the water on his back to remove the blood, then rubbed one of Mama Valérius' salves made with sage and garlic on the lacerations. Luckily, Erik had not touched the drawer with her maquillage—her rouge and other pots were still there as well as all her remedies. At her touch he groaned and arched his back, but did not move away as she applied the salve. She held him to her, until his breathing was stronger. Finally, he slept. She surrounded him in a circle of her arms, his horrible, dear face exposed to her. She felt warm and safe like she used to feel before. Her bloodied, ripped peach night rail reminded her that their lives were not like before.

Many hours later she felt him pull away from her, he grabbed his mask and left her room. She collapsed on her mattress, falling into an unsettled, dreamless sleep. In the morning, there was no breakfast tray. The waste bucket had not been replaced and was nearly full. She waited for but by mid-morning had to use it. It nearly overflowed and the odor of feculence saturated the air.

He appeared a few minutes before midday with a tray of bread, cheese, apples and a glass of water half spilled on the tray. He was hunched over, a shoulder on the door frame supported him. The pain showed in his eyes. He left, only to return a few moments later, with a fresh bucket. Christine begged him to let her put more of the healing oil on his back, he ignored her and picked up the fetid bucket, slushing the contents on his way out, leaving the fetid odor behind. She heard the clank of the turning lock.

Twice he tried to get up and failed. His arms lacked the strength. He finally rose a little from the mattress and pushed away her arms. He placed the mask back on his face. Groaning, Erik managed to crawl out of her room on all fours. Her salve made the pain bearable enough to move. Several times he dropped back to all fours on the way to his room. Somehow, he managed to creep into his coffin and he lay on his face. The mask nearly suffocated him and he slid it off. He needed to rest, to heal, but the Voice whispered to him and filled his mind.

There you have it, Erik, the proof you demanded. She ripped your flesh to save the boy!

This was what YOU wanted.

She makes Erik cry.

I forced her to hit me to satisfy your thirst for blood.

Ha! And you ended up getting the most satisfaction; sleeping in her arms.

I have a right to, she's my wife.

Then you should have forced her to satisfy your

needs. You prefer taking your pleasure from a few blows.

She already gave all her love to the boy. I have to be satisfied with her leftovers.

You are satisfied with so little... but, I am not.

You wanted blood; I gave you blood—mine! You cannot have her!

I am not satisfied!

You cannot have her!

By the time he awoke, it was near midday. He was exhausted from fighting with the Voice. Erik tumbled out of the coffin and dragged himself to the kitchen. He wanted to, but didn't have the strength to cook anything for her. He cut her a thick chunk of bread and a wedge of cheese, at the last minute he included two apples. He could barely straighten his back at all, so he walked hunched over, balancing the tray and clean bucket, as best he could to ease his pain. He managed to open her door and pushed the tray and bucket into her room. Teary eyed, Christine offered to put more salve on his back when she realized he couldn't straighten up. It would have felt wonderful to have her rub it in, to have her touch on his back again, but he rebuffed her offer and the pleasure it would have given him. The waste bucket half emptied along the way and when he could not carry it any longer, he left it along the way and half bent-over as he was, shuffled back to his coffin. The Voice wanted her pain, but it would have to be satisfied with his.

Chapter 23

Desolate

Erik threw open the door to her room and marched in. Christine sat at her desk writing. "You frightened me!" she said, turning around startled. For three days he had walked around hunchbacked. He would not allow her to help him in anyway and insisted on suffering alone as his back healed. She suffered as well, knowing his pain was her doing. She had nearly killed him, to keep him away from certain death at the Chagny manor.

"You need to be cleansed."

"If you would provide me with some water…" she began to say, mortified that her hygiene had gotten to such a state that he had to mention it again.

"It is Erik's job to care for you."

"I would appreciate a sliver of soap, a basin of

water, and I will do it myself."

"Only a basin? Have you seen the state of you?" She felt her face flush. She could not blame the smells on the bucket. It was empty. In a fluid motion, he grabbed her by the wrist and pulled her out her room and into the hallway. She gagged. The smell outside her room was even worse. There were several of the buckets she had used there lying about. Their contents made a muddy slush on the floor. He pulled on her arm again and they crossed the parlor, which was in better condition and through the front door. For an instant, she thought that he was taking her upstairs. She took a deep breath of the fresh, mossy air from the lake. To think, that she had once thought that smell unpleasant. She looked down at herself and what she was wearing, but she smiled at the thought of seeing the sunlight again. *Maybe I will see the sun today.* Hope surged in her heart.

As they neared the boat, he rushed past it. It surprised her to find herself flying in the air and it was not until she felt herself drop into the cold water, that she realized what he had just done.

"I can't swim well, Erik. Get me out," she screamed, thrashing about in the water. He did not move toward her, but rather looked past her and began to argue with someone on the other side of the lake.

"I will see to her. She is my wife. Go away."

She craned her neck as she struggled to get closer to the shore, but saw no one there.

"Erik!"

Her eyes searched for the stranger that had come down before, knowing it was futile. Of course, there was no one to help her five floors below the opera house.

He extended an oar to her and she held on as he pulled her closer to shore. Once she was close enough, he took a handful of her hair and kept her suspended with her head above the water.

"He is right. You must be purified, it is for your own good," He pushed her head under the water. She came up spluttering.

"Erik, no!" she screamed and struggled to get out of the lake

"Your piddling about with the boy has made you foul."

He dunked her again. She was terrified, and held on to his sleeves as best she could. He brought her up and she was able to catch her breath.

"Get me out, I can't..." she spluttered.

Before she could finish her plea, he pushed her under again. She heard a snarl muffled by the mask as he dunked her. Christine felt herself loosing strength, her hands slipped from his sleeves. There was nothing else to hold on to.

"You must be cleansed, so he won't hurt you," he growled as he pulled her up for a third time.

"Who? Who wants to hurt me?" she croaked in terror as she caught her breath.

He raised his arm slowly, eyes lost in the distance

and extended a bony finger toward the rock face.

"The Voice," he said deep in his throat and his eyes opened in horror.

She clung to his arm and blinked, trying hard to see someone where Erik pointed to. Suddenly, she felt his long fingers grip her skull like a cap.

"Erik, stop you're hurting me."

Holding her head tightly, he submerged her head, holding her under the water. She struggled, became disoriented and breathed in water when she should have expelled her breath. Her nose burned, as she desperately clawed at his hand. Erik was drowning her!

In desperation, she opened her mouth to beg him to stop and swallowed water. She was holding her breath and her chest felt like it would burst, her eyes could only see the dark water surrounding her. Very far away Erik was saying something, but she lost interest in her struggle. At last, she felt him pull her up and drag her out away from the lake. He patted her back forcefully until water came up in a gush, like vomit. Erik, sat holding her limp form on the rocky shore, shushing her as she coughed and spit out more water. He continued to rub her back until all the water was out. Her lungs pained her and, she could not breathe in enough air to satisfy her. He sang to her in his most angelic voice, interrupting his song twice, to argue with someone across the lake, that only he could see. Erik was out of his mind! She shivered in his arms as the cold water sluiced off her body. "Erik will not let you get catarrh. I will take you inside and warm you up. He has gone too far now!" he said softly, glaring into the far recess of the lake. He picked her up and raced across the home with her in his arms, entering his room. His black coffin gave her the usual chill as they neared it.

"Don't be frightened, you are cleansed, he is appeased for now."

He placed her in the coffin and walked away. Her fright was so great, that at first no sound came out of her mouth as it opened wider, but then as if it were an explosion she began to scream and climbed out of the casket, nearly overturning it.

He glared at her. "I thought you would be warmer in my bed, than out here in the draft, while I got you a towel. Why fear my coffin? It is not for you." He snorted. "It is I, who will reside in it soon enough," "Now I have a wet bed for all my consideration," he said coolly. "He will not like that."

Erik placed a towel around her shoulders and walked her to her room avoiding the soiled areas in the hallway. A short while later he was back and shoved two more towels at her and gave her a hot drink.

"There is no more bedding in the house, so take off your wet gown and wrap yourself in this," he said, giving her his dressing gown.

She took off her wet night rail, which did not look any cleaner in its wet state, dried herself and sat on her mattress wearing his dressing gown—it smelled of him. She pulled it around her in comfort. Erik stood by the open door staring at her, his arms limp at his sides. He threw her the door key. In a barely audible voice he whispered, "It is the only copy. Do not let me in again, no matter what I say. I will leave your food in a tray outside your door. Take it when I am not near the door. Leave your bucket out when you wish me to change it for you."

"Erik, please let me stay out with you. Look at it. We need to clean out home."

Before he closed the door behind him, he turned to her, his eyes dull and sad behind the black mask. "I can no longer promise that I won't hurt you. The Voice is here and he is stronger than Erik."

"What voice, Erik? There is no one else here!" Dread gripped her heart.

"Did you not see him by the lake? You cannot hear him then? Why would you? You do not want to hear that voice! It would take away your peace. Just…keep your door locked." As soon as he was gone, she closed the door and took up her rosary to the mattress with her. She said a long litany of prayers until she fell asleep.

Christine sat on her mattress, the poison vial Erik had given her as a wedding present in her hand. He had told her to use it to kill him and save herself if he became too unbalanced. She turned the liquid over in her hand. It was warm amber, like Erik's eyes when he had loved her.

She pulled on a red string which broke the wax seal. Who knew what he would do to her next? Last night he had spent half the night begging her to let him in, then the other half telling her how refreshed she would be if she slept in his coffin.

"My coffin is very comfortable, I will let you know. You can invite the vicomte to visit you, with my full permission. Let him complete the job, I so rudely interrupted. No pesky skirts to lift this time," he laughed, making her skin crawl. "Have you ever heard of a husband that is as kind and considerate as I am?" His voice dripped sarcasm. "The vicomte, can make sweet, sweet love to my wife right in my coffin...and for the grand finale..." He laughed. "Slam! Slam! Slam!" he repeated over and over again, laughing each time he said it as he walked away.

Her deception and mendacity had driven him insane. Erik was demented, but she loved him no less, so there was no question of poisoning him. She opened the vial and smelled the repugnant liquid. The smell made her insides quake. It would taste as dreadful as it smelled. She wondered if it would take effect immediately as he had promised or she would linger for days in pain. She put the bottle to her mouth and inhaled the noxious fumes in the back of her throat before the liquid hit her tongue. A nausea shook her from head to toes. Christine chided herself for her weakness. With shaking hands, she again neared the vial to her mouth and gagged again. *I have to do it before Erik kills me, maybe he'll lock me in that monstrous coffin and sit by talking to that man he sees.* She got courage from her thoughts and tried bringing the bottle up to her mouth again, but before she was even close a tremor shook her and the bottle slipped from her shaking hand, smashing on the floor. She stared at the debris, teardrops falling. *My fate is in your hands, as it has always been.* She picked up her rosary and asked God for forgiveness for what she had been about to do. An alarm from a tunnel sounded, startling her. *Hafiz!* She remembered their conversation and looked around for something red to wear, but Erik had burned all her clothes. If she just blurted out to Hafiz that she needed help Erik would just kill them both. She held her face in her hands and wept. *How do I let him know I need help?*

Louis, Erik's father, again sought out information about Erik from Mme. Giry. When neither Erik nor his wife were seen by either Mme. Giry or her daughter, in over two weeks, she finally told him about Erik's relationship with Hafiz and gave him the man's address. Used to dealing with the nobility in Persia, Hafiz was surprised and duly honored to have such a guest as the Marquis du Bourdeny in his home.

Hafiz welcomed Louis, into his home with all the solemnity he could muster. His lordship, told him he had attempted another visit to the lower cellars on his own, but was confounded when Erik did not answer his cries from the edge of the lake. The man was sick with worry for his only son's welfare. Louis implied, rather than said to Hafiz, that Erik might have gotten the impression that his wife and the vicomte had resumed their previous relationship. Hafiz did not tell the marquis, that if Erik had found Christine in the vicomte's arms, or any other such scenario, Christine Daaé must already be dead. He agreed to go visit Erik, with the intention of calming him down and quietly recovering the young singer's body. Hafiz's heart felt heavy with guilt, he regretted not visiting more regularly, but the couple had seemed so enamored during his last visit that he had wanted to give them more privacy. He had been too quick to unshoulder his self-imposed responsibility.

Once used his usual tools to get into the home through the back door, he found the monster of Mazandaran, thinner than he had seen him in years. The cloying smell of death and decay hung in the air. Erik was as disheveled as their home. It did not appear as if anyone had cleaned in a long time. Flies buzzed over their heads freely.

"Where is Christine, Erik?" the Persian asked, fully expecting Erik to point to a bloodied, festering bundle in a corner. Erik wore the black porcelain mask he had worn in Persia during the executions. It added to Hafiz's feelings of dread and sorrow. Hafiz had always found that mask disturbing and it brought back detailed memories of the blood baths in the palace at Mazandaran that made him shiver.

"What do you want with Erik's wife?"

Hafiz hated the muffled, inhuman sound that emerged from behind the mask. "Do not play games, Erik! Where is Christine?"

"Why should Erik answer your questions in his own home?"

"I want to greet her as I always do." Hafiz tried to remain calm.

"She is busy," Erik answered, looking away from him.

"Never so busy that she won't to greet me. She would be very upset not to have shared a cup of tea."

Erik looked uneasy. His daroga's nose never failed him. He was too late.

"She is in her room. She may be taking a nap."

"She will not sleep tonight if she sleeps at this time. It is best to wake her up." Hafiz prayed the sleep Erik referred to was not the eternal sleep.

"Fine, then Erik will tell his wife that she cannot rest, all because the nosy daroga of Persia demands her presence and a cup of tea," he barked, storming off toward the bedroom.

Erik's clothes hung on his frame. Hafiz knew that Christine was feeding him well and that Erik ate every last morsel she prepared for him. The monster was referring to himself as "Erik." In Mazandaran, he had heard Erik speak of himself in the third person, after a particularly gruesome spree of killings in the palace torture chambers.

It was a jolt when she appeared a few minutes later. Christine lived! Her face was almost transparent with two purpled bruises under her eyes. Her hair was bedraggled, uncombed for days or weeks. She wore Erik's dressing robe and it trailed to the floor, he could see a dirty ripped neckline peeking through. She was not wearing red. Had she forgotten their conversation? He knew she owned a red dress and shawl. Though the one detail was missing, everything else in the home spelled trouble. She sat staring into his eyes without saying a word, her own almost unblinking.

"See, I told you she was fine. Tell him you are fine, Christine."

"I am fine," she repeated tonelessly.

Erik narrowed his eyes in her direction, but said nothing else.

She remained standing next to Erik staring at Hafiz. On closer inspection, he noticed that she had smeared a careless slash of red lip paint across her pale lips and wore more rouge than usual.

The moment had come! The end to the mission he had imposed on himself so many years ago in Persia. He had to tread carefully, since the enemy was as cunning as all his past enemies put together. He was dealing with a coiled cobra, a monster that he had allowed to live and escape Persia.

It was not just his life that was in peril, but Christine's as well. Would he need to end the monster's existence at that moment? Could he? Not likely. He swatted at a fly and missed.

"Make us tea, Christine," Erik uttered sweetly.

Without a word she walked toward the kitchen,

and from behind Erik's back, she mouthed to Hafiz, "*Help me!* Hafiz kept his face blank.

"Well, so who else are you hounding these days?" Erik asked him in a tight lipped carefree voice. He turned to face Erik.

"One day you *will* hurt my feelings, Erik, but luckily for you, that day is very far away." He managed to smile and tried to keep up his part of their usual banter, while his heart thudded wildly in his chest and his mind ran circles inside his head.

Christine brought back the tea service and, while she poured, he noticed very mild discolorations on her neck. They were oddly placed and did not appear to be from a lasso. He did not rule out fingertips. *I should shoot him now and let it be over with.* Hafiz tried to swallow as he patted the small gun he always carried in his secret pocket. His lordship would not appreciate that.

As Christine sat drinking her tea, she allowed Erik's dressing gown to fall slightly open leaving the blood stained gown to show. She looked straight into the Persian's eyes. Another signal!

Was Erik so far gone that he did not realize how his wife looked?

He dared not acknowledge her signals in any way for fear that Erik would notice. It was too perilous. Hafiz sat back, stretched his legs and brought his cup up to his mouth as slowly as he dared—giving the thoughts in his head time to settle down. The air was heavy with a stench from the hallway. As if their sanitary had backed up. Hafiz could barely put the cup to his mouth.

"So, Erik, are you going to share some of those famous cookies today?" he asked swatting at another fly.

"There are no cookies! Drink your tea quickly and be grateful for that," Erik said brusquely.

Hafiz noticed, that they did not sit near each other. Erik was talking non-stop about all kinds of trivial matters, talking to no one in particular. He did not refer to her once or talk about anything they had done together. His eyes, like hers, were red-rimmed. Christine sat quietly. She brought the cup several times to her mouth, but not once did she open her mouth and drink. He had to get Christine out and then keep her safe, because Erik would hunt for her to the ends of the earth. Hafiz was developing a plan in his head, but he would need the help of the marquis to carry it out.

As soon as the Persian left, Erik rounded on her. "Why did you sit there without talking? He came to chat with you."

"You will not listen to me, so why should I bother speaking?"

"You sat there like a tomb slab. Erik told you to smile." he spat at her.

"I did my best." She crossed her arms, mulishly looking away from him.

"You must not try to deceive Erik. It would not fare well for you or that little Persian rat."

"It does not fare well for me now," she retorted.

He glared at her. "Return Erik's robe to him. Wear the gown you bought for the boy with Erik's money. Dream of making love to your vicomte while Erik watches. Erik wonders, would your lover still want you if he saw you today?"

She threw the robe at him. "You are acting like an animal. You almost killed me in the lake."

"Now, you realize it, you foolish girl. It took you this long to see what you married!"

"I hate you," she said, slamming the door in his face and locking it carefully.

For the second time that night, he came to her door and implored her forgiveness, beseeched her to open the door and talk with him. In her mind, she still had a vivid picture of her ordeal with the bugs and her near drowning in the lake. Tonight, he sounded different. He sounded gentle, like her old Erik.

"Sweetheart," said the beautiful voice coming through her door. "What did you refer to me as, when you first met me?"

"The voice? My Angel of Music," she answered shakily.

"Yes, that is who I am. I am your Angel! Won't you open the door to your Angel of Music? We can sing together."

"Erik? I am so confused. What do you want?" She wanted to open and fall into his arms. She wanted everything to be as it was.

"Do not open the door!" His voice took on a new frantic tone, sounding strangled to her. "Don't you wish to sing with me?" the gentle voice was back.

"What would we sing?"

"A little song your Don Juan has composed for you."

"Don Juan is your composition and you said I should not listen to it."

"Not that!" he growled. "We will sing a requiem together," the sweet voice said.

"A requiem…for whom?" She heard his laughter. "Da, da, da, da Daaé" he sang as he walked away from the door, and her skin crawled. *Do not open the door, no matter what I say.* That was what he had told her. She would keep the door closed until Hafiz could rescue her. She got on her knees and prayed for herself, her husband's sanity and her marriage.

Christine was on the fourth decade of the rosary when she heard the alarm in the tunnel Hafiz used. *He has come for me.* She could not envision the likelihood of Erik allowing her to walk away with another man.

She heard Erik curse and a door slam, then silence. She began to despair when she did not hear Hafiz. Had Erik hurt him? She put her ear to the door and heard a very soft knock at her door.

"Christine?" It was Hafiz. "Quickly, open."

She opened her door to find his dark face covered in perspiration, his green eyes glowing. Hafiz looked at her in her stained and ripped night rail. She had forgotten that her left breast was almost completely exposed. She pulled up the neckline and held on to it.

"Hurry, dress quickly, I don't know how long he will be away."

"But how did you…?"

"There is no time now. I will explain later. You do not have time to pack." She saw his eyes catch the half full bucket by the door. His lips compressed as his nostrils flared and he looked away without another word. She was past feeling embarrassed about a bucket of waste.

"I have nothing else to wear or to pack, Erik burned everything." Her hand reached out and she grabbed her rosary from the dresser. "It is all I have."

His eyes opened in comprehension. He gave her his jacket and led her away in her filthy night rail.

Before she entered the tunnel, she gave her home one long last look. Would she ever return down here to a loving home with Erik or was everything they had built destroyed? First, she had to survive and then she could help him from wherever she was. With the same passion she with which she had once promised herself to Raoul, she now promised to return and rebuild their home. Hafiz touched her elbow, and she followed him quickly into the darkened tunnel.

Erik heard the alarm from the tunnel Hafiz used. He went out to tell the Persian he was not welcome back on the same day, but instead of the Persian he had found a large dead rat near the alarm—electrocuted. *A French rat not a Persian rat;* he laughed at his own joke. He resolved to talk to Sebastian about tightening his watch on the critters.

The moment he reentered the house, he knew. It felt cold, empty. His heart skipped, and began to thud uncontrollably in his chest. *Christine!* He ran to her room, only to find the door unlocked, the room empty. His foot crushed the remnants of the poison vial. He walked through the house, knowing that he would not find her and felt compelled to seek her out anyway.

"Christine! Christine!"

His voice bounced against the cold walls. *She's safe.* A smile spread on his face, as sobs racked his thin frame. He continued his quest, looking in every room several times. An intense spasm tore at his chest, and her name escaped from his lips once more, "Christine" before falling to his knees in the middle of the parlor.

Alone again!

Damn you, you drove her away!

You allow a whimpering boy, just out of short pants to take your wife? You would have been better off if they had made you a eunuch in Persia.

What difference now that I have lost her. She may hate me, but my Christine is safe from you.

If I can't have her blood, then Paris cannot be!

So be it. Christine is on the Chagny estate, well away from Paris.

Nothing mattered now, why bother to fight. He would not be responsible. He walked into the torture chamber and released a trap door on the floor. Erik descended to the musty cellars where he had kept his new barrels full of gunpowder, so very many of them.

End of Book One

About the Author

Caridad Martin grew up in New York City after leaving her native Cuba. She started writing at age seven and has continued creating people on paper that talk to each other—she refuses to admit that sometimes on a silent, moonless night, she listens in on their conversations. Online, she has written novels and short stories since 2005 under the pseudonym of Phantasmarose. This is where the idea for the Masque series was first born.

She is a voracious reader and at home can be found in one of two places: reading in her favorite chair or pottering around the garden. She has traveled extensively throughout Europe, Latin America, Taiwan, and the Philippines. She lived in Colchester, England for several years. She loves camping and in the US, she has traveled coast to coast backpacking on her own and in an RV with her family. She is an avid collector of wine and lanterns and put her collection of both to good use when Superstorm Sandy hit the East Coast.

Caridad lives in New Jersey, where she can watch the ebb and flow of New York Bay. Her family puts up with her eccentricities and her need to hide away for hours writing. Her oversized black and white Coon Hound lies nearby, snoozing.

Caridad would love to hear from you. You can contact her at www.caridadmartin.com and at Twitter @CariMartinWrtr.

Please review the book at your favorite online retailer it feeds my muse!

Masque: Forge

A Gaston Leroux Phantom of the Opera Romance series

-Book Two-

Caridad Martin

Chapter 1

The Scourge of Paris

The wooden high back bench he sat on was uncomfortable, as was everything in his room. It was meant to remind him of the reality of life and to prepare him for the next life. *She is safe!* His head leaned back heavily into the chair back. *Now, I can die. My coffin is but a few feet away, and when my time is near, I will crawl in and just lie there. It won't take long without her. I do not need strength to care for her. Food is of no use to me now. All I need to do is stop the water. That will do it. One morning, I will not have the strength to lift the lid and at last it will be over. Let her be happy with her handsome boy. Knowing her jubilant should make me happy, even as it kills me.*

Soon, we will let the grasshopper loose, Erik. For Paris it will be a very special masquerade, everyone will wear a death mask!

Have I not already provided you with a plethora of bodies, heads, and blood?

I want the boy and so do you!

Erik took the vicomte's picture from his pocket and stared at it, a mix of emotions running through him, each darker than the last. With a snarl, he began to crush it in his hand, then stopped, not sure why he placed it back in his pocket.

He will not be in Paris when the grasshopper hops. What will you do about that?

I will go find him. He has to die before the grasshopper hops. He will hang from my lasso.

The Punjab lasso is much too coarse an instrument for such a handsome young man. Use your dagger to slice his face off. Will she still love him or choose your ugly face over no face at all?

I want her to be happy. But I want her for me ̄I am her husband. She must chose me!

Sebastian had already distributed the barrels all over the city. Erik had one last trip to make before he set off the grasshopper.

And then Paris will truly be La Ville-Lumière, the city of lights!

While planning Christine's rescue, Hafiz explained to Louis that the first place Erik would look for Christine was in his home at the rue Tivoli so he could not take her there. Louis offered them the perfect sanctuary, a small house he owned on the outskirts of Paris near Courbevoie. Erik had no idea the house even existed. The house was plain and unassuming. It was well set back on the grounds and easy to overlook. Louis mentioned, with a gratified smile, that he had used it in the past to enjoy the company of reputable women who were not society ladies. A few society ladies who did not wish to be ruined had also been guests.

On the day he saved her from Erik's house Hafiz took Christine directly to Louis' house. On arrival, Hafiz noticed that the house was in slight disrepair and assumed that Louis no longer made frequent use of it. A skeleton staff was kept there and had obviously been alerted to prepare the house for visitors. The house had been aired, the furniture dusted and clean. The white walls though dingy, were free of cobwebs. A few vases were filled with fresh flowers. Christine did not say a word during the trip. She was barely aware of her surroundings as they entered the house. A maid showed her to her room and a short time later came out with the bunched up night rail and his coat. The woman eyed him suspiciously, then said, "The lady is in the tub, Monsieur. But she is in need…" the older woman hedged. "She needs everything Monsieur. She don't have a stitch on!" Hafiz refused to give her the pleasure of an explanation, so he nodded and took the night rail from her hand. If there had been a murder to solve, he would have had at least ten ideas in his head. What to do with a…an unclothed woman, had him baffled. Relief washed through him as Louis was let into the house by the butler at that instant.

Not long after he entered the house, Hafiz had informed Louis of the immediacy of Christine's personal needs and to make his point displayed for him the night rail he had found her wearing. At present, he said, the girl, sat wrapped in a sheet in her room. Right after he sent word to his staff to ready the house for guests, Louis had asked Lady Alexa to purchase ready-made essentials for the girl and have them delivered expediently to the address he gave her, although he knew Lady Alexa was well familiar with the address, since she had once been a guest there herself. She had assumed the items were for Louis' latest fling—he did not let her know otherwise. Lady Alexa, was well paid for her services. Due to her present financial circumstances, she welcomed the extra Francs—the job was accomplished as agreed, but she let Louis know, that she felt poorly used by him.

Philippe and Louis discussed what the former had come upon on his return to the Giry parlor. Louis was horrified. His only son had married an opera floozy of the lowest order. As much as he wished the little baggage, as far away from his son as possible, right now he needed the girl alive so that she could save Erik from total madness. If eventually she proved to be an albatross around his son's neck, then he would use every connection he had to cut her loose from Erik, perhaps even send her to America. How both Erik and Raoul had gotten so deeply involved with a scattered-brained floozy of such questionable morals was beyond him. Louis wondered, how many other well-heeled men she had sniffed around at the Garnier. The package with Christine's essentials, arrived on his heels.

"What have I done?" the Persian gasped. Hafiz dropped his copy of *Le Siècle* onto his lap and removed his reading glasses. With a trembling hand, he mopped his forehead using a large white handkerchief. He picked up his newspaper again and reread the headline.

Three More Indigents Found Dead

An unknown individual, nicknamed the "Scourge of Paris" by the Paris police, has been cleaning the Parisian streets of its more dubious elements. Last night, two more derelicts were found outside the La Tavern Gauche. "These men had been drinking cider all night long, and became argumentative toward the end of the evening, the bartender commented. This makes eight unexplained deaths this week. In a statement, the Chief of Police, Pierre Lamatie, said there is no known connection between the victims since the incidents happened outside taverns in different parts of the city.

"Mercy! How many more bodies do you need to quench your thirst, Erik?" Hafiz put down his newspaper. If Erik was at this level of violence and madness, there was nothing he, Hafiz, could do at this point. If he told the police about Erik's home, many fine men would perish. By now, he was certain, all the tunnels were booby-trapped. He did not want the police trapped in collapsed tunnels, or drowned, in suddenly rising waters, on his conscience. Erik's underground home must be rife with new trapdoors and deadly illusions. Even he, would not dare walk in, without Erik by his side.

There was, as there had always been, only one solution to this crisis ‾ Christine Daaé! Could she somehow reach his frail mind without endangering herself? Hafiz could not find it in his heart to ask her to risk herself that way. After what she had endured in the house by the lake, she deserved a little peace in her life, a chance to be happy.

They sat in a side parlor, since Louis did not want Christine to be aware of his presence in the house. They drank coffee, Louis' heavily laced with brandy.

"Are you absolutely sure it is he?" asked Louis.

"Yes, my lord, I am certain of it from the descriptions given in *Le Siècle*. They were all strangled in a bizarre manner. In Persia, he was known as a master of strangulation. His weapon of choice has always been the Punjab lasso. He is a master in its use.

"All the victims were strangulated with a slim rope. In one case the victim was decapitated perhaps the individual tried to fight back. The weapon suspected was a thin double coil of rope, la loupe, in other words, a garrote. Erik's, I might add, is a Punjab lasso made of catgut, but the police would not be able to discern that."

"So you think it is *not* him?" Louis asked anxiously.

Hafiz hated to squelch the hope in those eyes. "Oh, it is Erik all right, but he is working with an accomplice, someone who was or is a Legionnaire. Some of the killings happened simultaneously in different parts of the city, My Lord."

"Ah, please dispense with the 'my lord'," Louis said, waving some sheets of paper in the air. "These might bring Erik to reason."

The Persian wondered if anything could bring Erik to reason, except a bullet straight through the heart. "What are they?"

"Last night, before he left, I acquired these letters from Philippe; Raoul left them behind. They are written by Christine, telling Raoul she wants nothing to do with him!" Louis explained. "I must admit that I am baffled by this girl. It was my impression that the girl was still in love with Raoul. I will go meet with my son, and if he can reason and I deem it safe, we may have to return her to him. Good God, over eleven dead in less than two weeks!" His expression was grim.

"I'm certain there are other bodies not found

yet," said the Persian with a shake of the head, his dark green eyes glazed over with memories.

"What do you think? Will she return with him?" asked Louis, nodding in the direction of Christine's room.

"She walks about like a shadow. I doubted her affection for him when I first heard of the impending marriage, but I have seen them together in that underground home of his; they looked the picture of domestic bliss." A fleeting smile appeared on his lips. "I do not know what he may have done to her, but have no doubt she would gladly jump at the opportunity to return to him."

"I will go through on the rue Scribe and call for him on this side of the lake. I must plead for his wife's innocence," Louis said with a snort.

"You won't know his state of mind when he first sees you. Keep one hand up by your eyes. Like this," Hafiz showed the older man. "It's the only defense you'll have against his flying lasso. Do not forget."

Hafiz did not question her openly, but his eyes probed her every move, allowing her to pine quietly. On the third day, she gave up her silence and began to relate to the Persian her experiences with Erik after the disaster of her meeting with Raoul.

"The night before you came for me was the worst of all. I think the pain of thinking me unfaithful drove him completely mad. One moment he was my

Angel of Music and the next Don Juan from his composition. He would entice me to open my locked door them order me not to listen to him and keep my door shut. He said terrible things to me, things I could not repeat."

He listened in dismay to the monstrosities Erik had put her through and pitied her. "I am so sorry, Christine. I thought love had changed Erik. I should have monitored the situation closer. I can't ask for so great a sacrifice from you. As soon as he hears of all this, I am sure the vicomte will take you far away and…"

"What?" She looked at him, baffled. "I want things to be as they were before I went to that accursed meeting. Hasn't Raoul caused me enough grief?"

Hafiz could not believe his ears. Trying as hard as he could, he could not close his mouth. "I just heard you tell me the most horrific stories. And now you say you want to go back to the man who almost killed you? What makes you think he won't kill you when you go back?"

"It was jealousy that made him do those things. He would not let me explain that he had no cause to doubt me."

"I was not at the Giry apartment at the time of the incident but … well at the risk of sounding indelicate you were seen to encourage the vicomte to take certain liberties." His dark skin prevented his blush from showing, but he felt the heat.

She went on to explain the incident. It made him

want to throttle both Raoul de Chagny and his gossiping brother. Her cheeks were flushed, but she continued, "Raoul told me he wanted Erik to see that he had marked me!" Her voice grew in strength. "Hafiz, I need your help. Erik needs to hear the truth about that day. Will you help me?"

"Yes," said Hafiz, with a heavy sigh. He prayed they were not both making a fatal mistake.

Once again Louis ventured to the lower cellars and called to Erik from the side of the lake on the rue Scribe. As had happened the last time he had been there, there was no answer. He left the cellars and returned to the most logical place where Erik would want to gain access; the Chagny manor.

As Louis neared the Chagny home, peculiar sounds drew his attention to the stables and unnerved him as well. Louis walked toward the noise in the chilly breeze of the early morning hours. As he arrived, he could see a pair of legs thrashing on the ground uncontrollably; the gurgling had stopped. The guard lay on the ground, his head in an odd position; the vacant eyes bulged. The tongue had grown too large for the mouth, and so it protruded and hung lazily between the lips. Just behind him, at one with the night, were eyes, invisible to all except to one who had eyes exactly like them. In a sudden panic, Louis grabbed at his throat. Then, remembering the Persian's words, his hand went up on the side of his face between his ears and eye.

Enveloped by the night's shadows, a man's figure backed away slowly until the two glowing eyes were pinpoints. Louis had an instinctual desire to run away from there to a place of safety, inside the house. By the height of the shadow, he guessed it was his son coming to kill Raoul de Chagny!

"Erik! Raoul is not here if that's who you came for." He was grateful his voice emerged stronger than he felt.

"How do you know I did not come for you?" Erik's voice floated to him.

"I'm still alive!"

Erik laughed. "Touché! He has something of mine and I came to collect payment. Where is he?"

Louis could not imagine what kind of payment Erik would demand. He was grateful both Chagny's were away. "His brother sent him to England."

A grunt, then Erik said, almost inaudibly, "She's gone with him."

"If you are referring to your wife, the answer is no. Raoul left two days after the unfortunate incident; she was still with you at the time he embarked. You may look in the house if you wish. Philippe is away on business as well."

"Why do you stay with them?" he asked, looking at the well-manicured grounds with disdain. He moved slightly closer, allowing enough light to shine on his eyes so that they glowed.

"Philippe has always offered me his hospitality

and I enjoy his company."

Erik lowered his eyes for a moment. "You would not have enjoyed a stay in my dungeon. Not after coming from such a grand home as yours."

"You have a fine home, Erik. I did visit you, if only for a few moments. At any rate, before he left, Philippe handed me these. I think you will want to take a look."

Erik moved slightly more into the light. He was dressed in black as usual. A moonlit shimmer gleamed on his shoulders. "Why would I want anything from a Chagny?"

"Because they are messages sent by Christine to Raoul Chagny!" He extended the letters in his hand to Erik. His son did not take them at once, rather he unfurled his fingers slowly, almost fearfully, taking them finally with trembling fingertips.

"Why would I want to read her love letters to him?" he spat out.

"The content will be a revelation to you."

Pointing to the folded papers in his hands, he asked, "Have you read them?"

"Yes."

Erik looked at Louis through narrowed eyes, took the letters with him and walked into the open, toward the light.

Louis stood by, waiting as Erik unfolded the first letter and read.

My dearest Raoul,

I write to you with a heavy heart. It seems that you have chosen to ignore my former note to you. I write again to say that I am married, that I care very much for my husband, and will not ever consider leaving my home. I am happy where I am.

If you still wish to meet with me, we can meet, and it will be to your face that I will repeat that I am indeed, happily married.

Let us keep our memories, and perhaps one day in the company of our respective spouses we can laugh at our foolishness and hug once more in genuine camaraderie.

Until then, your faithful friend,
Christine

Erik stared at the piece of paper held in his trembling hands. He knew Christine's handwriting and it was written on the paper he had given her. Erik fell to his knees. He examined the letters and lifted his mask a little to put them closer to sniff ‾ Christine's own smell without cologne. "She wrote him that she was happy … happy in our home … and that she cared for me," he said in an agitated voice.

Erik read the second letter through tears and was unable to read the other two. Louis heard him exhale noisily and catch his breath again. He watched Erik, remaining on his knees, began to weep.

Shaking the letters in his hand, he looked up at his father, unaware of the tears falling from the mask's edge. "Damn that boy! She was more than clear in these letters. Even the early ones." He started to reread part of a letter again, but his vision was too blurred by tears. "You say his brother gave you these? Why would he?"

"Philippe wants his brother to be rid of this delusion, he wants to see him carry forward with his life. And he knows you are my child."

"You've told people about me? He … he knows about this?" he asked, astonished, pointing to his face. Acknowledging him on paper was one thing, but to actually let others know that he had fathered a deformed creature was something Erik had never expected.

"Of course I told him. I will not hide you!"

"If the boy knew how she felt, why did he continue to pursue her? Why insist on meeting with her?"

"He's in love with her. Wouldn't you have wanted to see, and speak to her, for yourself? He thought you were forcing her to write those letters."

He opened the letters again. "She had not planned to leave me for him! She didn't want me dead."

"You misinterpreted the situation."

"Some of it. She let him make love to her. I saw him…"

"It doesn't add up. Does it make sense that the same woman who wrote these letters would turn around and make love with Raoul in that apartment? If she wanted him, why not leave with him and enjoy his kisses at leisure. For God's sake, he offered her marriage. All she had to do was leave with him. He is titled, rich … unless you have told her about…"

"No, I have not. She hasn't a clue. I wanted her to choose me for me."

"Think clearly. Why would she want to return to you now, unless she cares for you?"

He let himself slide down the wall until he was sitting on the ground, knees by his chest, and his head in his hands, sobs choking him. "I would not let her tell me," he sobbed. "Oh God, I've destroyed my life. She never meant to leave Erik! She wanted me, do you understand that? Somebody wanted me, and I hurt her. It was the picture that pushed me over the edge. She had a picture of the boy in her dresser."

Louis joined him and sat on the cold ground next to him. "Erik, I have pictures and letters of a compromising nature. Some could lead to an international scandal. I should have gotten rid of them a long time ago, but did not. As we pass through life, we tend to keep memories — good and bad. Perhaps to remind us that we passed through this life and made a difference, learned something. That way when our children do something crazy, we can remember that we too did crazy stupid things and lived through it. I don't know why, but we all keep pictures and mementos from our past. Did you ask her why she kept the picture?"

"I did not ask her anything; I never let her talk or explain."

"She wants to be with you, this I know!"

"How do you know? Do you know where...? *You* have her!" His eyes blazed for a few moments.

"I kept her safe for you. She's with the Persian," Louis answered.

"They are not in his home," Erik stated.

"No. Before you ask, nor at the château." A contentious look in Erik's eye made Louis stand up straighter. It was a precarious moment and he could not back down.

"How can she want to be with me now? I hurt her!"

Louis was asking himself the same question, but according to the Persian, she did.

"The things I said! I was mad with anger and pain. She will never forgive me."

"I don't think it will be as difficult as you imagine," Louis answered solemnly, putting his arm around his son. He felt him tense, but then Erik relaxed and accepted the touch.

"Turn away; I need to clean my face."

"You need not hide from me, ever, but I will honor your request," Louis said, turning around to give his son privacy.

Erik removed the mask and wiped his face clean with a handkerchief. "I have made a mess of everything. I am a booby, an idiot. How do I get her back? I have no clue how to proceed."

Louis' eyes fell on the dead man witnessing their conversation; he averted his gaze from the bulging eyes.

Erik followed Louis' eyes. "There's another one back there." Erik's hand carelessly signaled behind him toward some bushes. The older man exhaled and closed his eyes.

"I want to see her tonight!"

"Do you want *her* to see you in this state?"

For the first time in days, Erik looked down at himself. He shuddered to think of holding Christine in his arms. He reeked of the pollution of death.

"I need to be with her."

"I will help you. She needs time to forget, to miss you. I will take you to Rouen. You can clean up, eat and sleep. No, don't protest, three days at most and then, I will take you to her. We ... um ... need to take care of this." He would have preferred to walk away and ignore the bodies.

"My man will take care of things here."

Louis noticed a second shadow moving in the dark. He had been right, if Erik had intended to harm him, he would have been dead by now.

Erik called out, "I am returning to Rouen with my father. It ends here, tonight. All of it! You stay behind and clean up."

Louis thought he heard a slight groan of disappointment, but the breeze carried the sound away.

Available
Summer 2015—*Masque: Forge*
A Gaston Leroux Phantom of the Opera Romance series, Book Two

And coming soon—*Masque: LeBeque*
A Gaston Leroux Phantom of the Opera Romance series, Book Three